A PRINCE OF THE BLOOD

A PRINCE OF THE BLOOD

RAYMUND EICH

Cover art: Distant Castle: Image ID 146982265 | © camilabo | depositphotos.com; Man with Sword: Image ID 279635398 | © MerryDesigns | depositphotos.com; Queen: Image ID 237812828 | © iordani | depositphotos.com.

Cover design, book design, and aircraft carrier logo are copyrights, trademarks, or trade dress of CV-2 Books.

ISBN 978-0692454152

Third CV-2 Books trade paperback edition: March 2024

 Created with Vellum

CONTENTS

To Miranda

O brave new world, that has such people in't!

AUTUMN

The Palace

Silence filled Keladon's ears as he crossed the threshold into the chamber. His intuition told him the true purpose of the two men who'd summoned him had naught to do with curing the presumed infertility of the king or queen.

The two men waiting in the chamber wanted him for something else.

After Keladon stepped fully into the chamber, the servant manning the door from the outside swung it shut behind him. For a moment, the only sounds came from a fire crackling to his left and rain outside the windows high on the wall to his right. A man then spoke, his voice quiet and creaking with age. "Please lock the door, Your Illustriousness."

Keladon looked behind him. A ring bearing a dozen keys dangled from one positioned in the door's lock. He turned the key halfway, then moved closer. The zone of Blocked Sound encompassed the bolt and the inner mechanism of the lock. He rested the fingertips of his free hand near the lock, straddling the narrow crack between the door and the jamb. A final twist of the key drove the bolt fully into the jamb and sent confirming vibrations to his fingertips.

Five paces from the door, the two men waited for him. To the left, clad in the simple brown doublet and tan breeches of a prominent commoner, sat Melos. At his neck hung a medallion showing a pillar holding up a crown, the emblem of his position as Master of Offices. He had a full head of white, close-cropped hair and a face wrinkled like old parchment. His gray eyes, however, remained clear under heavy lids that showed he saw everything and forgot nothing. Melos was a crafty old man, in office under three kings, survivor of a civil war and untold numbers of conspiracies. No one loved him, and all feared him. A few murmured words to his clerks, and the palace guard or the King's Justice could carry anyone to a dungeon cell, or the headsman.

Sweeping red motion came toward him from the right. Norobom, Duke of Vonen-Kiget, stood tall and broad, with untamed blond hair and expressive brown eyes. He wore the asymmetrical gray coat of a battlemage: the right panel slanted from a few buttons near the throat to a single button at the left hip, and a rounded shape bulged under the coat over the lower right abdomen. Like all other noble battlemages, he declined the right due his station to wear a sword in the palace. Distinctive to Norobom was a red cape, held in place at his neck by a golden clasp embossed with a circle-with-a-handle depiction of a magegem. Also distinctive was his aura of assured command. Even those who did not know him guessed he was Commander of Battlemages.

Keladon bowed his head slightly. "Good afternoon, Your Grace."

Norobom gave a wide smile and swept his arms around Keladon, then slapped him on the back. "Good to see you, old friend." His voice echoed despite the thick, ornamented wallpaper lining the walls. "I still think fondly of our campaign together. Would we could ride into battle again and burn down our enemies, side by side."

The other's reference to the campaign against the Peluraki froze Keladon's face into a polite, artificial smile. "I too have fond memories from that time." He disengaged from Norobom's embrace. "Sir, and goodman Melos, shall we get to our business, before the yellow magegem fueling Block Sound spends all its energies?"

Norobom frowned for a moment. "Melos's palace mages have many more yellows in the vault... and they are irreplaceable." With his left hand, he reached into his jacket and pulled out a glassy, yellow ball with a flattened base and a handle on top. He set the yellow magegem on the floor to the left of his chair, then sat, flinging up his cape's hem of golden thread over his chair back. He waved at another chair facing him and Melos. "Take a seat, if you please."

He sat. From the way the light from a chandelier overhead and the fireplace to the side colored the yellow magegem, Keladon estimated the charge remaining in it. He compared that with the charge drained by Block Sound each second, and calculated the spell could run another forty minutes. Norobom went on. "Our summons was a false pretense to bring you to the palace."

Annoyance at being compelled to leave his peaceful researches at his estate and journey hundreds of miles washed through Keladon, but he kept his face still.

"I see you already guessed," Norobom said. "Of course it's true the king and queen have no children, but as best we know, both are fertile."

"Then what could my magic do?" Keladon asked.

Another smile from Norobom. "It's not your magic we need."

"What, then?"

Norobom turned to Melos. "Goodman, would you tell our guest our purpose here?"

"We need a man," Melos said, "a man of noble blood and the utmost discretion, to perform a task of the highest importance for our realm." His eyes narrowed to peer at Keladon. "Sir, we ask that you impregnate Queen Lilera."

Gooseflesh stippled Keladon's cheeks. Impregnate the queen!? Feelings churned inside him for a moment, until his mother's last warning to him, always in the back of his mind, settled them. *Avoid the intrigues around the palace. Never give your half-brother any reason to doubt your loyalty.*

After a couple of quick, shallow breaths, he breathed deeply and kept his voice assured. "I should think that would be a duty for King Raboros."

Norobom laughed. His baritone voice echoed off the plastered walls. "Discrete as ever, old friend! You must know His Majesty's tastes run counter to nature. Everyone in the palace does."

Outside, a gust of wind threw raindrops like handfuls of pebbles against the windows. Keladon huddled his shoulders. "I knew his desires inclined toward boys, but I have been away from the court for nearly twenty years."

"Have you reason to think his tastes have changed?" Melos asked.

"Since I inherited the estate of Korobei, I have heard nothing about where King Raboros now seeks his pleasure. Yet even if he took no pleasure at getting the queen with child, I would think him man enough to undertake the duty."

Norobom sniffed out a disdainful breath. "You think too highly of him."

"Sir—" Melos said sharply.

"Can he hear us in here?" Norobom looked down his long nose at Melos, and a sudden brightening of the fire reflected from the skin over his sharp cheekbones. "No. Let us speak frankly, then. King Raboros is addicted to his pleasures and scorns the fundamental duty of a king. It's his fault alone we're forced to ask Keladon to stand in for him."

"Duke Norobom's words are intemperate," Melos said to Keladon, "but they speak to the underlying truth. Your half-brother consummated his marriage on his wedding night, and perhaps five or six times over the following year; but after your father the late king entered the hall of Balar and Samala, he has not once lain with the queen, despite all our entreaties that he do so."

Keladon's aplomb had mostly returned. "Why is now the time for a champion to perform the deed on his behalf?" he asked. "The queen is only thirty-five."

"Both the royal midwife and Queen Lilera's attendants have made clear her tides of Samala come and go erratically, more rapidly than is usual for her age," Melos said. "The midwife predicts the goddess will finally ebb the tide within five years."

"And the longer we wait, the greater the likelihood she would bear a lackwit," Norobom said. The rain came down harder, rattling on the cobblestoned walkways in the palace's central courtyard outside the windows.

Keladon gritted his teeth. Better to find someone else to do it. "Your words are true, goodman and sir, but only regarding Queen Lilera. The king could petition the priests of Balar for a divorce, on some ground, true or not—"

"We have considered that approach," Melos said. A breath sagged out of him and his shallow chest sank further under his simple doublet. "Matters of state make it too complicated to pursue. The Peluraki king would protest if Raboros cast aside his sister."

Norobom snorted, waved his hand. "The Peluraki are toothless. Let them squawk. We slaughtered them twenty years ago, didn't we, Keladon? We can do it again."

Chill gripped Keladon as Melos glowered at Norobom. "Since then the Peluraki have found magegem caches—"

"—we still have better battlemages—"

Keladon eased back in his seat, grateful their argument focused them on each other. Twenty years ago, he had been a different man. Never again would he wield the reds of the battlemages. Never again would powerless men fall by the thousands to energies flung from his fingertips.

"—and finding another wife for King Raboros would not solve this problem," Melos said. Norobom glumly settled into his seat. The old man turned to Keladon. "He would refuse to do his duty with the next wife as well, which would put us against this same impasse in another twenty years."

"I see."

After a silence, a crumbling log rustled in the fireplace. Melos went on. "Keladon, you are our realm's acknowledged master of the peaceful uses of magic. Know you some magic to aid us?"

Norobom leaned forward and vigorously shook his head. "I tell you, there is none."

"Duke Norobom, your mastery is of red and yellow magegems, is it not?"

"I am aware of spells requiring the other colors," Norobom said with a glower at Melos, "though I lack the fullness of my old friend's knowledge." He swept his hand toward Keladon, then leaned forward, his brown eyes intent. "There is no way to make King Raboros a man whose spine stiffens when he thinks what lies twixt a woman's legs, is there?"

Would there were. "The Jeloreans charged the magegems with no such spells," Keladon said. "Nor have I or my assistants crafted such a spell from the commands we have learned."

"As I told you, Master of Offices," Norobom said.

Keladon thought more, and raised his hand with a feeling of sudden relief. "I can give some of my assistants the task of studying whether such a spell is possible, and composing it if it is." It might be a waste of part of the annual allotment of magegems granted him by his late father's will, but it could keep him free of this palace intrigue after all.

Melos leaned toward Norobom. "If His Illustriousness believes such a thing might be possible—"

"We shouldn't chance it." Norobom pouted and shook his head. "Even were it possible, we can't know the spell to make the king into a man could be prepared in time before the queen's womb rusts over."

Stiffly, Melos settled back in his armchair. Candles around the room and the fading fire shadowed the deep lines of his face. "I know spells exist that can force a man to do a mage's bidding," he said.

"Compel Truthful Answers is the only one we know," Keladon said.

Melos frowned. "Is it? A blue magegem carries within it the power to make rats dance and cats swim. How is a man different from such a beast?"

Keladon felt another moment of hope, but his knowledge of Guide a Creature's Movements welled up from his memory and crushed his hope. "The stronger an animal's mind, the more energy the spell would have to draw from the magegem to overpower it. A man's mind would consume a fully charged blue magegem within a few seconds."

"In the vault, we have enough blue magegems," Melos said.

"But as our guest reminded us when he entered, the stock is limited," Norobom said. "The Jeloreans took the ability to make and charge magegems to their funeral pyres, and we haven't yet learned that ability from the codices they left behind." He jerked his gaze to Keladon. "Have you proven me wrong, old friend?"

Keladon shook his head. "We have hypotheses of how to charge magegems, but no proof."

"Making more magegems can be a task for another day," Melos said. "King Raboros needs an heir now."

Norobom jumped to his feet and lifted his shoulders and chest. "Keladon is right about the limited number of blues, but he left out the key objection. Are you fool enough, old man, to guide the king's movements against his will? What sovereign could tolerate the shame of being enslaved, if even for a few minutes, by a lesser man? After you exhausted every blue in the vault, the king would regain his powers, and then have you and the mage hanged near to death, then resuscitated in order to hang you again."

Melos leaned back. "You both speak wisely. Magic will not help us."

Norobom flipped up the tail of his gold-trimmed crimson cloak as he sat. "Only you can, Keladon."

Keladon glanced past the two courtiers to the wall behind them.

There hung an equestrian painting of his father, handsome and resplendent, a young duke pursuing the throne in the interregnum following the death of Larabos IV, the son-less king. "Noble blood and discretion, you said, Master of Offices? I can't be the only man with both."

"You have the most noble blood of all," Norobom said in a commanding tone. "The blood of a king."

"A king," Keladon said, "who came to the throne because one unmarried daughter survived Larabos IV, and a clash of arms with the girl's other suitors had to give someone the throne. My father was born to inherit a dukedom. So too were you, Norobom. Do you wish to take Raboros' place in the queen's bedchamber?"

Briefly, Norobom's eyes bulged, but his usual expression of confidence and power soon returned. "Your father made himself a king. That makes his blood even more royal than if he'd happened to be born a son of old Larabos."

Find someone else to get Queen Lilera with child. Murky fears of conspiracies pushed Keladon's back against the chair and froze his tongue.

"As for discretion," said old Melos, "if you delivered this stroke of state, would you tell a soul you were our next prince's true father?"

He could lie and say he would... in which case he knew too much already. He would not leave this room alive. But even without that cold calculation, he would have told the truth. "I would not. I am loyal to King Raboros."

"But what if a foe, say, King Aril of the Peluraki, were to capture you, and his mages Compelled you to give Truthful Answers?" Melos peered at him.

Keladon grimaced. "I would resist until the pain from telling falsehoods overwhelmed me. Being a mage would not shield me from that spell. But they would have to have some suspicion about the next prince's true father to capture me, let alone ask me the question. I would not give them any reason for suspicion. Would you, Master of Offices? Or you, Commander of Battlemages?"

Keladon put as much steel into his gaze as he could and swept it between the two courtiers.

"I am loyal to King Raboros," Melos said.

"As loyal as you," Norobom said to Keladon.

Another rustle of a crumbling log, and glowing embers drifted up the chimney, entrained in the hot air of the fire. Keladon asked, "What does Queen Lilera think of your plan?"

Norobom sniffed out a breath. "Our Peluraki prisoner will do as she's told."

"We have broached the subject with her," Melos said. "She consents. She has known from a young age she was fated to bear a child for reasons of state. The men of the Peluraki royal house trained her well."

"She could give her Peluraki kinsmen knowledge of her child's true father," Keladon said. "What mischief could they work with that?" Maybe this objection would free him from their intrigue. Tension eased from his chest and shoulders.

Melos shook his head. "We let her receive and send letters to King Aril and other Peluraki personages. We of course read what comes in and, if needed, rewrite what goes out. When she meets with a Peluraki emissary, or any of her brother's subjects who wish to pay her their respects, she is attended by a multitude of servants, at least two of whom are agents of mine fluent in her native tongue. If she speaks the wrong word to a visitor, my agents would run the visitor through in front of her. The Peluraki will not learn her child's father is a man other than King Raboros."

"Of course," Keladon said. He heard the resignation in his voice.

"You seem unwilling to do this task for us." Melos frowned. "Like your half-brother, do your tastes run contrary to nature?"

"Don't insult our guest," Norobom said.

Keladon replied to Melos, "My tastes are those of most men."

The old man looked unconvinced. "We know you have fathered no children."

Melos' words rubbed at a sore spot in Keladon's mind. Though no prince, he was still the son of a king, claimed by his father, and granted a lifehold on the small but prosperous estate of Korobei. "You know I have never married. After my father claimed me, I could not take a wife from the lesser nobility. To take a wife from the highest born would enmesh me against my better judgment in my in-laws' intrigues."

With a laugh, Norobom said, "You make not marrying sound a bad thing." His smile turned to a puzzled look, crinkled eyebrows and a deep crease across his forehead. "But we spoke of children, not marriage. You must vent the pressure in your groin somewhere, wife or no, and if seed falls on fertile ground, it will sprout."

"I have needs like any man," Keladon said, "but no desire to father bastards." He would not wish a child to grow up facing the scorn he had encountered in his youth. "In one of the villages near Korobei works an artisan skillful at making assurance caps from lamb entrails."

"Then why do you squirm in your seat to avoid answering us with 'yes?'" Norobom asked. "Forget your village harlots and foolish peasant girls. You can plow the furrow of a queen!"

Keladon let out a breath. His last line of defense was a bluff. "There is a spell other than Compel Truthful Answers that could disrupt the secrecy this scheme needs. Have you heard of a spell castable using a green, Scald the Cuckoo's Egg?"

Melos squinted in thought. "A petty earl, from near the Pelurak border... what was his name?"

"Hardly important," Norobom said. "A year ago, give or take? Through that spell, he found the son born to his young wife wasn't his. He killed her, then raised her adultery as a defense when her relatives had him summoned by the King's Justice."

Keladon's hopes shrank. All would depend on how much they knew of the ingredients of that spell. "My point should be clear. Through magic, one can find a child is not sired by his putative father, and disfigure that child for the rest of his life, for all the world to see. Should that spell be turned onto the next prince—"

"Pardon me, old friend," Norobom said with an air of theatrical innocence. "I don't know all the details, and perhaps I'm mistaken, but doesn't that spell require an ingredient from the putative father?"

His bluff had been called. Keladon took a deep breath, then rested his forearms on the arms of his chair. His gut felt exposed, but he refused to cover it with his hands. "It does."

Melos peered at Norobom and Keladon. "What ingredient? Don't hold this information from me."

"Yes, Keladon," Norobom said, smiling. "Tell us both."

A deep breath failed to still Keladon's unease. "It requires the putative father's semen."

Norobom smirked and leaned back in his chair. Melos gave Keladon a dispassionate look. "Raboros would not deliver his semen to a mage capable of casting that spell. You are bookish, and from that I could guess you were perhaps a fool about people's minds, but I am certain you know your brother would not give another the power to destroy his legitimacy and that of his dynasty."

"I know it."

"Finally you speak bluntly," Melos said. "Now, tell us, why do you resist our request? The kingdom needs an heir. You are the best man to provide it one."

Melos was right. The last king to die without an heir had left behind a chaos that was mercifully short-lived, thanks to an alliance between Keladon's father and the first men to tap the rediscovered power of the magegems. But now, four decades later, so many mages had been trained, and so many scattered vaults had been found throughout the kingdom, that another interregnum would descend into bloody stalemate, benefiting only foreign kings, and vultures.

"Provide it one?" Norobom asked from deep in his chair. He shifted forward with a lively grin. "Or be one?"

Sweat dewed on Keladon's forehead and nape. "What do suspect me of, sir?"

"Suspect? Old friend, fear not. You know we cannot be overheard. No one will take my words as indication you conspire against the king. All I mean is you and the king are the only claimed sons of old Radobom. If the king died without a surviving son, some faction among the nobility would settle the crown on you by default."

"I would not want it."

"Oh?" Norobom said, eyebrow raised. "Truly?"

His feelings roiled, but Keladon pushed them down and gazed levelly at Norobom. "Truly."

Sadness filled Norobom's face. "Then the blood of the kingdom would be on your hands."

"How? I do not follow you."

"Enough of the ambitious would bend their knee to a claimed son of Radobom to maintain the kingdom's peace."

"Claimed? Who would declare a bastard his king? Would you?"

Norobom's breezy confidence flickered for a second, then returned to the fore. "Old friend, most of the highest born have as little mettle for a civil war as the basest peasant. But if the throne had no heir, a dozen of the highest born would vie for the empty throne with large armies and thousands of reds. Civil war would despoil provinces and send tens of thousands to their pyres. Would you want that?"

Scholars working at his estate, and goodmen plying their trades in the nearby towns, came to Keladon's inner eye, suffused with the golden glow of autumn sunsets and turning leaves. "No," he said. "I want prosperity for the kingdom, but I do not want the crown." A new thought troubled him, but it would not be enough to free him from their plans. "I will bed Queen Lilera as you ask... provided the king himself tells me he approves."

Melos's eyes briefly widened. "Why should that be necessary, sir?"

"As you recall, I grew up in the palace. I saw men convinced they acted with royal favor end up at the headsman."

"You fear King Raboros would consider you getting the queen

with child to be an intrigue against him?" Melos said. "He approves both our plan and your role in it."

The fire had faded. Embers glowed at the bottom, but only a few lazy tongues of flame licked over the shriveled, blackened logs. "So you say."

"You don't trust us?" Norobom asked. "I can understand you not trusting Melos—only a fool would—" He smiled arrogantly at the Master of Offices. The old man responded with a look barren of feeling. Norobom spoke further. "—but Keladon, you and I trained side by side, campaigned side by side, and toppled towers and slew Peluraki side by side."

Keladon let the words fade before replying. "Twenty years ago."

Norobom's eyes narrowed as Melos spoke. "Very well. If that is all you require, King Raboros will assure you of his will with his own words."

Hinges groaned and brass pulls squeaked against their brackets as two footmen opened the double doors leading into King Raboros' lesser audience chamber. A herald waiting with Keladon took two steps into the chamber, thumped the padded end of his walking stick against the hardwood floor, and bowed. The herald spoke the formulaic words requesting a nobleman's admittance in a deep, booming voice.

Despite the herald's entry, conversations went on, and someone within the audience chamber laughed. The sound echoed off the high walls and ceiling. "His Illustriousness is admitted," came a bored reply.

Keladon's rarely-worn sword bounced against his hip as he entered. He had practiced swordsmanship for many hours in his youth, but he only carried it now as a badge of rank. Tall windows to his left let in the light of a sunny but cold afternoon. Across the central courtyard of the palace rose the west wing and the gray stone keep of the old castle behind it. The sun's bright rays caught the contours of the audience chamber's textured wallpaper and a massive painting of Keladon's father, regal yet fleshy with middle age and decades of rich living, accepting the submission of Peluraki emissaries in baggy, mud-stained tunics at the end of the war.

The doors thudded shut behind him.

Below the painting, ranked daises bore a collection of standing men. Melos and Norobom were among them, along with two palace mages wearing blue doublets and empty magegem slings at their hips. Also present were two hard-eyed men wearing baggy, plain doublets whom Keladon took to be Melos' agents.

Keladon did not know the others by either name or role. Most were young and slender noblemen, with rouged cheeks and curly hair. Their dapper attire took the eye away from Norobom's customary red cloak. Their swords had ornate basket hilts with gold filigree and emplaced jewels, and their doublets, brightly patterned, had multiple slashings revealing flounced sleeves.

Some of the noblemen gave him scornful looks tinged with wariness. Keladon read their sentiments out of long habit: a bastard, but sired by the late king, and slayer of more men in an hour than a pretty sword could pierce in a lifetime. Unexpectedly, though, some gave him a look of appraisal, flicking up and down his body, such as other men gave bawds and serving maids. Keladon ignored them until they returned their attention to uppermost dais, and the man seated in the room's only chair.

The circlet crown lay aslant King Raboros' brow. Keladon had not seen his half-brother in over fifteen years, and studied him as he took slow steps into the room. He could not remember Raboros' past appearance with any exactitude, but he must have looked more vigorous than he did now. Middle age had worn him down faster than their father. His nose looked thick, jowls sagged under his jaw, and wrinkles splayed from the corners of his eyes. His hair looked as black as dyed leather, so falsely colored it emphasized, not refuted, the features showing his age. A bulky purple doublet, slashed in two dozen places and puffed with silk, hid Raboros's torso, but when he shifted his weight, it became clear he had added perhaps two stone of weight over the years. He watched Keladon with an expression of mild distaste.

Are you annoyed I ask a favor of you, half-brother?

A long, narrow table, its surface incompletely covered with a black velvet cloth, had been set across most of the room's width. Various objects had been lain on it. Keladon glanced over them to confirm Melos' palace mages had done as he'd asked.

Two magegems, one blue and one green, sat just to the left of the table's center. He envisioned the fingers of his left hand curling up and around the handle of each one in turn. The blue was a rich, deep azure, untouched or nearly so by any mage in the thousand years since its charging. Not so the green; it had faded to the color of moss growing high on the shaded slopes of hills. Whether a Jelorean or some more recent mage had tapped its stored energies he could not say. A glance told him it would have enough remaining power to work the demonstration that was the official purpose of this visit.

The objects on the table other than the magegems would be acted on by the energies he would tap. Two earhorns, a pair of hand mirrors, a pot of soil about nine inches in diameter and a foot high, and a cut white rose with six inches of stem. A large water jar stood next to the table. The water surface lay only a few inches below the rim. The jar stood two feet high and a foot and a half in diameter, with long rope handles slack against the sides.

Keladon stopped at the table, glad for the distance it imposed between him and Raboros' hangers-on. He bowed the proper distance. "I thank you for extending me this courtesy, Your Majesty."

"Our predecessor on this throne granted you an annual allotment of magegems in his final testament. It is fit you show us spells you may work with them." Raboros idly waved his fingers. "Proceed."

"First, I shall demonstrate Grow From a Cutting." Keladon picked up the rose stem with his right hand, deftly avoiding its thorns. He plunged the stem's cut end into the pot of fresh soil. "I will need—" He eyed the water jar, guessed its weight, glanced around for servants. "—two strong footmen to add water, slowly and steadily, when I give the word."

Two bulky servants strode forward. Though broad-shouldered, their tight faces, and the faint slap of water against the jar's wall, revealed they struggled with the jar's weight.

Keladon reached for the green with his left hand. The glass was smooth and cold. His fingers curled around the handle until he could feel it in the proper position against his fingers.

"*Jojipo bobi yuloto,*" he told the magegem in Jelorean. *Attend me.*

The green grew slightly warmer. He closed his right thumb and forefinger around the rose's stem and continued speaking in Jelorean. "*Target your energies upon the rose I touch.*" The rose shimmied for a moment. "*Grow the target, flux three-hundredths of a boil per drop of time, begin.* Start pouring water," he said to the footmen, "with a flow no stronger than your first urine of the morning."

The footmen tipped the water jar toward the planted stem. They poured it steadily for a few seconds, then sloshed water over the pot of soil and onto the table runner and Keladon's hand. One of them gasped in surprise. The stem had begun to grow.

"Mind your task," Keladon said. The footmen steadied the jar and the flow grew even again.

Stalks sprouted from the stem, and soon turned into stems themselves. Leaves feathered out, elongated, twisted to show themselves to the windows. The main stem thickened, gently pushing Keladon's thumb and forefinger apart. He touched his little finger to a growing stem, then waited for an opportune moment to release his hold on the main cane and quickly grasp another, closer to the growing rose bush's periphery. The air around the bush turned hotter and more humid.

The footmen's job grew easier as the water jar neared empty. From his spot to the side of the dais, Melos stood taller and peered at the pot. "Where is all the water going, sir?" he asked. "You have poured in enough to soak the soil."

"The plant consumes water as it grows," Keladon said, "and

releases more through its leaves." A drop of sweat ran down his fore-head into his eyebrow. He kept his gaze on the growing rose bush as he spoke. The first flowers began to bloom. "Stop pouring. *Stop growing the target, no flux. Release the target. Release your attention from me.*"

The handle of the magegem instantly cooled. Keladon removed his hands from the magegem and the rose bush. As he withdrew his hand from the rose bush, a thorn caught it. A drop of blood welled amid the distended veins and fine hairs on the back of his hand.

He stepped back and bowed. "The spell is complete, Your Majesty."

Raboros studied the rose bush for a moment. An uncertain expression passed his face. "A clever trick, certainly." His voice trailed off.

A young man wearing a paisley doublet with an open pane over the heart stepped forward, his face mirthful. "Your Illustriousness," he said, drawing out the uncommon and relatively low style of address, "you have worked a barren miracle. You have created roses for us, but we lack any fair ladies to give them to." He angled his head from side to side, inviting laughter at his jape. Most of the other young men gave it.

"Fear not, Dobak," Raboros said. "We shall bestow our guest's bounty on our well-formed lads." Another round of laughter followed. "Who here merits a rose?"

Arms rose to form a barren forest of rich fabric and puffed silk. Voices babbled out, "I do," "me," "clearly I—"

"We hear each one of you," Raboros said. He turned to a short, slender footman. "Have you garden shears handy?"

The footman's eyes widened and he quickly, deeply bowed. "I do not, Your Majesty."

"You knew a mage would work a trick with a flower from our garden, and yet you failed to provide garden shears?" A vein of anger lay within the king's voice.

Keladon winced with sympathy for the footman. *I told no one what spell I would work.* He leaned forward and opened his mouth, wanting Raboros to see he needed to speak. The king's glower remained on the bowing servant.

"Your Majesty," the footman said, "I shall send a houseboy to fetch a pair as quickly as he can."

"Do so." The footman backed toward a swinging door at the side of the room. "When we have a pair of shears, Dobak shall select be the first to select his rose, followed by...." Raboros reeled off a half-dozen names. "What shall we do, lads, while we wait for our servants to do as they're told?"

Dobak bowed to the king and set his hand amid the ruffles of his shirt over his heart. "I have a question for our guest, Your Majesty."

"You may ask it," Raboros said, and picked up a wine goblet.

Dobak turned an imperious gaze on Keladon. "Grateful as I am to His Majesty for his munificence in granting me the first fruit of your effort, a rosebush seems a trifling way to waste some of our irreplaceable magegems. I should think Sodelerak has enough roses."

Before replying, Keladon glanced at Raboros. The king seemed not to see the goblet still in his hand, seemed not to hear the conversation. Keladon's hand drifted to the outside of his sword's plain steel basket hilt. "The rose bush merely demonstrates the power of Grow From a Cutting."

"Have you used this demonstration on the tavern wenches in the towns near your estate?" Dobak asked.

Keladon swallowed thickly. "My purpose here was to work a spell with results readily discernible to all—"

"—meaning, even those as ignorant and foolish as us?" Dobak asked. "Is that what you think of us?" He swept his arm to take in all the men in the room except for the servants, Melos, and Norobom. The angle of his elbow showed he included Raboros.

Keladon blinked, and sweat formed on his nape. "—discernible to those who serve our kingdom in ways other than working with magegems." His words sounded stiff.

Raboros slumped against the side of his throne, with heavy

eyelids and his chin propped on the heel of his upturned hand. "Yes, yes. But Dobak has a good question. What value comes from making rose bushes?"

"The spell applies to all vegetable matter, Your Majesty." Keladon breathed more calmly. With that clarification, Raboros should see the value in it.

Instead, the king's eyebrows lowered in puzzlement.

"Your Majesty, if I may," said Melos, "the spell could be used to replant fields burned by raiding parties. A single stalk of wheat could be multiplied to save a village from starvation."

"Saving villages?" called a dandy from the crowd near the windows. "Surely we must have better things to do with our magegems than *that*." In a softer voice, barely overheard by Keladon, he added to his nearby peers, "Old Melos wants to save his cousins."

"Or is our guest the one with common cousins?" said another. "Only his mother's word got him claimed by the late king." Laughter broke out around him.

Another sycophant, his hair red and curly, shook his head. "A village starved to death cannot pay tax," he said, in a voice, though quiet, that carried through the room.

Raboros looked to the ceiling, plainly bored.

Norobom strode forward and thrust back his shoulders. A ripple passed down the length of his red cloak. "In addition, the spell my former colleague has shown us would also serve our forces when campaigning in hostile lands," he said. "Throughout history, many a campaign has been lost because men could not be fed. Foraging armies are as locusts. With this spell, we could replenish fields previously foraged by our armies, and remain longer in battle against our foes."

A bustle came from the side door. Raboros looked up, his face more lively than it had been since Keladon had entered. "Yes, our garden shears have finally arrived! Excellent! Houseboy, go to the bush on that table and cut the rose chosen by each of our lads as he comes up."

The houseboy did as he was bid. A young boy, with a smooth face and innocent eyes, he kept his gaze turned to the floor as Dobak and the other sycophants came toward the table. Keladon retreated a step, and his grasp tightened on the outside of his basket hilt.

Dobak pointed at a large bloom that had just begun to open. As the houseboy reached for his selected rose, Dobak shook his head. "You're a pretty one, aren't you?"

The boy's hand trembled, and he pulled the shear back from the stem. He bowed his head again. "My Lord, I don't understand."

"I see you know to work the naïve act. Get to cutting me my rose."

The boy reached quickly for the stem and cut. He winced when a thorn caught his fingertip, but he kept quiet. Head bowed, he handed held out the rose.

Dobak snatched it from his trembling hand. "Boy, mark my words. Wait, you don't know how to mark, do you? Remember this. If ever I catch you letting the king see your face full-on, I'll put a scar on each of those lovely cheekbones and the king will never look at you again." Dobak passed the rose to his left hand, then fondled his sword's hilt in warning.

He breathed deeply from the flower, gave Keladon a cold smile, and turned to the daises. Dobak tucked the rose behind his right ear and winced faintly as a thorn drew blood from his scalp. He climbed to the dais below Raboros' throne and knelt. "I am humbled by Your Majesty's gift."

"You have earned it, Dobak," replied Raboros. "Oh, how you've earned it."

Would there were a way to move beyond this sycophancy. Raboros might be inclined contrary to nature, but there's no need for him to conduct court like this. An anxious feeling gripped Keladon's chest. He studied a smudge on one of the mirrors to try to derail his thoughts. *Sodelerak would be better off had Larabos' daughter been the mistress, and my mother, the queen.*

Keladon squeezed his eyes shut for a moment, stepped back, took a breath. He glanced up and Norobom caught his attention. His former peer in the battlemage corps was the nearest to a friend he had in this room. Norobom gave his head a minimal, resigned shake. *Fool, are your thoughts too plainly visible?* Keladon's body stiffened and he blanked his face. He barely breathed for a moment, until it became clear the king and his dandies had attention only for their own crowd.

The houseboy cut the last rose from the bush and backed away while the hangers-on returned their focus to the king. Raboros leaned forward and looked past them all. "What other tricks can you show us, squire of Korobei?"

He won't even call me 'son of Radobom.' Keladon inhaled deeply to push down his resentment. "Your Majesty, there are two more spells I wish to show, spells that may be useful in finding the secrets of your enemies. Pass Light and Pass Sound."

"Two?" Raboros clearly sounded annoyed the number was so large.

"I may work them at the same time, Your Majesty."

Melos spoke up. "Is that safe?"

Keladon took another breath. "It will be safe." The worst that could happen would be an accidental touching of charged objects, but the king wouldn't be holding any of them.

Unless you asked him to—

Do you want to visit the headsman? another part of his mind replied. Keladon's pernicious thoughts shrank back to wherever they lurked.

Raboros drank more wine. "Proceed."

To a footman, Keladon said, "I need two houseboys." He remembered Dobak's threat to the most recent servant. "I'm sure the one who just attended us has been assigned to other tasks by now, so any two will do, no especial requirements." He put a little emphasis on the final words.

The footman's eyes briefly showed recognition of Keladon's meaning. He bowed and backed out of the room, soon to return with two houseboys, both plain looking. One had gangly arms and misshapen teeth; the other, a face scarred by childhood pox.

Keladon gripped the blue and tapped its energies. With a few words of Jelorean, he sent energy flowing into the earhorns, then the two hand mirrors.

"I will hand each of you two objects," Keladon said. "Do not touch them together. You would get a painful jolt."

Keladon gave the gangly one an earhorn and a mirror. "Go into the concourse," Keladon said.

"'Concourse,' Your Grace?"

Some of the footmen hissed. Melos narrowed his eyes. Norobom only responded by quirking his mouth, though he had most cause for offense—he was the only duke in the room.

"You may address me as 'Your Illustriousness,'" Keladon said. "Take these items into the hallway." He waved with his right hand toward the double-doors.

"Yes, Your Gr—Illustriousness." The boy nodded nervously.

"If no one is about, hold the mirror up to the paintings along the wall, or the gardens seen through the windows. Turn the earhorn toward your feet. If you see other people, tell them you wish to speak to them in the name of—Melos, Master of Offices." Not Raboros', because he would not tell the boy to speak for the king without the king's word; not his own, because he wanted his name out of the minds of the palace's habitants. "Turn the mirror to them and ask them to speak into the earhorn."

"I should put it in my ear, Your Illustriousness?"

"No, hold it in the air near their mouths. Are my instructions clear?" The houseboy nodded. "Then go." The gangly boy left, and other servants swung the double doors shut behind him.

Keladon turned to the pock-faced boy. "Take the remaining mirror and earhorn to the foot of the daises, and hold them up for the king's inspection."

"By your command, Your Illustriousness." He took the items from Keladon and went around the long table.

"Honored gentlemen," Keladon said to the sycophants, "I suggest you take up positions where you can see the face of the mirror beheld by His Majesty. I also must ask you to be quiet. Although I can make the audible demonstration louder, it would more rapidly waste the energy of our irreplaceable magegem." He glanced at the blue under his fist. It looked dimmer already, but he had to be seeing things. He'd barely tapped it.

The houseboy reached his position and held up the mirror and earhorn. Keladon's admonition had been unnecessary. The gaggle of hangers-on fell silent.

"That's the painting in the corridor of Balar and Samala," Raboros said in a ragged whisper. "We see it in the mirror as plain as if we stood in front of it." He looked at the closed double doors. "There's no trick of reflected reflections here. Your magic carries the sight between the two mirrors as if they are the two sides of the same window." He lifted his hand, pointed his forefinger to the ceiling. "Shh."

From the earhorn came the gangly servant's voice. "I say, speak to me in the name of Melos, Master of Offices."

"What knave does he speak to?" Raboros asked, peering at the mirror. His sycophants gave looks of regretted ignorance.

In reply to the houseboy's question, a curt voice said, "The old man would never give you a command directly."

"It wasn't him directly," replied the gangly servant, "but it was His Illustriousness, Keladon, so—squire of Korobei."

"Kela—what is this you hold? An earhorn?" After a moment, the other person's next words came faster, as if the pause had compressed them together. "Does a mage listen to me? Melos himself?" The curtness dropped from his voice. "My Lords, I am a mere servant, I know nothing of your ways, should you choose to entrust this houseboy with your powers—"

"Enough." Raboros flicked his hand at the air, then rubbed his temples. "We have no need to hear more prattle from lackeys."

Keladon spoke to the blue the commands needed to halt the

spells, then lifted his hand from it. The blue might have been a shade lighter than when he'd started his spells, but he couldn't tell for certain. His eyes weren't as sharp as they had been during his youthful days in the battlemage corps. He told the pock-faced boy to put the earhorn and mirror down on the table and bring his fellow houseboy in from the corridor.

After the boy left, Keladon bowed. "Thank you, Your Majesty, for the honor of demonstrating these spells."

"We see how they could be useful to our spies," Raboros said. "Melos, have you any comment?"

"I certainly agree, Your Majesty, our agents may well find them useful."

Norobom looked thoughtfully at the objects on the table. "Sire, these spells might have other uses that could redound to the glory of your kingdom."

Raboros' brow creased. He reached for his wine and said, "We leave such details to you, sir and goodman. Now, we must say a few words to His Illustriousness." He raised his voice to carry through the room, and his eyes looked less bleary when he locked his gaze on Keladon. "As is apparent to all, you are capable of deeds that we lack the ability to perform. Do you swear, before Balar, Samala, and all your ancestors feasting in their hall, to perform these deeds, and solely for the glory of our reign?"

Keladon stole a glance at Melos. Their gazes met and the Master of Offices briefly cocked his head while insistence showed around his eyes. He would get no private, explicit assurance from Raboros. These elliptical words were all the approval the king would give to being cuckolded by his bastard half-brother, and best he take it. Flawed as Raboros was, he was the son of the wife, the son who wore the crown.

Keladon bowed deeply to the king. "The glory of your reign is the paramount guidance for all my deeds, Your Majesty." He was glad the bow hid his face and any spoor from his lie. He acted for the good of the kingdom, not the good of this man born lucky.

"Good," Raboros said. "Now you may take your leave." The firmness of his gaze faded then, and though his lips turned up, he watched the hangers-on crowding the daises with unsmiling eyes.

A footman pushed the houseboys toward the table to gather up Keladon's implements, and the palace mages took custody of the magegems. Keladon worked his way through the bustle toward the rear doors, and from there into the corridor. Time to head to his guest rooms, and books by the fireside—

MELOS CAUGHT up with him near the painting of Balar and Samala. The Divine Couple welcomed the first man into their hall. The window lit up the portrayal of the first man's old age falling into his funeral pyre as his spirit regained its youth. Melos strove to catch his breath. "Your Illustriousness. A word. If you please."

"Of course, Master of Offices." The corridor was public, but without Block Sound, any room in the palace would be public. "May I express to you my gratitude to His Majesty for recognizing I take action on his behalf."

"You need me to confirm—" Melos' next breath came deeper and more slowly. "—what His Majesty said?"

"No." Keladon frowned. "I assumed you sought me out for that reason."

"I did not think I needed to. Rather, I ask you to come with me to the royal library."

"The library? For what purpose?"

Melos moved one hand near Keladon's elbow and gestured with the other. Keladon started walking. "The royal library is second only to yours regarding the Jeloreans' legacy. Our librarians recently found a codex containing spells unfamiliar to the mages employed here at the palace. We want you to study it."

"What sort of spell?"

"It requires a green magegem." Melos lowered his brows and glanced up the corridor. Two officials walked their way. They broke up their conversation and halted their progress to hail the Master of Offices.

Melos returned the greeting and asked a few questions about some matter of policy. Keladon kept silent until the officials moved on. Green was the color of medicine and living things. "Many sorts of spells use green magegems," he said.

"It is difficult for me to describe it," Melos said. "I lack fluency with the terms of your art. All I can do is show you."

They wound their way through the palace. They passed people of all stations, from houseboys and scullery maids, to clerks and skilled artisans, to noblemen in sumptuous doublets and bejeweled swords. All paused for Melos. The old man strode past the commoners and stopped for the nobles. The noblemen only spoke to Keladon as afterthoughts.

Their slow progress brought them to the south wing of the palace, then up three flights of stairs. A door opened, releasing the smell of paper and binding glue, and a glimpse of shelved books. Keladon felt at ease for the first time on this visit to the palace.

The library overlooked a small courtyard surrounded by the south wing. Shelves covered every square inch of wall space between windows and doors, and bowed under the weight of their books. Keladon squinted at labels glued to the books' spines, unable to read them from his distance, but more labels were glued to the shelves' front edges and bore texts written in a firm, precise hand. History, Theology, Logic, Rhetoric, Natural Philosophy—

A librarian in a plain yellow doublet and breeches stepped forward and bowed. "Sir, follow this man," Melos said to Keladon. He then drew from an outer pocket of his doublet a folded paper, sealed with wax impressed with the Master of Offices's sigil. "You may open this when you arrive at the room to which this man will lead you." To the librarian, he added, "Leave him to his studies in peace."

The librarian blinked, swallowed. "I—We have prepared the room for him."

Keladon said, "Lead me."

At tables near the windows, paper rustled as clerks, noblemen, and a few ladies turned pages. A few readers glanced up at Keladon, then returned to their books. One lady, though, skin pale and smooth as a marble statue, kept her gaze upon him. Her brunet hair, lustrous from the window's light. A thin white silken strip, pinned atop her hair and covering her ears, marked her as a widow. She smiled coyly at him and with smooth deliberation slid a leather bookmark off the edge of her table to land at Keladon's feet.

"Noble sir, pardon me," she said with an artful lilt in her voice.

He knew how the game was played. He bowed, picked up the bookmark, and set it on the table. "I am delighted to assist, my lady—?"

"Countess Dalasa. Are you Keladon, squire of Korobei? The great mage of both war and peace?"

"A mage, yes, but whether I am a great one is for others to say."

"I shan't detain you, noble sir. But will you be visiting the palace for a time?"

Even after he bedded the queen, Melos and Norobom would ask him to stay at the palace until the queen missed her next tide of Samala. Kept at the palace, and he had needs like any man; and this lady had needs like any woman. "A fortnight, at least. Till another time, my lady."

They parted, but her coy smile lingered in his mind's eye as he walked on.

At the final table in the room, just before a narrow door, sat two palace mages, one with graying hair, the other with crow's feet and a sizable paunch. The latter scribbled notes onto foolscap as the forefinger of his other hand tracked over the open pages of a beginner's treatise on blue magegems. Rare to see someone old enough to have wrinkles begin training in magic.

The librarian took a key from a pocket of his doublet and unlocked the narrow door. "Your Illustriousness, please enter."

Keladon went into a small room. More shelves, jammed with

books, covered the walls, save for the door and a window to his left. Although drawn curtains dimmed the light, the cramped space held books close enough for him to read titles as he waited for the librarian to light a candle. Of the books across the room, he recognized some from their size, shape, or the ornament of their bindings. This room held advanced works on magic. He had written a number of them, and his assistants, several others. Some were translations from Jelorean, but many were written, wholly or partly, in that tongue. Some related to the commands from which spells were built, and a handful taught techniques for crafting new spells.

A plush chair and a thick table filled the center of the room. A thin clank pulled his attention away from the books lining the shelves to the tabletop. The librarian had placed the key on the table, next to a book with a narrow leather bookmark. The only other item on the table was a piece of fabric covering a lumpy shape about a foot in each measure. "You may lock the door from the inside, Your Illustriousness," the librarian said. He left and shut the door behind him.

Keladon locked the door. He held his sword against his outer thigh and walked sideways around the table, checking the walls for small holes through which someone could see or hear what he would do, and finding none. He pulled the curtain back far enough to see a few servants' children chasing each other at the far end of the courtyard. Satisfied with the room's security, he sat down. The lumpy, covered shape sat near his left hand. He guessed what it was. No need to expose it yet.

He pulled the folded paper from his pocket and broke the seal. He guessed its contents before he unfolded it and started reading. A pass, authorizing the use of magic on the palace grounds by the bearer between the hours of three and six o'clock that afternoon. Signed by both Melos and Forek, the chief palace mage. His subordinates continually monitored the grounds for the casting of spells. Without a pass, a mage casting a spell in the palace could get thrown in the dungeons. Or worse.

Keladon pulled his watch from his pocket. Three-thirty. Presumably time enough to finish by six o'clock. He opened the book to see what spell Melos wanted him to cast.

Codex Doril-Haberiana, the title page read. *A collection of spells composed by the lost Jelorean masters, castable with the powers of a green magegem, discovered in a vault located in the vicinity of the town of Doril-Haberi in the Kingdom of Sodelerak, set and printed in Teisoret, capital city of said realm, in the 22nd year of the reign of Raboros, First of that name—*

Keladon turned the next pages, to the blocky geometric shapes of the Jelorean syllabary. The original document had been handwritten by some millenium-dead Jelorean scribe. Most likely the printer had set the pages of the codex in ignorance of the Jelorean language, simply copying the appearance of the syllabary's symbols. Without understanding what he set, the printer could well have introduced errors, or copied errors in the original, that a person fluent in Jelorean would have corrected. Keladon read the introduction to grasp the printer's understanding of the language, as well as the era in Jelorean history in which the original had been written. A few decades before the Jeloreans's final collapse, he assessed, and mentally corrected a number of obvious printing mistakes. The codex featured spells relevant to the physician's art.

His fingers found the leather bookmark. He opened the book, laid the front and back plates flat, and smoothed down the central crease with pressed-together fingertips. A memory came up of a dimly lit, sensual evening, his hands gliding over the warm, curved skin of a widowed lady whose name sadly eluded him.

His gaze went to the top center of the page, where the spell's name should be. His hands froze and his breath caught. He had never heard of this spell, but it made sense Melos and Norobom wanted it casted.

Father a Son.

Melos and Norobom? He wanted it too. If he could assure a boy, an heir to Raboros, would come from his current visit to the palace, he would return for the boy's claiming ceremony, and never return again. His thoughts turned, down a lane he had not let them go in the few days since the meeting with Melos and Norobom. He would be the father of Sodelerak's next king. Even though no one else could ever know his son's true father, he would. Wonder and pride swelled his chest.

Pride he could never show anyone else. The prudent parts of his mind quietly, calmly guided his pride like a tamed bull back to its corral.

He had work to do. Keladon read on. In keeping with the late date of composition, the spell's text assumed the mage knew which hand went where and when. *The magus is to grasp the sendpod.*

Sendpod? He puzzled for a moment before the most likely explanation, a printer's error, and a plausible correction occurred to him. *Seedpod* fit with the subject matter of the spell, but was it truly a late Jelorean term for *scrotum*? He knew the language well, but not with the mastery of a native speaker. Keladon rose. He'd seen a few Jelorean glossaries near the windows....

Half an hour later, and after a wary glance at his watch, he set the glossaries back in their places. The one with the most frank language dated back to the early years of the Jelorean empire, when *bullstones* was the most common term for testicles. The glossary from the late Jelorean period focused on technical terms relating to warfare, battle magic, and tax collection.

Assuming the intended word was *scrotum*, Keladon kept reading. The spell assessed animalcules in the male's semen (he wondered if the spell would work on animals as well as men) and rendered lifeless those that would impregnate a female with a girl-child.

The flux usable by the spell could no more than six-hundredths of a boil per drop of time. More than that and the spell would raise the temperature of the male's semen so much all its animalcules would die of heatstroke. Two-hundredths was recommended: a flux low enough for the pain suffered by the male to be tolerable, but high enough for the process to proceed quickly. The codex failed to guarantee success. *For a man who expels a typical amount of semen, maintain the spell for three hundred drops of time.* A little under three minutes, as time was counted in Sodelerak, but who knew how much was typical for a Jelorean man? *This will give him a son nine times in ten, if he impregnates the woman within two days.*

Presumably Melos had some intelligence the queen was near the peak of her tide of Samala. Or else he expected Keladon to repeat the spell as needed. Keladon reread the spell, then in his mind worked his way through its steps to be confident none were omitted by the author, and to know what he should expect at each moment. The testicles that could be lost to an error would be his own.

Time to begin. Although the room barred vision to anyone outside, as for sound, the books would muffle it, but the door would not.

Keladon pulled the fabric from the lumpy shape, revealing a green. He'd expected one, but still exhaled in admiration. The color was as rich as a well-kept lawn on a sunny spring day. A beautiful piece. He would wager it had never been tapped between its charging and the moment the palace mages had brought it up from Melos' vault. He didn't need so much charge—the mottled green one he'd just used in the king's audience chamber had more than six boils of flux left in it. Melos' palace mages would have told him that.

Melos wanted him to succeed.

Keladon's heartbeat slowed and pounded. What would Melos do if he failed?

He set his watch on the table, then untied the ribbons holding his breeches to his doublet. He had practice doing it himself, from visits over the years to prosperous young widows living in the vicinity of Korobei, but it would have been easier if Lar, his valet, were here. He worked his breeches and underhose down over his rump to mid-thigh and sat as if on a convenience stool.

His left hand gripped the magegem's handle. *"Attend me,"* he whispered. In the quiet room, the magegem would hear. Foolishness warmed his cheeks as his right hand cradled his scrotum. *"Target your energies on the seedpod I touch."* His chest tightened in expectation he had the word wrong and some disaster would lance his genitals. A pleasant tingle filled his scrotum and he exhaled in relief. *"Render lifeless any animalcules generative of a girl-child, flux two-hundredths of a boil per drop of time, begin."*

The tingle spread into his abdomen, behind the root of his manhood. It began to hurt. Keladon winced and kept his gaze on his watch. Three minutes. The pain grew more intense, switching from a tingle to pulses of pressure, like someone squeezed his scrotum. He loosened his right hand's grip but the pain clenched his fingers into a rigid claw. His breaths sounded ragged through clenched teeth. Two minutes to go—

The pulses of pressure increased in both intensity and duration. He pressed his lips together to keep from crying out, but he couldn't stop himself from whimpering. Sweat ran down his forehead and stung his eye. He blinked and shimmied his head and a drop of sweat flew to pop against the paper of the open book. He looked where it bled into the paper and read again that the level of flux he had chosen made the pain tolerable. Tolerable? Had the Jeloreans been made of stronger stuff than modern man, or had their mages reveled in the pain they could inflict under cover of their art? One minute and thirty seconds—

The pressure increased and the pulsing stopped, replaced by a monotonic agony compressing his scrotum and pushing against the root of his manhood. What mangling did his testicles suffer? His manhood, stupid thing, stirred and lifted off his thumb to stand against his abdomen. If the spell failed and he sired a daughter, would it be able to rise to another attempt to impregnate the queen? One minute to go. His lips remained compressed, but now muffled, high-pitched grunts, not whimpers, escaped them. Sweat ran down all his exposed skin and thick, unpleasant heat swaddled him under his doublet. Thirty seconds.

Spots swam in his vision, and the ticking of the seconds seemed to slow, like mockery from some cruel false Jelorean god. Fifteen seconds. *The end is in sight, remain steadfast—*

As soon as the last second ticked by, he whispered, *"Stop rendering lifeless any animalcules. Release the target. Re—* " Almost an error that would drain the magegem, and damage its storage cabinet and other magegems around it. *"No flux. Release your attention from me."* He pulled his hands away from the magegem and his crotch. Keladon slumped back in his chair. Sweat continued to run down his skin, and his burning genitals sat exposed to the room's air.

Cautiously, he looked down, expecting to see bruising and swelling. But his scrotum and manhood looked intact. Pain throbbed. He pulled up his underhose and breeches, but his hands shook when he tried threading the ribbons on his doublet through his breeches's matching holes. He caught his breath a few minutes before his hands held steady enough for him to work.

Breeches retied, he stood and started for the door. Each step hurt, and it seemed impossible his manhood would ever rise again.

A FEW HOURS LATER, Keladon sat near the fireplace in his guest suite. On a nearby table, an empty plate held chicken bones and sprigs of rosemary, next to a half-full goblet. The wine had dulled the ache pervading his entire crotch.

Knuckles rapped on the doorway to his suite. Lar, his valet, set down his darning needle and Keladon's spare doublet, and went to the door. After a short conversation, the door thudded shut and Lar cleared his throat. "The Master of Offices has requested your presence, Your Illustriousness, and has sent a footman to guide you."

He wanted the queen bedded now? Melos would give him no more time to heal? Keladon frowned, then set his annoyance aside.

Though his valet was a young man, with only two years in his service, he knew Lar enough to glean the valet's thoughts from his tone of voice. "You think the man without has some other purpose?" Keladon asked.

Lar looked surprised and contrite. "I only say what he told me, Your Illustriousness." A faint leering grin lurked around his face.

If he could misdirect his valet's curiosity about his doings, so much the better to keep this whole affair secret. "If you had to guess at his purpose, what would you say?"

Lar blushed. "Your Illustriousness—"

"I know you saw me return this afternoon on unsteady legs with my breeches poorly retied."

Lar's grin broke out. "It's not for me to ask who a fine lord passes his time with, Your Illustriousness. But is it the same lady as this afternoon?"

Keladon rose from his chair and rebuked Lar with his gaze. "A gentlemen protects the reputation of ladies."

"Of course, Your Illustriousness, my pardons to you and—"

"The door." Keladon maintained a haughty look. He strode toward the door and Lar scurried to open it for him. It would only take minutes for Lar to gossip to the palace servants that Keladon had taken pleasure that day with two different ladies of the court.

Once Keladon stepped out, the waiting footman bowed, turned, and started walking. Keladon followed. Candles in sconces mounted high on the walls lit the quiet corridors. A few other people were about, primarily servants carrying dinner trays or chamberpots. When the others came into view, the footman changed course at the earliest opportunity to pass through empty galleries or take stairways up or down. Mostly down: after a time, the footman pulled a hilted candle from his pocket, touched the wick to a flame in one of the sconces, then led the way down a creaky wooden stair into an unlit tunnel.

They kept on. Rough, striated stone formed the tunnel walls, and Keladon ducked his head in spots. The ceilings ranged from brick to plaster, both materials dark with years of candle and lantern soot. Despite more twists and turns, Keladon gauged their direction as westward, toward the base of the old castle.

·   ·   ·

THE FOOTMAN STOPPED at a closed door, knocked twice, and stepped back. From inside came the sound of a key working a lock. The door swung open, spilling lamplight into the tunnel. The footman bowed to Keladon and swept his arm to indicate the open door. Keladon stepped through, and the footman shut the door behind him.

Melos stood next to a tall, wide rack bearing kegs of strong-smelling beer. His lantern rested in the cleft formed by neighboring kegs. Though less dank than the tunnel, the cellar was as cool and, outside the reach of the lantern, as dimly lit. "Your Illustriousness, are you ready for your task?"

Keladon glared. "My testicles still ache. I understand the window of good chance at success is a short one, but couldn't it wait a day?"

"This evening is the best chance we shall have for the next month. I could not grant you your desired audience with His Majesty before this afternoon. If you had not sought that audience, we would have had you do your work in the library yesterday." Melos gave him a cold look.

Keladon crossed his arms. "Tell me what to do, and I shall get to my task."

"Follow me." Melos walked around the racked kegs. Candlelight cast dancing shadows across thick exposed beams running the length of the ceiling. Gray stones formed the opposite wall of the cellar, and over most of it, cracks ran through the mortar joining the large stone blocks. Melos trailed his fingertips over the wall, found a block at about chest-height, and pushed. His feet slid backward and he stiffened his legs. He pushed again and his legs trembled. He stepped back and his torso heaved with exertion.

"Perhaps you retain the strength I have lost," Melos said.

Keladon stepped closer. "Here?"

Melos nodded. Keladon braced his right foot against a keg, and pushed his right arm against the stone block.

A section of the wall swung inward on grumbling hinges. The opening had jagged outlines from the uneven sizes of the blocks making up the hidden door. A cold draft touched Keladon's hands and face and set Melos' candle flickering. The candlelight revealed the top steps of a dark wooden stairway. "Down," Keladon said, "and then?"

"When your father built the new wings of the palace and joined them to the old castle, we marked all the junctions in the tunnels and secret passages the king needs to follow to reach the queen's bedchamber. The symbol you should look for is a horizontal line of green paint, long as a man's forearm, at eye level. The line has a sharply angled hook at the end in the queen's direction." Melos handed him the candle. "Go, now. The king has heeded my request to remain alone in his chambers for the next two hours, and Queen Lilera's servants have been barred from her private rooms until I give the word. When you are finished, swing the conception harness down from the ceiling and tie her legs to it for twenty minutes. Then come back here. I will be waiting."

The boards creaked under Keladon's feet. After the last step, the tunnel bent to the right. His candle soon revealed his tunnel ended in a T-intersection with another. A step closer brought into view a horizontal line of green paint with a hook pointing to the left. The intersection smelled of stale beer. Shards of a broken mug lay in a kicked-together heap on the floor under the guide symbol.

Someone had disfigured the guide symbol. Charcoal lines fleshed out the symbol with a glans, a penile shaft, and a scrotum sprouting hair. All three of the defacements had been drawn by different hands. The servants must have known for years that Raboros never visited the queen in her bedchamber, and they could mock the royal couple in this way without fear of rebuke. *Misdirecting Lar was wiser than you knew.*

He turned left and took a step before a question stopped him. Could he find his way out of the tunnel? How many mug shards and defaced guide symbols were down here? Probably few, but why not make this site even more distinctive? Keladon stepped closer to the

defaced guide symbol and extended the candle toward it. He hesitated at the immaturity of what he planned, then shook his head and
chuckled at himself. It fit perfectly with the coarse boyishness of the
graffiti. He touched the upper edge of the candle at the urethra
drawn in the charcoal glans. Molten wax, milky in the candlelight,
dribbled down the wall and quickly solidified. He set off in the
queen's direction.

The remaining length of tunnel was free of interlineations and
spilled beer. The floor rose and fell, he guessed to avoid tunnels at
other depths. The mouths of cross-tunnels welled up in the darkness. He paused at each opening to listen for footsteps or a person's
breaths, but heard nothing more than dripping water and scurrying
rats.

The guide symbol directed him into yet another tunnel, but this
one soon turned a corner to a narrow flight of stairs. The boards had
been built with care and did not creak under his feet. The stairs kept
climbing. The stone walls gave way to plaster with peeling white-
wash. The stairs switched back and forth at small landings, and
Keladon paused at a couple of them to catch his breath before
climbing further.

The stairway grew even narrower; Keladon raised both his
elbows a few inches away from his body and his sleeves brushed the
plaster. His father had grown stout late in life. How had he made the
climb to Larabos's daughter? Perhaps he hadn't. His father's
appetites had remained vigorous despite his age, and Keladon's
mother had surely not been his only mistress.

He reached another landing and looked around for the next flight
of stairs. He found none, only a narrow door lacking a handle. It
lacked hinges on this side. His breaths came heavily, but no longer
from exertion. Keladon extended his hand and pushed the door
open.

· · ·

AFTER THE CANDLELIT gloom of the tunnel and the staircase, the Queen's bedchamber dazzled his eyes. On lowboy tables stood stacks of books. A vanity bore two candelabras, flanking a magnifying mirror and small boxes spilled over with face powders and jewelry. Thick rugs of Peluraki design, displaying images of peasants working fields, covered the floor in overlapping profusion between the door he'd entered and a four-post bed. Drapes covered the windows and more Peluraki rugs, these showing hunting scenes, hung on the walls. From between wall hangings peeked thick stones and rough mortar.

THE PELURAKI PRISONER had a velvet-lined cell.

Queen Lilera stood at a reading table with her back to the door. A thick dress of blue velvet followed the lines of her figure, and pins studded with diamonds clasped a blue veil to her dark blond hair. She closed her book and he bowed as she turned toward him with a rustle of her skirt and petticoats. "Your Majesty, I am Keladon, son of Radobom and squire of Korobei."

He held the bow, waiting for her response. The pattern in the rug showed a farmer standing behind an ox team, plowing a field in the shadow of a Peluraki castle. Memories of trampled fields, of tumbling stones, of screaming men came to him.

Queen Lilera spoke in a measured tone. "My late father-in-law sired a hundred bastards, yet Melos and Norobom sent the butcher of Sherbal Ford to my bedchamber."

Though she pronounced the placename with a Peluraki accent, he instantly knew what she meant. Memories of the final battle of the campaign rushed into his mind. Keladon maintained his bow, and the fingers of his left hand curled slightly while his right forefinger twitched. The Jelorean words *Burn At Distance* sounded in his mind's ear. He shut his eyes to push the memory away. "You may call me what you wish, Your Majesty."

"A queen does not need a bastard's permission to do that," she said. "Rise. I would look on your face."

He stood and met her gaze. He had only seen her once before, when he stood in the back of the hall at her wedding to Raboros. She had been pretty then, in a timid girlish way. Now, though, her mature beauty sent shivers over his neck and chest. The intervening decades had given her the assured gravity of adulthood. He could not look away, even though her face showed disgust.

"I could look on you and almost believe you are a man like any other. But I know you are not. Tell me, how many sons of Plurach did your powers send to their graves at Sherbal Ford?"

The memories grew strong. He sweated despite the cool room. "Need we speak of such things, madam?"

"Do you want to do what Melos and Norobom asked of you?" She crossed her arms and gave him a haughty look. "Tell me how many sons of Plurach you slew that day."

He wanted to look at the floor, the bed, anything but her eyes. He took a deep breath and met her gaze. "Between four and six thousand Peluraki foot and about six hundred knights, madam. Roughly another two thousand more foot drowned attempting to flee across the river."

"Eight thousand six hundred in sum?"

He had worked the numbers in his head on many night in his prayers to Balar, nearly two decades ago, at a time when he still prayed. "As best I recall, madam."

"So few? In your camp, after your half-brother took me as his prize, your compatriots spoke as if you had turned a hundred thousand daughters of Plurach into widows."

Keladon shook his head. "Men brag, madam. I didn't ask them to, then or since."

"Oh yes. I know you resigned your position as a battlemage, and you've retired to your estate to peacefully work magic. You're the butcher with a conscience."

"Madam, I slew men, highborn and low, who happened to serve

a king not my own. I take no glory in it. I have vowed to never do it again."

"You have? You don't need to." Queen Lilera coldly regarded him. "You were richly rewarded for your butchery. You have an estate for life, leisure for your researches, and all the books and magegems you need. Renounce all those fruits, and I shall believe you are contrite."

"I lack a taste for blood, madam, but I am fortunate I can use my skills and knowledge to serve Sodelerak in other ways. Just as you have been asked to serve Sodelerak—"

"I have been forced to serve Sodelerak by wearing its crown in public when your customs demand it. Your power, bastard, wrenched me from the loving embraces of my father and brother and trapped me in this tower—"

"Trapped? You have freedom—"

"I do? Yes, I may freely walk the tower, the west wing of the new palace, and the courtyard within the west wing. If I pretend Melos's spies are not watching me from a distance, I can pretend to myself I have the liberty of the outer gardens and two of the new palace's other three wings. And since my father-in-law died, I have been freed from your half-brother's uninterested poking between my legs. But those things are not freedom. You know that as well as I. The only freedom I have is the freedom to refuse you." Queen Lilera's eyes flashed with anger and challenge.

He remembered her earlier words. "I gave you the answer you sought, madam, about my deeds at Suherabal Ford."

"I said not answering me would deny Melos and Norobom the result they wanted. I did not say answering me would grant them it. They sent the one man I will not consent to lie beneath."

Don't take this guff from any woman, part of him thought, *not even the queen*. He could wrestle her to the bed, force up her skirts, and have his way with her. Neither Raboros nor the courtiers would be troubled, and Queen Lilera could not hate him any more than she already did.

But a woman with cause to hate a man could redirect her hate to his unborn child. A peasant woman around Korobei could find silphium or pennyroyal in the woods and ingest it to kill a child and expel it from her body. Melos would try to stop Queen Lilera from receiving such an herb, but were she motivated enough, she could get it, and the loss of the child would appear to arise from natural causes.

Also, even if she could not hate him more for taking her by force, he would hate himself. It wouldn't be the same as using magic to kill, but would still be a barbarous use of the advantage in strength nature had given him. A gentleman had no need for such recourse.

"I don't know that refusing me is your only freedom, madam, but you do have it. May I sit?" Keladon gestured at a nearby divan.

She inclined her head to allow him.

As he sat, he glanced at a stack of books on a nearby table. Frothy novels, written in the past few years, set in a Jelorea that never was, about a courtier who worked as a spy, whose magegems never ran out of charge and could inspire any woman to lead him to her bedchamber. He quirked his lips in passing. The situation binding Queen Lilera and him had no room for such fancies.

"Although you have that freedom, madam, exercising it will gain you nothing. However many bastards and cuckoo eggs my father might have gotten on wenches and other men's wives, I am the only one he claimed. For that reason, I am the only man Melos and Norobom will permit to stand for your husband in this task."

Queen Lilera set her fists on her hips and leaned toward him. "They shall be gravely disappointed. I will not lie beneath you."

He would hate to subject himself to Father a Son another time, but he would not let her see that. Keladon stretched his hands along the divan. "Madam, if you turn me away tonight, I shall come back in a month, and if need be, every month after that."

"I will never lie beneath you."

He shrugged. "If not me, madam, then you will lie beneath no man."

"Do you mean those words to frighten me?" She laughed coldly. "They fill me with joy."

With an exaggerated sigh, Keladon waved the back of his hand at the stack of frothy novels. "Madam, unless you have addled your mind with these absurd fancies, my words should frighten you. Every month that passes without you conceiving a child will make it more likely Melos will pressure the king to divorce you and find a wife more pliant and in the full bloom of fecundity."

She glowered. "Neither my husband the bugger, nor the old man who tells him how to wear his crown, would ever dare. If they cast me aside, I would tell everyone from the highest lord to the lowest knave why my husband never fathered a child. My brother, King Aril, would rouse the lions sleeping in the hearts of the sons of Plurach at the insult to a daughter of their royal house. Would my husband allow you to remain at peace at your little estate, when war would be unleashed on your kingdom and your peasants would hear for the first time their king is inclined contrary to nature? Or would he force you to become a butcher again?"

His legs stiffened as if to push himself away from her words. "The peasants and goodmen of Sodelerak would believe their king is a robust and virile man, and blame you for the failure to produce an heir." He gave her a calm look. "They would reject your rumors of the king's inclination as Peluraki lies. Those of us who know better would keep quiet for the sake of our kingdom, our positions, or both."

A passing doubt was visible on her face. "The other kings would side with Plurach against my husband."

Keladon turned a wry eye at the stack of novels before speaking to her. She spoke from more blindness to reality. "The kings of Dosoten and Rak-pawindu know the truth already. Their emissaries have seen King Raboros hold court often enough. But both those kings have unmarried daughters who either cannot or are unlikely to inherit their thrones. Those girls would be pawns for the gambit." Lilera too had been a pawn, a sacrifice offered by her father to give him more time to develop Plurach's pieces. Keladon kept that thought to himself. "Melos would counsel King Raboros to take one or the other of those girls, thus cementing an alliance with her father against Peluraki aggression."

He leaned forward. "Though there would be no Peluraki aggression. Your brother has had cause to declare war several times during his reign, yet never has. Pelurak has some battlemages now, but we have more, with better training, and more caches of magegems to tap." He paid little attention to his own words, and much to her reaction. How much might she know of her brother's war capability? From her face, she either was so apprised she knew he spoke the truth, or so uninformed she feared he did.

Queen Lilera looked down to sturdy peasants in the rug, and her eyes glistened in the candlelight. He remembered again the timid girl brought before the altar of Balar and Samala to wed his half-brother. But her sadness and resignation soon softened, making way for her face to show a haughty, regal bearing. His heart lifted in his chest. "You shall be the most lucky bastard any king ever fathered. You shall lie with a queen and live."

AFTERWARD, he swung the legrests of the conception harness down from the ceiling. The hinges groaned from long disuse. Flecks of rust fell like a flurry of bloody snow. Once the legrests were unfolded, her legs remained solidly on the mattress.

"Your legs, madam?"

She left them on the bed. "Do what you must."

He lifted her legs and leaned them against the legrests's padding. The light of a small candle made her skin milk-pale. Sadness panged him. He was not the monster she thought him to be, and seemingly nothing he could do would change that. Yet he had to try. He buckled a padded strap across her shins, an inch above her ankles, careful to make it secure but not too tight. She would be comfortable... at least as comfortable as anyone could be with her legs raised straight in the air for twenty minutes.

He slid across her bed and reached to the floor for his doublet and retrieved his watch from its pocket. Because she remained nude, he would as well. After sitting cross-legged on the bed, he set the watch near him and squinted at the time.

"You need not stay," Lilera said. She stared expressionlessly at the ceiling. "But have the manners to tell Melos to alert my servants when I may be freed of this thing."

"I put you into it," he replied. "It would be fitting for me to release you from it." He gestured at the bed. "May I sit?"

She looked at him with distant eyes, and the sadness panged him again. "Can I stop you?" she said.

Uneasily, he sat. A minute ticked past. The curves of her body, capturing shadows cast by the candle, drew his gaze and repelled it both. To leer at the queen would dishonor them both, but he would never get another chance to see her nude body.

Her stare turned keen and she studied her legs and the contraption of iron, wood, and leather binding them, and relief filled Keladon when she said, "Would there were some magic to spare me this."

He looked away from her and at the bed curtain, in the direction of the table next to the divan bearing her foolish books. "Magic is not the easy matter some puffed novels make it out to be, Your Majesty."

A fraction of her earlier anger returned to her voice. "I am aware of that, squire of Korobei. Do you think all I have learned is from trivial entertainments?"

"I only know what books you have—"

"From a bowl of apples, you pick the one pear." She kept a haughty look on him as she pointed at different spots on the bed curtains, indicating different tables he'd glimpsed around the room. "I have books on the histories of Jelorea, of Sodlerach since the rediscovery of magegems, descriptions of magegem vaults and caches, *A Primer on the Capabilities of Magegems* by Telapuj...."

His cheeks suddenly burned. "My apologies, madam. Clearly you have a stronger grasp than most of what magic can and cannot do." Memories of Raboros' boredom during the afternoon's demonstrations came to Keladon. "Particularly, Telapuj's *Primer* is the best introduction for people untrained in the art."

"You draw that conclusion in great measure because he spent eight months researching that book at your school?"

She had studied her books closely indeed. His thoughts whirled, and he covered them with a light tone. "No. Only in small measure."

Lilera almost smiled, but her face soon grew clouded. "I well know there is no spell to enhance a woman's fecundity. The Jelorean magelords cast spells for their own needs. Plainly women meant nothing to them. If a woman could not conceive, what of it to them? If she conceived, but could not give birth safely, what of that?"

"Your thoughts on the Jeloreans fit with mine, madam."

Lilera turned her hauteur upon him. "So why have you not composed a spell to replace—" She waved her fingers at the conception harness. "—this thing?"

His genitals shrank from a sudden cold feeling. "Madam, I assure you—"

"How difficult could it be? Say *Jojipo bobe yulato*, and then the Jelorean for 'make the animalcules in semen swim faster.'"

Keladon drew in a breath. "First, madam, you have mispronounced the words for 'attend me.'" He enunciated, "*Jojipo bobi yuloto*—"

"When counting your flaws," Lilera said, "I missed your pedantry."

"If you ever have the chance to use a gem, madam, you will thank me for my pedantry. If a mage mispronounces the command to attend, the gem will do nothing. If a mage mispronounces a command in the midst of the spell, the gem could inflict grievous harm."

Lilera looked chastened.

Keladon went on. "Second, the gems only respond to particular

Jelorean words. A green understands the word for 'animalcules,' but won't understand any words to make them swim faster. Though you have it right we can compose new spells, we are limited to use of the words the Jeloreans taught the gems."

She lay silently for a time. "Thank you for your explanation, sir. All I have known is what I have read, but much wisdom remains unwritten, and no one has ever spoken to me of such matters."

Longing sounded in her voice and saddened him. But what could he do to sate it? Yet should he not try? He checked his watch to cover his thoughts. "Your time on the harness has ended, Your Majesty." He unbuckled the strap holding her legs.

She lowered them to the bed. Her face lost expression. "My shift, please."

"Of course, Your Majesty." He hesitated. "You sound less pleased to be free of the harness than I would have expected."

Her thoughts left faint traces on her face. Finally, she drew a breath and turned to him. "You were supposed to be a monster, squire of Korobei."

"What am I instead?"

"The only person to converse with me about weighty subjects since... since...."

The sadness Keladon felt out of sympathy for returned, this time joined by the disdain Keladon had felt for his half-brother that afternoon. He could forgive Raboros for not seeking the pleasures of the flesh with Lilera. But neglecting her mind and spirit had left her a worthless asset, a rusting sword or a granary full of fungal rot.

He climbed off the bed and stepped through the curtains. Naked in the queen's bedchamber; a story he would take to his grave. Birds fluttered and cooed outside the windows as he retrieved her shift. "Perhaps we could converse again, Your Majesty."

She paused with her shift halfway on, still obscuring her face. "How?" A plaintive note cracked the word.

"I will stay here at the palace until we know our—encounter— has proven fruitful." He felt foolish to use the euphemism. He pulled on his garments as he kept talking. "That will take at minimum two weeks. I would be honored if, during that time, you requested, through Melos, that I demonstrate my arts to you." Another thought came to him. "As part of the demonstration, madam, I could guide you as you cast a spell."

Her eyes widened with a mix of delight and alarm. "Am I capable?"

"I should think so."

"Do not flatter me." Her voice climbed in pitch. Why did she expect flattery again? Had she ever received it here in Sodelerak? "I have never heard of a woman commanding a magegem."

"The magegems attend whomever commands them. They do not heed their wielder's sex. Among the researchers working at Korobei are several priestesses of Samala."

"I am no priestess," Queen Lilera said, "of your goddess or of mine. I am a base woman who happens to be one king's daughter and another's wife."

"You have read about the magelords. Whatever your sins might be, compared to them, you are a saint." Keladon looked deeply into her eyes. "You are amply capable of commanding a magegem."

A hopeful look lightened her face, but she flung it away with a shake of her head. "Melos would never allow it."

Melos did not trust her, of course, but: "The magegems do not belong to him. They are Raboros's property."

Her eyebrows arched. "Are you naïve?"

"I know Melos commands the men who guard the door to the magegem vault," Keladon said. "Yet wouldn't he open the vault if your husband ordered him?"

"You are naïve. Raboros would never order it. After I was forced into his possession, he set me on a high shelf to collect dust while he plays with his dolls. He would gain nothing by allowing me to touch a magegem."

He wanted to tell her some sweet lie, but they both knew the truth. "Yes, but he owes me."

"Owes?"

Keladon spread his hands to indicate her bed and their recent use of it. "He asked me to provide him with an heir. He should be grateful."

She peered at him with a mix of compassion and warning. "How did you survive growing up in the court? If you are not naïve you are dangerously close to it."

"I avoid the intrigues of the palace. Your husband has never had cause to doubt my loyalty. Asking him a favor is not disloyal—"

"It would be worse than a crime," Queen Lilera said. "It would be a mistake. He already will look for a reason to destroy you. Don't give him one for something as foolish as asking to give me command of a magegem. I am not worth your life."

Keladon bowed. "As you wish, Your Majesty. But I urge you to continue your studies of magic. The mages at my school spend years in study before they first cast a spell. I will send you copies of all the primers and beginners's tomes in my library, and we can converse by letter until a time may come that Raboros would give you opportunity to cast a spell."

"Melos will read every letter between us."

Her headboard's ornate geometric carvings in Dosotenese style, the fashion twenty years ago, caught his attention. "I will write knowing he will read what I say." He studied her face. "You fear my half-brother would take my letters as a reason to destroy me?"

"Yes."

"Cannot the queen command me to correspond with her? Only Raboros could countermand you, but we both know he would not bother to do so." A tug in the back of his mind told him he needed to return to the cellar where he'd left Melos. "I would I could stay, but your husband must be tiring of his enforced solitude."

"Yes, he must." Lilera studied him in the dim light. "I too would you could stay."

"Madam, please consider commanding me to write you

regarding the subject of magic. You have both curiosity and a keen intellect to study it."

"You flatter me, sir," she said, her voice hollowly formal.

He sought the right words to share his feelings, and found some that at least hinted at them. "I came here tonight not knowing what kind of woman you are, but I leave proud to call you my queen."

WINTER

Interlude

L ilera pulled her shawl tighter around her shoulders and huddled deeper into the settee. The frigid night seemed to seep through the stones of the wall. The hanging tapestries could not block it and the fire crackling at the hearth could not dispel it.

She hated every season of her confinement, but winter most of all.

Yet this winter held a warmth coming from her soul. Her stomach had finally settled after the first nauseated months of pregnancy. Her child had not yet moved, but she knew he was there, quietly growing in the shelter of her enlarging belly. He would move when he was ready. Though he had been put into her by a cursed destiny she could not resist, she found herself loving him.

Him? Yes, him. An intuition had struck when she leafed through a codex found in a magegem vault near the town of Doril-Haberi. The royal midwife, who came every week to measure her belly and peer up her skirt, wearily shook her gray head every time Lilera told her. *You can't know*, the midwife always said, and Lilera always replied with a regal smile.

She had another book on magic open across her knees. This one held all the commands known to be heeded by green magegems, each command followed by paragraphs of commentary by Keladon and his colleagues. A few interleaved pages held commands and commentary they had discovered since the tome had been printed and bound.

Why is it necessary to learn each command by itself? she had asked in a recent letter to him. *It should be sufficient to remember each spell as a whole.*

His reply had been polite, though pedantic. *First, knowing the commands of each spell is like knowing the letters of an alphabet or the symbols of the Jelorean syllabary; it makes it easier to read whole words in the latter cases and cast entire spells in the former. Second, it is necessary to know what each command is capable and incapable of doing, in order to aim it at the proper target and expend the optimal amount of energy to have an effect without wasting the irreplaceable resource. Third, and I cannot emphasize this point enough, the Jeloreans did not compose all the spells that can exist. The commands may be combined or rearranged in novel ways to compose new spells. We are on the cusp of a new age of magical capabilities and commands are the fundamental particles of those capabilities.* She had pictured him pausing with his quill over the paper and had smiled at his next words. *Have you continued your lessons in Jelorean elocution?*

The memory of his letter, and of him, warmed her. Her gaze flowed across the Jelorean symbols without reading. After a moment, she caught herself. Keladon had spoken to her as someone with a brain in her head and satisfied a long-felt craving of her body. Yet to imagine something more might come of those things was pure girlishness. Their encounter had proven fruitful, he would train her from a distance in the theory of magic, and she would remain trapped in the palace. He had the liberty of the kingdom, and all the tools, pennyroyal and assurance caps, needed to dally with its ladies. He would soon forget her. Sadness nibbled at the edges of her mind.

She turned her attention to the book. Yet here, too, she indulged in foolish longing. She could practice speaking Jelorean, memorize lists of commands, even imagine curling her fingers around a magegem's handle, but Melos would never permit her to cast a spell. She should tell Keladon to save his attentions for students who could someday become mages—

A faint rustle came from outside the window. She looked up and listened. A beak tapped the glass and wings flapped against the window's stone frame. Many years of habit gripped her. She closed the book, set it down, and went to the window.

Step around the window drape. The moonless night left the bird barely outlined by starlight. Anyone about? No sign, but the rest of the palace lay too far away and below to say for certain. Guilt tightened her shoulders. *Come to the window more often when there is no messenger, to make your presence here unremarkable to Melos's spies.* Open the window. To the east, the city of Teisoret was as quiet and dark as it could get. Scoop up the bird. A red-breasted starling, of course, native to Plurach, but its winter moult had shed its color and added white spangling to its plumage. A casual observer would not notice it a stranger to Sodlerach. Its heart raced and it shivered from fear, cold, and the magical energies that had compelled it to journey hundreds of miles from her brother's palace to her window. Its black eyes darted around the room as she carried it back to the settee.

She sat with the bird in her lap. The message capsule had been clasped to its right leg, as usual. Release the clasp. The message capsule fell and rolled down into the gap between cushions. She would find it later. Lilera took the bird back around the drape to the window. Put it out the window. She was certain none of the birds ever made it back to Plurach, but in this weather, it would die before it could get to any shelter in the Forest of Larabos. It would probably die on her ledge, fall to the grounds, and be eaten by some cat.

Pity touched Lilera, but her brother had long impressed on her the need to rid herself of all evidence of his letters to her. He knew what was best. She set the bird on the ledge and quickly swung the window shut. She shivered all the way back to the settee and her fingers trembled as she dug the message capsule out from between the cushions. It took a few minutes standing by the fire to feel warm enough to face Aril's message.

Her magnifying glass lay in its proper place in her sewing box. The rubies on the gold handle glinted in the candlelight. At first touch, the handle chilled her fingers. She set the message capsule on the lid of her sewing box and pressed the heel of the handle down on it until the thin porcelain broke. After picking out the tiny, tight roll of paper, she swept the porcelain fragments into her hand and tossed them into the fireplace.

Back on the settee, she picked up the tome on yellow magegems. A moment of guilt pressed her lips together. Using Keladon's loan to her this way.... She unrolled the message and used the weight of the magnifying glass to press it flat against the tome's rigid cover.

My dearest sister,

The Sodlerachan ambassador finally delivered the news of your pregnancy to me and the Councilors of State. The Councilors were all truly surprised, and I am skillful enough at dissembling that I appeared surprised. "Pregnant? How can that be? My brother-in-law is a bugger!" Oh, how I secretly exulted at the ambassador's discomfort at me baldly stating the open secret!

Yet for a fat Sodlerachan, he is an adequate diplomatist. He put on a dissembling face of his own. "I don't what you mean, Your Majesty. Regardless, Queen Lilera is three months with child."

I thanked him for his news and prepared a letter to you that should arrive by diplomatic courier within a fortnight. Add as many days as your jailers usually take to read your mail to receive it.

But, here, I can speak honestly. As you concluded from my earlier words, I knew before the ambassador's audience that you are pregnant. I also know that your husband is not the father of your child, and instead, a secret cabal of his advisors forced the bastard of Sherbal Ford upon you. My agents in your husband's palace gave me this intelligence.

Many feelings swirl through me when I contemplate your pregnancy. I feel shame you have been forced into this situation. Not because you bear a cuckoo's egg—men only condemn women who bear another man's child out of the hope it will keep their wives from doing the same. Not even because the true father is a bastard himself. He is the son of a king, after all, and showed his mettle in battle against us. I feel shame because Father and I could not earn the victory needed to decide your destiny; instead, defeat compelled us to hand you over to be bred to a Sodlerachan.

Was it her brother's place to decide her destiny? The question sounded in her mind for a moment, before other parts of her smothered it with unease. Old habits gripped her limbs, her emotions, her thoughts. She would not question Aril's words again.

Why had she doubted for even a moment that she should do as he commanded? Keladon's letters? They were no different than the base novels of a romantic Jelorea that never was; a source of idle wishes. She should have ordered him to leave her in the conception harness rather than let him sow delusions in her mind.

She returned to the letter.

Yet I also feel happiness at the opportunity your pregnancy gives us. Through my agents, I have plans afoot to turn the birth of your child, should it be a boy and your husband's putative heir, into a disaster for him and liberation for you and your blessed-to-be-half-Plurachan child. I can say no more now, for the precise steps of the plan are not yet finalized, and given the distance between me and your husband's palace, my agents must take some actions on their own. Should one of my agents approach you, and ask you to take certain steps at certain times, do as he says. Your doing will benefit your family of birth and your native land.

My love for you, dearest sister, remains as strong as it was in our childhood days together.

Yours, ever,

Aril.

Lilera spent a few moments with her eyes shut as she longed for

Plurach, the old palace, her place in her family. She remembered childhood summers, when shafts of golden sunlight slanted through the high windows of the grand hall while she and Aril played. A deep breath, and she put the longing aside just enough. Feelings must not be indulged when work must be done.

Following long habit, Lilera read the letter, then shut her eyes and tried to recall it word for word. It took her four times instead of the usual two. The midwives had never warned her pregnancy would dull her wits. She then picked up the magnifying glass, creased the paper lengthwise to expose it as fully as possible to its environs, and cast it into the fireplace.

SUMMER 1

From Korobei to the Palace

L ate in the afternoon of the second day of their ride from Korobei, Keladon and Lar entered Harumal Wood. The fallow fields of the last village, splotched bright green by clover, ended abruptly at a pair of signposts on either side of the road. Into each gray granite post had been chiseled the royal arms, now worn down by years. A royal wood, its exploit forbidden to commoners. Though with no more barrier than the granite posts and infrequent inspections by the district reeve, the common folk of the nearby village no doubt regularly violated the ban.

A year ago, he would have sympathized with peasants sneaking into the wood to take a few rabbits or fell enough trees to build an altar to the Divine Couple. Now, Keladon sourly puckered his lips. The wood and the game dwelling in it only belonged to King Raboros for now. In due time this property would pass to Keladon's—nephew.

Only five people in the world know you are the father of a future king. You should rejoice in the latter fact, not feel disappointment in the former.

A few more paces took them into the wood. The thick canopy of oaks dappled the road with sunlight. The deeper parts of the wood beckoned with cool greenery. Vines climbed their trunks and sent runners along the roadside in thick green bands. A chattering jay landed, rustling a shrub's branches. Rabbits scampered in the undergrowth nearby, and deeper in the wood, a larger animal snapped fallen twigs.

"Will we make Haru town by nightfall, Your Illustriousness?" Lar said. He labored under a heavy pack containing most of their baggage. The end of his walking stick beat a slow rhythm on the packed dirt of the road.

From the back of his gelding, Keladon peered down at his valet. "We shall. Do you fear the wood at night?"

"I've heard tell of bandits about, and now, with so many fine folk on the way to the palace for the newborn prince's claiming ceremony—"

"The reeves and local lords have swept from these woods all the bandits who arose in the years between Larabos' death and Radobom's coronation," Keladon said. "And should bandits be about, I have ample means of defense." His sword hung from his waist, and more importantly, a bag hanging from his saddle's right front horn held four fully-charged gems, two greens and two blues. Though the gems had no role in combat, brandishing one should scare off most attackers.

The walking stick thumped twice on the packed dirt. "As you say, Your Illustriousness."

Keladon ignored his valet's doubtful tone. They walked on. The road wound a bit as it climbed a gentle slope. From ahead came the groaning crash of a felled tree. After cresting the ridgeline, they would have two miles of shallow descent to Haru town. Months of traffic since last winter had pounded the dirt into a firm and mostly even road, marred only by pats of ox dung from journeying carters. "We will make faster time each day of this journey than we did through rain and cold last autumn," Keladon said.

"Earlier to each night's inn," Lar said, "where the lasses will be wearing lighter garments, and the news of the prince's birth will make them more willing to shed them."

Keladon made no reply. Ever since his evening with Lilera, his usual pattern of dalliances had failed to satisfy him, and by late spring, he'd entirely given them up. Every day, he thought of Lilera. She had developed a strong understanding of the theory of magic, as well as of spells that could be cast by a green. They shared letters as teacher and student, and someday, he hoped, would share them as friends. His heart quickened with another thought. Perhaps, in six months or a year, should Melos want assurance against a disaster striking the prince, he would get another night in Lilera's bedchamber. But that would be all he could ever know. Nothing else could come of his longing for her and he should set it aside.

They crested the ridgeline and started downslope. The road curved sharply to the left. Keladon followed the road and stopped his horse. The tree he'd heard fall—a young maple with smooth, greenish-brown bark—lay across the road. One end of the trunk bore the chiseled marks of an ax.

Keladon twisted in his saddle and looked at the wood on either side. Lar's words about bandits returned to mind. "You may be righ—"

A faint whizzing sound came from his left, then pain bloomed in his upper arm. A quick glance showed no tear in his doublet's sleeve and no blood, but spots swam in his vision. He couldn't move his arm. A slung stone had broken one of his bones, and every passing second brought the bandit in the woods closer to seating and slinging the second—

Keladon pulled his left foot from the stirrup and slid down the gelding's right flank. From the trees to the left of the road came the clack of a stone against a trunk. His horse remained stolid, poor beast. Despite the pain from his arm, Keladon kept on his feet when his boots landed on the road. His right hand worked at the knot holding the bag of magegems to the saddlehorn. Finally he released the bag and clutched its neck in his right hand. Though tight, his grip didn't hurt enough to distract him from his broken arm.

Lar crouched and cast about wide-eyed glances.

"Pretend to run off," Keladon told him. His teeth clenched and sweat dewed on his forehead. "No bandit would chase a servant when his master lies wounded. Hide as close as you can. I may need you to distract the bandit when he comes close to steal the gems."

"Your Illustriousness?"

"Do it!" Keladon slumped to his knees and, with a loud groan, pitched down and twisted to his left. His scabbard cracked and his sword bent, and his weight fell on his broken arm. He groaned again, louder and with feeling, and rolled onto his back. He pushed his right foot against the road, raising his knee and lifting his right hip. He cried out more and memories of the dying, screaming Peluraki footmen shadowed the back of his mind. The day at Suherabal Ford had been even hotter than today—

Partially hidden from the bandit by his hip, his right hand loosened its hold on the magegem bag's neck. He grabbed his left wrist with his right hand and wormed it into the bag. He knew the magegems he carried by the fine details of their handles. A green, still well charged.

"*Attend me,*" he murmured. He set his right hand on his left upper arm. "*Target your energies upon the broken bone within the arm I touch. Heal Bone, flux six-hundredths of a boil per drop of time. Begin.*"

The pain did not cease. It grew even more intense for a time as the spell's energies pulled fragments of broken bone together and whipped their vital essences into healing. The heat of the spell's energies added to his torment. He cried out more. Would his plan work? All depended on the bandit coming close enough to touch. Clearly the knave would when he realized seemingly-wounded Keladon clutched the magegems. He wished greens worked at a distance, as the other colors could.

Brush at the roadside rustled. The bandit strode into view. His narrow eyes sent wary glances up and down the road, and his thin, pale mustache made Keladon think of a rat's whiskers. He wore a brown jerkin mended with green patches, dirty-kneed green peasant trousers, brown boots, and a soft green cap. All together, his clothes blended into the colors of the wood. He could have shadowed them from the moment they passed the signposts.

The bandit's sling cradle lay on his left shoulder, with one of its two cords hanging down his torso nearly to his knee. He held a sword in his right hand. No fancy nobleman's rapier, the bandit's sword had a simple crossguard and sharp edges from hilt to tip. An antique design, but the blade looked straight and it reflected a flash of the dappled sun.

Keladon's arm still ached, but the pain had lessened. He groaned once for effect, then murmured *"Stop healing, no flux, release the target,"* followed by some louder words in Sodeleraki for the bandit to overhear, vague prayers to Balar and Samala.

The bandit stopped a pace from Keladon's feet. He aimed the tip of his sword at the bag of gems. "Take your left hand out, Your Illustriousness, or I'll run you through by the time I count five."

Keladon kept his gaze on the bandit's face. Lar remained out of his peripheral vision. "If I take my hand out," he said, keeping his voice tight, sounding pained, "you'll run me through by ten."

The bandit looked thoughtful for a moment. He shrugged and drew back his sword for an underhand stab at Keladon's guts—

Wood thwacked against the back of the bandit's knees. He stumbled backward and turned. His sword waved for balance. "Be gone, knave!" shouted Lar. He swung his walking stick at the bandit's sword hand. The bandit dodged, but the motion left him unsteady on his feet.

Keladon pushed himself up with his right hand, then stretched out and dove for the bandit's ankle. *"Target your energies upon the man I touch. Paralyze Four Limbs, energy one-quarter boil, now!"*

The bandit's legs crumpled. He dropped face-first onto the road as the sword clattered out of his hand.

Keladon stood up and caught his breath. His half-healed left arm twinged. He would finish healing it in a moment. The energy he had channeled into paralyzing the bandit from the neck down would wear off in about ten minutes. "Lar, you honor me with your service."

The valet looked bewildered. He blinked a few times, then bowed his head. "I am honored to serve, Your Illustriousness."

"How much rope have you in your pack?" Keladon asked, and received no sign the valet heard. "Lar, rope, how much?"

"Oh. Twenty feet, give or take."

"Turn him on his back. Bind his hands in front of him, then tie the other end to a horn of my saddle. Empty his pockets and take his sword."

As Lar worked, Keladon returned to casting Healing of Bone on his left arm. As the energies throbbed, he mused on the paralyzed bandit. The man thrashed his head uselessly and spat at Lar, who cuffed his cheek in response. The bandit had known Keladon's title, and his calling as a mage.

Lar finished emptying the man's pockets and went to the gelding to tie the rope. Keladon stepped closer to the bandit. "Tell me how you came to attack me."

The bandit glowered. "I gain nothing by talking. You'll drag me to Haru town, where the reeve will hang me on the morrow."

"Too good a fate for you," Lar said. He pulled the rope tight, jerking the bandit's arms.

With a few words of Jelorean, Keladon returned the green to its quiescent state. He could move his left arm fully, but weakly. He went to the bag of magegems, on the ground near where he had lain, and swapped the green for a blue.

He turned to the bandit. "You can freely answer my questions," Keladon said, "or you can be forced under threat of pain." He swung the blue high with his left hand. Mistake—pain instantly filled his upper arm—he dropped his arm to his side. The single brandish would likely be enough. Most people knew mages could cast spells of punishment.

The bandit looked at the gem with contempt. "I've resisted ten times the pain your sapphire could inflict."

"How little you know the blue," Keladon said. His boots scuffed the dirt road as he stepped toward the bandit. He spoke the Jelorean commands to target its energies on the man. The blue could work at a distance, but the amount of flux lost on the way to the target rose rapidly with the distance from the magegem. The bandit winced a moment, presumably in response to the flux flowing at him.

"*Compel Truthful Answers, flux one-hundredth of a boil per drop of time, begin.*" Keladon peered at the bandit. "Who are you?"

"My name is Wotek." A commonplace name.

"Who am I?" Keladon asked. From how Wotek had addressed him, he already knew the bandit's answer.

"Keladon, squire of Korobei." Wotek's face showed more contempt. "Bastard of the late king."

"Did you attack me because you knew who I am?"

Wotek gritted his teeth. A drop of sweat ran down his forehead to the road's dirt. "Yes."

"What was your intent in attacking me?"

"To rob you of your magegems—" Wotek cried out. His face turned ashen. He clamped shut his mouth and thrashed his head.

The fact robbery was a lie told a great deal, but Keladon wanted the bandit's confession in his own words. He added authority to his tone and said to the bandit, "Answer or I will increase the flux, which will proportionally increase the pain."

"No."

"*Increase flux,*" Keladon said in Jelorean, "*zero-hundredths of a boil per drop of time.*" No point spending more of the magegem's energies when the typical man, ignorant of the Jelorean tongue, would hear the language spoken and assume the worst. Most men's own minds would increase the pain.

Wotek's eyes squeezed shut and his mouth locked open in agony. His neck clenched and his head arched back. Strangled noises came from the back of his throat. "To kill you!" His neck relaxed and his mouth eased closed.

"Who ordered you to make an attempt on my life?"

The bandit's breaths became choppy. "Old Atem."

"Who is Old Atem?"

"A crime master in Teisoret."

Keladon frowned. He had never heard of Old Atem. Why would a master of thieves and murderers want him dead? "What is his real name?"

Wotek shook his head. Fear lurked around his eyes. "I don't know. No one does."

"What does he look like?"

"I don't know, Your Illustriousness. I've never met him. I don't know if anyone ever has, he hides himself. He gave me the job through his subordinates. See, I tell you true."

"Why did he send you to kill me?"

"I don't know, Your Illustriousness."

Perhaps Wotek was the best man for waylaying travelers, or perhaps he was the only one available. "Why would he send anyone to kill me?" Keladon asked.

"I wasn't told, Your Illustriousness, and I know not to ask."

His mother's final words about intrigues came to mind. "Does he work with another in this task?"

Wotek shook his head and wriggled his arms, testing Lar's knot. "I don't know, Your Illustriousness."

"I see you are regaining feeling and ability in your limbs. Can you stand?"

"Yes." Slowly, Wotek sat up, then rocked back and forth until he could climb to his feet.

Keladon turned to Lar. "He will walk behind my horse to Haru town. Walk beside him, outside of range of his foot, holding his sword. If he should attempt to strike me or you, or even attempt to untie the rope, kill him." He remembered martial training in his youth and the boasts of swordsmen around the camp after Suherabal

Ford. "A sharp blow of the sword's edge across his kidneys will debilitate him for a mercy stroke to the neck."

"My hands are bound," Wotek said. "I can't do a thing."

"I shall not underestimate you," Keladon said. Nor would he underestimate the crime master behind Wotek. "Did Old Atem send other assassins after me?"

"I don't know." Wotek winced and grunted. "I should think not. He has used me for roadside work before and I never failed him before today."

Keladon stopped the spell and quieted the blue. Another moment and he returned it to his saddlebag. He retied the bag to the saddlehorn, mounted the gelding, and set out at a walk for Haru town. Wotek's face showed he knew his fate was the hangman's noose, but held still his chin up; he kept some slack in the rope and decided alone where his footsteps would fall.

The walls of Haru town cast long shadows across the fields and the road as Keladon, Lar, and the bandit drew near. A crowd of carts, carriages, and peasants on foot delayed access to the entry gate. They whiled away the time with gossip and laughter, reminding Keladon of the mood of the peasants around Korobei on the eve of the harvest festival. Loud, leering praises for the king and queen told him the mood arose from the news of the prince's birth. Keladon tossed a sou to the most presentable of the street boys wending through the crowd. "Alert the reeve's men the squire of Korobei captured a bandit in the wood."

A few minutes later, the crowd parted for pikemen in doublets, breeches, and the yellow sashes of the King's Justice. The pikemen took charge of Wotek and led Keladon and Lar to the reeve's station. The valet went off to find an inn for the night and a canal boat with a cabin for hire for the next leg of the journey. The reeve's assistants led Keladon to their master.

The reeve breathed heavily and the buttons of his doublet strained over his paunch. "Your Illustriousness, you were attacked in Harumal wood? I assure you, we've cleansed the wood of bandits."

A cautious intuition held Keladon's tongue for a moment. If word got back to Old Atem his hireling had failed, let him—and the man behind him?—think Keladon ignorant of his plans. "Are times desperate for the local peasants?"

"No, sir. But desperation is less likely than ambition to drive a man to crime. Everyone in the realm knows we finally have a prince, and many a lord and wealthy goodman is bound to Teisoret for the claiming ceremony. Glad you could snare him with your arts, sir, so you could bring him to justice. My clerk will write up your complaint against him, and we'll hang him on the morrow."

After Keladon gave the clerk a false story of a random attack on the road, the sun hung low in the west when he and Lar arrived at their cramped room in a local inn. After a meal of roasted chicken and mashed turnips sent up by the innkeeper, and a wash with a basin of cold water, Keladon stretched out on the lumpy mattress and fell asleep in moments.

FAR TOO SOON, the next morning flung bright patches on the wall across the room. His left arm ached where Wotek's stone had broken it, but he could move it fully as Lar helped him dress. Minutes later, they went to the canal docks. Most foot traffic in the streets flowed against them, bound for the plaza outside the reeve's station, site of Wotek's imminent hanging.

Parallel walls of stone block, fifteen feet apart, defined the sides of the narrow canal. The four long, slender boats drawn up to the landing all looked the same, save for artwork at their bow and banners hanging from poles mounted on the dockside. A half-dozen men-at-arms and four servants stood on the gravel landing near the *Rose of the West*. They surrounded a lady in an ornate white headdress and veil, the customs of widowhood distorted by vanity. Keladon didn't need a clearer look to identify her. The livery worn by her guards and servants bore a triskelion of golden sword-arms on a red, triangular field: the arms of Norobom's ducal house. Norobom's mother, the dowager duchess of Vonen-Kiget. He had never met her before, and she had no particular reputation he could recall.

As stevedores loaded the baggage of the dowager duchess and her entourage, the boatman doffed his cap and bowed to Keladon, resting his left hand on his thigh. "Your Illustriousness, my boat, my crew, and I are honored to serve you."

A few paces away, two guards and a servant lifted their heads.

Keladon gave them a glance, then returned his attention to the boatman. "Rise," he said. He gestured at the entourage crowding the landing. The guards and the servant worked through the crowd toward Norobom's mother. "Have you room for me and my man?"

The boatman had a face like an old parchment map. The web of wrinkles across his face flexed as he winced. "Your Illustriousness, your pardons, please. As I told your man, I have room for you, sir, but sadly, only one tiny cabin. Not enough for a lord of your stature and wisdom."

"If it will timely deliver us to Mitok town," Keladon said, "we will take it."

The dowager duchess came up with some members of her entourage. She remained silent for a time, and still pulled in the attention of the boatman and Keladon. Through her thin veil, her face clearly showed a haughty expression. "Bastard, you will not travel with me," she said.

A breath sagged out of Keladon. He hadn't encountered overt prejudice from the nobility since his return from the Peluraki war. Even before, during his adolescence on the margins of the court, noblewomen had rarely expressed it, and some had even extended sympathy to him and his mother. What woman could resist a king, even when she should? But when a noblewoman disdained his bastardy, his finest manners and his services to the kingdom in both war and peace could not melt her loathing.

An emotional shell hardened behind his face while he spoke in a light tone. "I would never interrupt a lady's repose, Your Grace. Fortunately, our host has a cabin for me separate from your own."

Two passing stevedores shared a glance of stifled mirth. The dowager duchess failed to notice, her attention locked on Keladon. "Do not mock me, bastard."

"I have merely spoken truthfully, Your Grace. I have hired passage from our host, as have you."

Her eyebrows rose. She called over her shoulder to her servants. "Get me a copy of the passage contract."

The servants rustled behind her. One, a man with lank hair matted by sweat, soon came forward with a binder roped shut around a sheaf of foolscap. He untied the binder plates and pulled from between them a sheet. "Here, Your Grace." He held the paper an arm's length in front of the dowager duchess.

She lifted the corner of her veil and peered down her nose at the contract. After the pallid sheen cast over her face by the veil, her blue eyes startled Keladon. She quickly scanned the foolscap. When she looked up, satisfaction played at the corners of her mouth.

"I hired 'cabins of number and type suitable for a duchess, or such as her or her agent, and the boatman or his agent, may mutually agree.'" She fixed the boatman with a stern gaze. "What number and type of cabin are suitable for a duchess?"

He blinked and nervously bowed. "Three, Your Grace. One, the most spacious and well-disposed, for Your Grace's personal use; one for your servants; and one for four men-at-arms—"

"I have six men-at-arms," she said, "as my servant no doubt told you." The dowager duchess dropped her veil and gestured toward the lank-haired man.

A nervous look crossed his face.

The boatman squinted at the lank-haired man. "He said no such thing."

She leaned forward. "Do you accuse me of a lie?"

The boatman bowed, wincing and pressing more weight on his knee. "I only report what your man said and did not say."

The dowager duchess turned to the lank-haired man. "Is

that—?" Cheeks red, the lank-haired man looked down and hunched his shoulders.

"We will address your failing later," the dowager duchess told her man. To the boatman, she said, "You should know I am no ordinary duchess. My son was instrumental in the victory over Pelurak two decades gone. Therefore, I deserved your fourth cabin from the moment my agent signed the contract."

The boatman bowed again. "Certainly, Your Grace, you are a lady of fine merit. All know your son fought well for our late king in the last war. No doubt I am mistaken, but many of us hear tell your son fought almost as well as—His Illustriousness." The boatman bowed deeper.

A few deep breaths rocked the dowager duchess's torso before she spoke. "If you cancel your contract with the bastard, I shall recompense you. If you choose to keep his custom, I shall cancel mine with you, and you shall have no recompense. Can you pass up the fare of three cabins hired by a duchess?"

"Money is like the waters of a canal lock, Your Grace," the boatman said. "It rises and falls. Yet if you wish to timely reach the palace for the new prince's claiming by King Raboros, you might deign to accept the terms your man agreed to yesterday." He stood taller and swept his arms to take in the entire dockyard. Crowds gathered to board the other docked narrowboats. Here and there, a few harried travelers, pleas in their gestures, spoke with the other boatmen.

The dowager duchess gave a sour look up and down the dock, then straightened her back. "I will board now, boatman. I wish to never see this bastard while we travel. And after I debark, remember this: in Vonen-Kiget, my son the duke can dispense justice as readily as the king." Her haughty gaze lingered on the boatman a moment longer. She strode to the thick wall of the canal, up two steps, and across the top of the wall. One of the boatman's sons, a tall lad with ropy arms, stood on the narrow deck alongside the boat's midcastle and offered his arm to her. She boarded unassisted and walked to her cabin with a confident grip skipping along a rail at the edge of the midcastle's roof. Her remaining servants and men-at-arms followed.

The boatman scratched under his jerkin's collar. "A minute, Your Illustriousness, and then I'll show you aboard."

"I fear you have made an enemy," Keladon said.

"The contract's on my side and Her Grace knew it too. As for her duchy, I can earn my keep without darkening its precious waters, after all you've done for me."

His tone made clear he meant more than hiring a cabin. Keladon squinted in passing. He knew people came to Korobei for help from his scholars, but he rarely dealt with them directly. "Remind me, if you would."

"Your pardons, please, Your Illustriousness. You and your assistants see so many supplicants you couldn't remember them all. Three years ago, we squabbled with the *Gilded Lily* because its crew stumbled its horse into our towline. Their lads swung a pole that caught my son—" He aimed his chin toward the boy on deck. "—to the side of his head. He started having fits. Bitten tongue, falls—he went over the side once and my other boys jumped after him. He thrashed so hard I feared he would take one of his brothers with him to the Divine Couple. Nothing's more frightful than thinking you might lose your child, my lord, not a thing."

"I understand completely."

"So our next chance, my wife took him to your school, and your assistants worked a magic that healed him. Thank you, my lord, Your Illustriousness. You've done my family more good than all the duchesses in the kingdom." The boatman squinted at the sun. "Your Illustriousness, if you would be so kind to board, it's near time to shove off."

Keladon and Lar spent most of the next three days in their cabin, a long, narrow room at the bow, four feet wide at the head of Keladon's bed and tapering to a point at the foot of Lar's bedroll. On the second day, Keladon realized Lar and the dowager duchess' servants had negotiated an arrangement to divide the abovedecks daylight hours between their employers. He had four hours a day to sit on the roof of the midcastle. On the canalside towpath, hired horses trudged along, keeping the tow line taut as the boatman's youngest son guided them. The boy might be ten years old. The horses moved more out of habit than submission to the boy's low whistles and mild taps with a whittled sapling. The boy's command of the team sufficed in mild conditions, but would it be enough if a crisis erupted?

When they neared a lock, the two oldest boys untied the tow line from the bow and lifted poles from mounting racks on the midcastle roof. They stood on opposite sides and pushed their poles against the canal bottom to guide the narrowboat into the lock. Scant inches lay between the sides and the stone retaining walls of the lock. Water drained out and the narrowboat dropped into the cool, damp pit of the lock. Midday sunlight gleamed on the moisture glistening on the lock's southerly wall.

Watching the operations of the narrowboat briefly took Keladon's mind off the fact a hired killer had been sent after him.

Why did Old Atem want him dead? In his thoughts, he laid over all his actions, in Teisoret during his visit to the palace the previous autumn, at Korobei in recent years. He replayed conversations as the narrowboat went along to the sounds of lapping water, clopping hooves, and buzzing gnats. He'd done nothing to turn a crime master into a murderous foe. Impotent outrage burned in his chest, but soon cooled as he thought more.

Old Atem was not his foe. Wotek the hired killer had been ignorant whether Old Atem worked alone. Murder for hire could easily be a part of his criminal empire. So who had hired him? One of Raboros' sycophants, bitter about some perceived slight? A highborn interested in the widowed countess—he dredged up her name, Dalasa—who thought him a rival for her affections? People at court were not so petty as to want to kill for such trivial reasons. Were they?

A foreign ruler? For twenty years, he had forgotten his battlemage days as best he could, but perhaps some king's councilors implored their sovereign to permanently retire the victor of Suherabal Ford, as a precondition for some adventure against Sodelerak.

King Raboros? Keladon felt chill despite the muggy air, until his thoughts grew clearer. If the king wanted him dead, Melos would have already issued the warrant to take him into custody.

At least his opponent on the narrowboat did not conceal herself. When they reached the canal-docks at Mitok town, he stayed in his cabin while the dowager duchess and her entourage debarked. The day was still early, and he instructed Lar to hurry to the docks along the Derepar and find a boat bound for Teisoret which he would not have to share with Norobom's mother.

THE VALET FOUND ONE, a three-masted barge whose captain swore he wouldn't let a single cabin to the dowager duchess. But when Keladon and Lar reached the wharves along the riverfront in mid-afternoon, a first glance made it doubtful he would have any cabin at all.

An exuberant crowd in oft-patched garments, yet with more baggage for their number than the dowager duchess's party, mobbed the foot of the gangplank. Keladon overheard their conversations, regarding shows and marks, and saw enough mirthful faces and women wearing jerkins and hose to identify them as a band of entertainers. A midget, a giant, a slender woman with sandy-brown curls, a sad-eyed woman in a skirt. Their impresario, a barrel-chested man whose mustache's ends fell below his jawline, bowed deeply, with ornate flourishes of his hat, when the captain led Keladon and a few other noble passengers, as well as some wealthy commoners, through the crowd and aboard. One of the commoners, a stout, sweaty man in a brocaded doublet, a merchant or prosperous tradesman accompanied by a bored, homely wife, nervously touched the outside of one of his pockets, as if assuring himself a purse remained there.

By early evening, the barge had put ten miles of the wide, sluggish Derepar behind it. A stiff southerly wind bowed the sails and the lines creaked as a crewman led Keladon and Lar to the captain's drawing room. The other noble passengers arrived soon after. As their servants stood along the wall, Keladon and the lesser nobles consumed three bottles of wine, followed by a dinner of cold tomato soup seasoned with rosemary, thick slices of crusty white bread and cured ham, and a dessert of strawberries and dipping cream.

Keladon expected to suffer through the evening, but one of the noblewomen, a dame of an estate fifty miles upriver from Mitok, steered the conversation toward his work at Korobei, away from the men's inclination to ask about the Peluraki war. Keladon warmed to the topic, and his tone revealed his optimism regarding how magic could improve the lives of all estates of Sodeleraki society. "All the horses of the team would be stronger, to better pull the carriage of—our future king."

The view outside the portholes turned dark, making the river seem to stretch to the horizons, by the time the captain led a toast and departed. The dame's husband suggested a game of ruff and honors, and Keladon surprised himself by joining. They dismissed their valets—Keladon read on Lar's face a desire to get to know a lass from the entertainers' troupe—and sat at the table.

Keladon reached for his goblet when a sudden fear froze his hand. A master criminal from the capital would be unlikely to recruit a country squire to kill him, and how could Old Atem know which boat he took to Teisoret? He dismissed the fear as excessive, but still took slow sips of his wine, wanting to maintain his wits. No need for it. His companions drank heavily, and he made a few intentional misplays and slurred his speech to make it seem he had drunk as much.

After the game, he went on the deck through a pleasant cool night to the fore stair. Down a flight, then his cabin behind the second door. He pulled from his pocket a key the captain had given him and turned it in the lock. The bolt did not snick back from the jamb. Unlocked. Lar—

Brow furrowed, Keladon opened the door, and froze halfway. The brocaded doublet of the man on the bed marked him as the stout, sweaty merchant who'd boarded after the nobles. For an instant, the merchant's eyes remained closed and his face, slack with pleasure, until his head lolled toward Keladon. Eyes suddenly wide, he jerked his leather-shod feet from the floor and slid backward on his rump, pulling at his breeches as he moved. His manhood, glistening in the glow of a single candle, showed for a moment.

"Who dares invade my cabin?" Keladon shouted.

The merchant rolled off the bed. His fist turned white around gathered fabric from his breeches. "Your pardons, Your Grace, Your Highness, your pardons—" Eyes turned down, cheeks red, he hurried past Keladon, shrinking away to avoid brushing against a nobleman and scraping the doorframe for his troubles. His footsteps pounded down the hall.

Keladon stalked into the room. "And you, brazen wench? What have you to say for yourself?"

The other invader of his cabin had not moved from her kneeling position at the side of the bed. A thick, curly mass of sandy-brown hair hid her downcast face for a moment, but then with a little toss, her hair fell back from a long face and thick, painted lips. She gave Keladon a look of false naiveté.

"This cabin is occupied?" The tenor voice, and the play of a laryngeal bulge, made clear this person was a man.

"Out!"

The other stood. A slight figure, half a foot shorter than Keladon, a bold manner lurked around his eyes in stark contrast to his smooth skin and youthful lines of muscle and bone. "My lord. Is it so bad as that? If you let me work my magic on you, I promise you'd never go back to the slop twixt a woman's legs."

Stunned by the man's gall, Keladon couldn't speak as a male voice came down the corridor and to the door. "Balar's balls, what's—" The impresario froze, and for a time his only movement was a quiver of the tips of his mustache. "Vos, what have you done?"

"I entertained a fat moneybags, Toreb."

"In the cabin of a highborn one?" The sound of fear strained Toreb's voice. He bowed deeply to Keladon. "Your Illustriousness, I beseech you, let me make amends in some manner—"

"Amends?" Keladon shouted. "He picked the lock. I can have him flogged a burglar, and if anything is missing, hanged a thief. Do you think this affront can be amended by anything less?"

Toreb looked alarmed. "Your Illustriousness, he is impulsive and foolish, but I swear he meant no offense." To Vos, he said, "Did you even know whose cabin you invaded?"

"No. I just knew we couldn't go to my fat moneybags's. Wives fail to understand—"

"Silence," Keladon said. He gave Vos a further glare for emphasis, then turned to Toreb. "What is Vos' game? No doubt you know it."

"I know not what more he might do beyond, ah, entertaining various men. I swear it, by the Divine Couple."

Keladon glowered. "Vos is either a hired gunsel, or a pickpocket who distracts his mark with—" He waved his hand. "Whichever it be, he will empty his pockets, and every sou that falls out, I will return to the merchant. And, goodman—" He pronounced the word mockingly, "—you will never again feign ignorance of his actions."

Toreb nodded deeply. "He will empty his pockets, Your Illustriousness, to ensure no coins have fallen in them."

"My exchanges are fair!" said Vos. "I'm worth every sou they pay me."

The impresario sidled past Keladon and, from a thick fist, jutted a finger at Vos. "Shut up. Toss your coins on the bed."

"Toreb—"

The impresario pinched Vos's ear and twisted.

"Ah! Stop! I'll do it."

Toreb released Vos's ear and pushed him back half a step. Vos pulled a small purse, then another, from pockets of his jerkin, and dumped their contents on the bed. He turned to Toreb and Keladon. "There, that's all."

Keladon folded his arms across his chest. "The hidden pocket as well."

Vos pouted a moment, then slid his hand into his jerkin. He brought out a long, narrow purse, then gaped its mouth like a fish to disgorge coins one by one.

"Take your man and be gone," Keladon said to Toreb, "while I remain in the mood to forgive. Are you bound for the festivities at the palace in celebration of our new prince? I will warn you, most noblemen would demand a harsh punishment were their quarters debased like this."

Toreb bowed with a mawkish doff of his hat. "We are bound for the palace, Your Illustriousness, as you surmise. I will keep Vos in check. I overflow with gratitude for your clemency and your advice." He put back on the hat, then turned to Vos. His profile hardened and he pinched Vos' ear again. "Stupid fool, we're getting out of here and never coming back." He went toward the door, tugging Vos after him.

"Careful, you'll bruise my ear, and you don't want that—"

"If you have a bruise, cover it with powder and your hair...." Toreb and Vos went out of earshot down the corridor.

Vos's carefree attitude toward other people's money came back to Keladon with a start. He checked the wardrobe in the corner, where Lar had hidden bags of coins and magegems under spare underclothes and a travel pack. All still there. He relaxed, but only slightly, then scooped up the coins from the bed and went out. After locking the door behind him, he searched for the merchant.

As he stalked the halls and decks, his anger at Vos ebbed. The gunsel was a pathetic figure, but any more so than the sycophants of King Raboros's court? Only an accident of birth made Vos susceptible to the King's Justice. Underneath the cloak of nobility, Dobak and the other hangers-on were no different.

And the kingdom's crown prince, his son, would see them, when looking for paragons of nobility and virtue to learn from.

If the Divine Couple truly existed, Sodelerak must have committed some grave, unidentified sin, to be cursed with a king susceptible to the vilest of influences, influences he would parade as commonplaces before his heir. In his pocket, his hand played softly with the coins Vos had yielded while his thoughts ran on.

Another king than Raboros could not be worse.

At the railing, he stopped and took a breath of warm night air and let the treasonous thought fly away with his exhalation. He soon found a sailor who gave him directions to the merchant's cabin. Keladon descended two levels and rapped his knuckles on the appointed door. A weary servant opened the door a crack, and his eyes shot up. "My lord, how may I help you?"

"I would speak with your master."

"About what matter, sir?"

"He will know."

The servant eased the door shut. A few moments later, it swung open. The merchant walked out with straight shoulders and a level gaze, until his servant shut the door behind him, leaving the merchant alone in the corridor with Keladon. The merchant cringed and stooped. His voice came in a whisper harsh with self-loathing. "My lord, most noble sir, I beg your forgiveness. He told me the room was unoccupied and the captain had given him a key. I swear on every brick in the Divine Couple's hall, had I known, sir, I would never—"

"I hold you blameless," Keladon said. He pulled the fistful of coins from his pocket. "Here is the money stolen from you."

"Sir?" the merchant said.

"Take it. I have no need for it."

The merchant held out his hands. Keladon dropped into them the clinking mass of coins. With deft movements of his thick fingers, the merchant sorted and counted them on his palm. Relief washed over his face. "Sir, thank you."

"Shall I speak to the captain, or will you tell him of this wrong?"

The relief drained away. "Tell him?"

"Aboard his boat, he is as powerful as a reeve. Do you want Vos clapped in irons and handed over to the King's Justice when we reach Teisoret?"

The merchant's face paled further. "Sir, please, there's no need for any more inquiry into this. Thanks to you—" He raised his hands full of coins. "I've been made whole. I only want to put tonight's misadventure behind me."

His thoughts from above deck swirled through the back of his mind. Keladon leaned closer and murmured, "It makes me no mind if you lie to your wife about your inclinations in order to protect her, or to protect yourself. But if you are careless in how you satisfy your inclinations, the truth will come out."

The merchant bowed. "I hear you, sir. I shall be discreet."

Keladon had his doubts, but he had done all he would to save the merchant from himself. He went back to his quarters to find the door unlocked. Had that impudent gunsel invaded his cabin again?

He flung the door open to find Lar glumly awake on his roll at the foot of Keladon's bed. Lar jolted to his feet. "Sir, is something amiss?"

Keladon shut the door and locked it. "You don't know what happened?"

"After you gave me liberty for the evening, sir, I went into the troupe's part of the boat, seeking out the songstress, Nera. I only just returned—"

"Without success, I take it?"

"Another in the troupe said she pines for Toreb, the troupe's master. Perhaps her mind will change once we arrive at Teisoret. They'll be performing at the palace, she tells me." He gave Keladon more attention. "Sir, if I may, what did happen?"

Keladon rehearsed his encounter with Vos and Toreb, then readied for bed. Sleep took a time in coming, as the prospect of encountering the two entertainers spiked him with anger. But the next day and the rest of the trip, the entertainers left Keladon untroubled. When the boat arrived at Teisoret docks on the third morning aboard, he would be the first to debark while the troupe waited below.

Nearing the docks, the city stretched as far up and down the river as he could see. Downriver, wooden buildings leaned over the bank, and rust streaked from nailheads down boards weathered to gray. Upriver, walls of brick and mortared stone thrust up from the river's edge. The plaza at the docks teemed with motion and noise, the profanity of stevedores, the calls of bawds and carters, the clop of hooves, the squeak of wheels, the nervous murmurs of lesser nobles in the city for the ceremony. Smells of mule dung, sweat, and netted fish flooded Keladon's nose.

Worry hunched his shoulders. Old Atem could lurk a few hundred paces away. Or he could be here in the plaza now, with a gang of hired killers. Sweat ran down Keladon's nape as he studied the crowd. Most were uninterested in him, and the few others took notice of his obviously noble attire and hurried on. He craned his neck for a time, then said to Lar, "Are my tools near the top of your pack?"

Lar looked surprised that he asked about the magegems. "They are, Your Illustriousness. Do you wish to hold them?"

"I wish to know where they are should I need them."

"As you say, Your Illustriousness." Lar's eyes widened with delight. "Finally, a free carriage! Shall I hire it?"

Keladon nodded. Lar scurried forward to haggle with the driver. Above the low roofs, on higher ground about a mile distant, stood the gray pillar of the old castle and the long, whitewashed wings of the new palace on leveled ground at the castle's foot.

"Straight to the palace will cost you four crowns. Not a sou less," the driver said.

"Bah!" Lar said.

"Crowded as the city is, bumpkin boy, you think you'll hire a carriage cheaper?"

Keladon came closer. "We'll take that price," he said, "provided you stop and wait for us at the Temple of Samala."

The driver double-took, then bowed and flourished his arm. "As you wish, my lord."

Keladon idly watched the crowds flowing through the streets. He had routine business with the temple. Because the possession of gems on the palace grounds was a crime, he would deposit his in the temple's vault, just as he had done the previous autumn.

Despite the crowds, they reached the temple within fifteen minutes. Lar transferred the gems to a burlap sack and stuffed wool padding around them. Alone, Keladon left the carriage and climbed the worn marble steps leading to the chapel.

A few congregants knelt at the altar as a priestess in a blue robe recited the mid-morning prayer. More priestesses waited at a side door near the back of the chapel. One noticed him and came his way. Sudden nervousness caught his breath. Kala. The gray streaks in her hair and the smile lines in her face showed wisdom and worldliness. They had spent a few pleasant hours together the previous autumn, and he would now trade them all for ten minutes' converse with Lilera.

She smiled. "Greetings, Keladon, friend of the goddess. I expected you would come and entrust us with your treasures."

"No one is more trustworthy than your sisterhood."

Her eyes narrowed slightly, but her smile soon returned. "Follow me to the vault."

She found a lamp and led him down a set of stairs to a basement, then a dozen paces along a brick-walled corridor. They came to a thick stone door. Kala reached into her right sleeve and pulled out a key on a chain. She unlocked the door and reached for the handle. The door swung in with an ease that still surprised him despite seeing it the previous autumn.

Inside, the vault's side walls each held an array of locked boxes. Kala used her key on one of them and pulled out a logbook and a rack bearing more keys. She made a note in the logbook, pulled out a key, and relocked the box. A few paces down the wall, she unlocked a box, opened it for him, and set its key inside. "We shall always keep your secrets," she said. She went out the vault's open door and held the lamp so only it and the end of her arm were visible to Keladon.

Keladon slid the sack of gems into the box, then locked it and returned the key to Kala. He waited in the corridor while she locked up the vault. Perhaps she would let their autumn dalliance remain in memory, he hoped.

Hope is for fools, a part of him responded.

On the stairs heading back to the chapel, she glanced over her shoulder. "Will you be in Teisoret for long?"

He affected a sad head shake. "After King Radobom claims the new prince, I must return to Korobei. My scholars are making great strides in understanding the tools of my trade and we are on the cusp of breakthroughs."

After a moment, Kala said, "The goddess admires your dedication to your calling. Yet the claiming ceremony will not be for five days. Have you tasks about the palace before then? Or will you have time to take your leisure?"

"Affairs—matters, I mean—at the palace require all my attention until the ceremony."

They reached the side door to the chapel. With a guarded expression, she blew out the lamp's flame. In the sudden dimness, lit only by a curtained window, she said, "The goddess admires honesty more than any other trait."

Why did he reject her interest for the sake of an impossible longing for Lilera? Yet he did. "I would matters allowed me the freedom to take my leisure. However, I am bound to attend them."

A look of disappointment flickered away from her features, to be replaced by the mask required by her calling. "May the goddess bless your actions, Your Illustriousness."

SUMMER 11

The Palace

A few hours later, early evening stretched the shadows of an apple orchard across the gardens between Keladon's window and the north wall of the palace grounds. Amid the gardens was a grassy sward where he had trained with a sword long hours of his youth. His watch showed seven-thirty, though he felt more tired than he normally would at that hour. Travel had worn him down with strange beds and thronging people, and his rooms, smaller than his ones last autumn, crowded him with low ceilings and shabby furniture in a style old when he had lived in this wing as a boy.

Above all, underneath those things like a monstrous fish at the bottom of a river, lay the knowledge someone wanted him dead.

Three loud knocks sounded on the door. Lar hurried over while Keladon remained at the window. Beyond the garden wall rose the tops of tents, pitched on a mustering field unused since the Peluraki war. The nearby inns must be swollen with travelers. How many thousands of people had journeyed to Teisoret? How many hundreds would be admitted to the palace with only cursory glances by the Royal Guard? Which one would be Old Atem's next assassin?

"Your Illustriousness," said Lar, "I am honored to pray admittance to your presence by Melos, Master of Offices."

Surprised, Keladon needed a moment to answer. "Goodman Melos is admitted." What brought old Melos to his rooms? Had he heard from the reeve in Haru town of the attack in the wood?

Melos shuffled in, face as lined and eyes as droopy as ever. A palace mage accompanied him, a youngish man with jowly face and flat eyes, and a tied roll of papers tucked into a loop on his breeches.

"Good evening, Master of Offices," Keladon said. He tried to sound more energetic than he felt. "To what do I owe the pleasure of your visit?"

"We have a number of things to ask of you, Your Illustriousness. First, I hear from the armorer that your sword was bent and you sent your man with it for repairs?"

"It wouldn't do to appear at court with a bent sword," Keladon said. He'd sent Lar to the armorer a few minutes after being shown his rooms. The old man would have prattled for hours about the old days of Raboros' reign and Keladon's youth, had Keladon gone to him himself.

"If I may, sir, how came it to be bent?"

Keladon angled his head. "You have not heard about the attack I suffered in Harumal wood."

The palace mage looked shocked. Even Melos raised an eyebrow. "No, sir. What happened? What came of it?"

"A bandit no doubt noticed my attire and thought to score an ample purse. I bested him and bent my sword in the process, then marched him into Haru town where the reeve hanged him."

Melos shook his head. "An attack on a king's claimed son is a grave matter. The reeve in Haru town should have reported it to the Master of Reeves, who should have reported it to me."

"Perhaps the reeve in Haru town gave it no especial consideration. Roadside banditry has never been fully eliminated."

"His task is to report any crime against a king's claimed son. I will decide whether to give it any especial consideration. Thank you, sir, for bringing it to my attention. Now, let us turn to the second thing I mean to ask you. You may recall the second demonstration you gave in His Majesty's small audience chamber last autumn?"

Lar went about the room, lighting lamps on side tables. The new glow pushed the deepening shadows of night from their faces. "Yes," said Keladon.

"I have thought of it often as I have guided the preparations for the newborn prince's claiming ceremony. We will hold it in the pavilion in the palace's central courtyard, where roughly two hundred of the most highly born may see it closely. Another thousand or so of lesser rank will be admitted to the courtyard and have a chance to glimpse it. But thousands of the city's common folk and people from the provinces have come for the festivities without any chance to view them. Given that this is the king and queen's first child, born after many years of marriage, and against a backdrop of rumor that impugns the dignity of His Majesty, it would be desirable to make the event visible to as many as possible."

"You would use Pass Light and Pass Sound to project the images and speeches of the ceremony beyond the walls." Keladon's eyebrow rose and his cheeks tightened in delight. "A clever thought. You should have trained as a mage."

"Duke Norobom conceived the notion, not I." The palace mage shifted forward as Melos added, "Though I have confidence in Forek here and his subordinates, we are five days from the claiming ceremony, and should you be willing to assist us...."

Worries about Old Atem and further attempts at murder receded from Keladon's mind, replaced by the chance to do something of value. "I would be glad to. I welcome a purpose to leave these rooms."

"As you say, Your Illustriousness," Melos replied, "though I should think it likely a man of your stature has already found another purpose in the lap of a highborn lady of the court."

"I have not made any such plans," Keladon said. "Depending on how much work Forek and I might have before us, I may not have time to make any, either." A yawn pushed his jaws open.

"You have had long days of travel." Melos turned his head to Forek. "Would the morning be timely enough for His Illustriousness to meet with you in earnest?"

Forek nodded with quick, jerky shakes of the head. "Though, Your Illustriousness, would you have time to review the work we have done so far?" He pulled the roll of papers from its loop and with both hands held it out.

"I shall," Keladon said. They made arrangements to meet in the central courtyard the next morning, and Melos and Forek then left.

Keladon drifted to the window and stared at the apple orchard, now lit only by flickering lamps hung on posts by the gardeners. Should he have rejected the offer? He already had a purpose to leave these rooms—hunting down Old Atem. But Melos was right: projecting the claiming ceremony to the crowd would redound to the glory of King Raboros. Helping plan out the tools, gems, and spells required would honor his mother's last words.

And depending on the order of protocol in the pavilion and the courtyard, a projection might be the only way he would see Lilera and his infant son.

THE NEXT MORNING, Keladon arrived at the central pavilion later than he wished. The interior spaces of the north wing had been redivided since his youth. Forek and a trio of younger palace mages waited near the east steps of the pavilion and swept impatient expressions from their faces as he approached. Forek bowed deeply and introduced the others. Keladon missed their names, and thought of them as Hooded Eyes, Narrow Chin, and Long Face. The latter had gray hair and looked familiar. After a moment, he remembered Long Face had been one of the palace mages waiting in the library while he had cast Father a Son.

Keladon handed over the rolled plans as Forek asked, "May we show you what we have done so far?"

The steps creaked as they climbed. The pavilion floor was a circle fifty feet across formed from narrow planks of tightly-joined polished maple. A waist-high railing ringed the floor. Every ten paces, poles punctuated the railing. A taller pole in the center held up the white canvas roof tied at its edges to the poles around the perimeter. Though mostly taut, the canvas had enough play for the wind to ripple it. The wind and the canvas's shade softened the full force of the morning's heat. Keladon glanced up and remembered the night he'd first lain with a woman, when his father had brought a team of trollops to a party under that same canvas in the hope one would catch Raboros' fancy. He shook his head to clear the memory.

At the far side of the pavilion, the claiming table and a statue of the Divine Couple had already been set up. Cloths covered Balar and Samala's faces and torsos, secured with golden cords around their waists. Thick oak beams formed the claiming table. Keladon's heart quickened. Was it? He knelt and looked for scratchings on its lower crossbeams. *I am Larabos futur king*, gouged with the tip of a knife by a boy a century ago. Yes, the same table on which Keladon had been claimed. More than large enough for an infant, but as a fifteen-year-old, his lower legs had dangled off the edge.

His knee creaked as he stood. Behind the claiming table and the statue, beyond the railing, past the sharp line of the canvas roof's shadow, flowerbeds and fountains punctuated the courtyard's lawns. The gray spire of the old castle rose behind the west wing of the new palace. Keladon looked out and up at a blue sky dotted with a few puffy clouds, then turned to Forek.

"I've looked at your plans," he said, "but tell me in your words what problems you face."

"Of course, Your Illustriousness. The Master of Offices asked us to project images that could be seen by as many outside the main gate as possible. To collect the images, we have three large mirrors—" Forek held his hands at greater than shoulder width.

"—mounted on stands with lockable gimbals. We'll set them here, here, and here." He pointed to spots on the floor between the claiming table and where the highest-born spectators would stand. "To show the images, we have created three arrays of the largest windowpanes the best glassblower in Teisoret could make, backed with the finest sheets of silver we could find."

The words fit with the plans Keladon had studied the night before. "The viewing mirrors fit together to show an image six paces by four, correct?"

"Correct. I'm wasting your time, sir, pardon me. The problem we face when we test the system is the projected image is poor. It's as if we see the collected image in twilight. All the people and objects are colorless and indistinct. We've tried increasing the flux between the collecting and viewing mirrors, but that doesn't help at all. It only drains the magegem faster." Forek looked hopeful. "Does the problem lie in projecting onto multiple viewing mirrors?"

"You cast the spell with all the viewing mirrors in their place? A frame around the entire array?"

"Yes."

"Then that's not the problem. Your problem is not enough light at the collecting mirrors."

Forek's forehead creased. "We do not follow, Your Illustriousness."

Keladon thought for a moment how best to describe it. "Light in a mirror is like water in a goblet, let us say. Fill a goblet with water. How deep is the water? Three inches, give or take?" Nods and mouthed words showed the mages followed him so far. "Now pour that goblet of water into a large tray." He spread his arms to their full span. "How deep would the water be in that tray?"

"Much less than an inch," said Narrow Chin.

Keladon shrugged. "We don't need to calculate the exact depth. You understand me, though, all of you?" Forek and his subordinates nodded. "The issue you face is that you're pouring light into a longer and wider mirror."

"Increasing the flux didn't help because there's no more light to send," Forek said. "So the solution is to collect more light from the scene we want to show."

"Exactly," Keladon said. "My simile breaks down at the fact, while a goblet quickly is filled with water and can hold no more, a mirror can hold a vast amount of light. A sunny day would not be enough to fill it."

"Let's think of ways to add more light to our collecting mirrors," Forek said.

"We could suspend braziers," said Narrow Chin.

"You'll hang fires over a crowd of highborn?" Long Face replied. "Don't be a fool."

Hooded Eyes said, "And it's already going to be hot at ten in the morning."

"Bring down the roof?" Narrow Chin's tone trailed off.

"Would only make it hotter," Long Face said.

Forek and his subordinates looked thoughtful. Keladon gave them a moment, but when they didn't speak, he broke the silence.

"The ceremony will be held at ten in the morning, you said?" He pulled out his pocket watch. "That's about this time of day." He stepped around the claiming table and robed statues, then down the pavilion's west steps. He felt the sun on his nape when he left the pavilion's shadow. He stopped on the grass a few paces from the bottommost step, where the cuckold's guard would stand during the ceremony, then shaded his eyes with his hand and squinted toward the sun. With his other hand, he cradled his pocket watch with his fingers and sent reflected sunlight under the pavilion's canopy. Forek and the other mages covered their eyes against the dazzle. "Mount some mirrors here where I stand, and mount more high under the canopy inside the pavilion." He pointed. "You can reflect sunlight onto the claiming table and people around it, which will then allow more to be collected from the scene." His left hand drew lines in the air to indicate the light path.

Forek nodded, then gestured his subordinates toward the center pole of the pavilion with a wave of the rolled documents. Keladon pocketed his watch when a motion in the courtyard caught his attention.

A short, wide man hurried toward him. His plain doublet was unbuttoned at the collar and sweat dampened its underarms. He wore a crisp white apron which he smoothed down with repeated wipes of his palms. "Your Illustriousness, my lord, a moment of yours, if I may?"

"I am busy, goodman."

The man drew closer. A final wipe of his hands, and he bowed. Sweat beaded atop his balding head. "Your Illustriousness, my lord, I beseech you, please use your powers to help an honest artisan who seeks only to offer his finest products to His Majesty and the court."

"State the matter—briefly." Keladon emphasized the last word with a raised forefinger.

The man bowed again. "I thank you for your audience, sir. I seek the assistance of a mage to help recover stolen property of mine."

"That property being?"

"Six paces of sheep intestine."

Keladon blinked, then opened and closed his mouth, uncertain of what to say. "Tell me your name and occupation, if you would."

"I am Yoret, maker of the finest sausages within a hundred miles of Doril-Haberi. I traveled to the capital at the request of no less a personage than Duke Norobom, Master of Battlemages, to make and present my products to His Majesty. I spent yestermorn in the markets of Teisoret, finding the freshest cuts of flank steak and pig heart, the most pungent spices, and the lengths of sheep intestine needed for casings. My process, unique to my shop, takes six hours to prepare the sheep intestine for use, followed by an overnight rest. Thin as gossamer and strong as cobweb. I am a meticulous craftsman, sir. I know to the ounce and inch the ingredients of my sausages. This morning I found six paces of prepared intestine absent from the resting vat."

"You ruled out simpler explanations? A kitchen cat? Someone

needing an assurance cap? A cook short of the ingredients for chitter-ling soup?"

The jowls under Yoret's wide jaw shook with a shudder. "A chef who would boil my casings with salt should be flogged. No, sir, I am certain the length of casing was stolen by one of my rivals to learn my secrets."

"You may well be right, goodman Yoret."

Yoret patted his damp forehead with the back of his hand, then bowed again. "If I may be so bold, sir, I have heard the practitioners of your art have the ability to find an object gone missing—"

"I cannot help you."

Yoret rocked on his feet, then bowed even deeper. "Sir, Your Illustriousness, I beseech you, and if I have offended—"

"You have not. Goodman Yoret, you ask the impossible. The spell to find an object gone missing requires a partner spell be cast on the object before it leaves." He came up with a metaphor. "The spell is a hound and must first have a scent to track."

A long, weary breath sloughed from Yoret. "I am lost, then."

Keladon frowned. "You are lost? Or one secret of yours? Is your casing the only element that distinguishes your work from others'?"

Thoughtfulness slowly pushed despair from Yoret's features. "You have given me much to think on, sir." He bowed once more. "I cannot express all my gratitude for your attention to my minor concerns. I seek your permission to depart."

"I grant it."

Yoret walked backwards with careful steps until he was well past the two paces required by custom. He then turned away and hurried to the east wing of the palace.

Keladon chuckled. Imploring a highborn mage's help for the sake of six paces of sheep intestine required a vast amount of cheek, but Yoret had seemed too consumed by his troubles to even notice. Though his obsession with sausage looked laughable from the outside, to Yoret it must seem the most right and proper thing in the world. A goodman indeed, a smallholder dedicated to his craft, the backbone of Sodelerak.

The mages under the pavilion watched Keladon with expressions of guarded curiosity. He had royal blood and some chance to indulge whims, but with the claiming ceremony four days away, now was not the time. Keladon lifted his shoulders and stalked up the steps two by two. "Now that we have the collecting of images sorted out, what can we do to improve the viewing of them?"

THE DAY PASSED QUICKLY—KELADON repeatedly surprised himself by glancing up to find servants and gardeners scurrying through the afternoon's growing shadows. By four o'clock the mages had done all they could. The glassblower would not be able to deliver the additional mirrors and mounts needed for Keladon's proposed solution until the next morning. Forek looked pleased. "We have benefited greatly from your wisdom, Your Illustriousness. Let us meet again tomorrow at noon and set the mirrors into place."

"Till then." Keladon followed a flagstone path across the courtyard to the north wing. Gardeners worked in a flowerbed with hoes and shovels. One gardener leaned on his shovel to rest and its center of gravity slipped away from him. The shovel clattered to the flagstones. The sound echoed through the courtyard.

Embarrassed, the gardened bowed deeply and repeatedly. "Your pardons, sir, I beg you."

Keladon waved his hand in idle forgiveness and started on his way back to his rooms. Yet after a few steps, he remembered his sword should be ready at the armorer's. He hesitated, weary from the day's efforts and wary of the armorer's rambling stories. *Go to your rooms and send Lar after it.*

You gave Lar liberty after he mended your stockings, another part of him recalled. *He'll be off chasing servant girls until the dinner hour.*

Keladon entered the palace, then made his way to the east wing and the armorer's shop. Near the front door, an apprentice worked a blade across a whetstone, *shrik shrik*, while the old man dozed in a chair in the corner.

The apprentice looked up and stopped. "My lord?"

"My servant brought in my sword yesterday for straightening. Is it finished? Bring it to me. No need to wake your master."

"Wake?" The old man stirred in his chair. "No, sir, I'm only resting my eyes to better hear the lad's work." He squinted at Keladon. "A sword in need of straightening, yes. What was your name again, sir?"

"Keladon. Squire of Korobei."

"Karelon? Oh, Keladon, Keladon. Keladon? Son of King Radobom? Why, sir, I recall when you were a stripling in ill-fitted boots bashing about with a wooden sword. You gained some skill with the real kind. Pity you chose to play with baubles, begging your pardon, sir. But you slew more of your father's enemies with the bloody bauble than you ever would have with a sword...."

"My sword."

"Yes, yes, of course, you're a gentleman who needs to be fully equipped for the ladies of the court. Now what did we do with it?"

The apprentice cleared his throat. "Master, you decided it was irreparable."

"Irreparable?" Keladon asked.

The old man paused in thought. "Yes, you remember truly, boy. After straightening, sir, the blade proved too weak at the place it had bent. It wouldn't do for a king's claimed son to carry a sword like that, ready to break in a fight. The sharper rump wouldn't make up for the shorter reach. Not proper. We had a sword we recently made for a lord I shan't name who suffered a sudden embarrassment of funds when time came to pay for it. A fine piece, finer than that gentleman deserved, I suspect, but no matter, we had it at hand and we offer it to you." The old man looked satisfied for a moment. "Well, boy? Fetch it for His Illustriousness."

"Yes, master." The apprentice scurried away.

Keladon put on a polite face and wished the boy would be quick.

While the apprentice retrieved the sword, the old man reminisced about the decades of boys he'd trained in the art of the sword. He forgot names and remembered as contemporaries boys born many years apart. Keladon felt more sympathy for the old man than he expected. Perhaps reaching middle years had shown him he too would suffer forgetfulness and loneliness some day. Or did he feel more attuned to the cycle of life since the birth of his—nephew?

The apprentice returned with the sword in its scabbard, then bowed and lifted it across his palms for Keladon's inspection. A handsome piece, with a plain steel basket hilt dimpled with indentations—

"Sir, yes, we took off the jewels the patron had requested. We couldn't justify their expense if we weren't getting paid. I didn't think you would mind. You dressed rather plain for a noble youth, and you always seemed a sober type.... What was I saying, sir?"

"You were saying it's a handsome blade. May I draw it?"

"Of course, sir."

Keladon took the scabbard from the apprentice's hands, stepped back, and drew the sword. He slid his feet and lifted his hands to the guard position. A few slices at the air, a few parries against an invisible foe. "Well-balanced. I am honored to receive it, goodman."

The old man smiled, wrinkles shifting like springtime ice on the distant southern sea. "I am honored to give it, sir. May the Divine Couple guide the arm that wields it."

Keladon belted the sword to his hip, then left the armorer and went into the maze of rearranged corridors in the north wing. Finally he neared his rooms. His steps slowed and his hand went to his sword. A sliver of daylight showed between the door and the jamb.

Had Lar returned? He listened, heard nothing. He eased the door open and went in.

The shabby sitting area was as he'd left it. But through an open doorway at the back of the sitting area, leading to his bedchamber, he glimpsed disarray. The wardrobe stood open and his spare doublets and breeches lay rumpled on the floor.

His heart pounded. Lar would not have left his rooms in such a state. What had the thief taken from the wardrobe?

Keladon hurried into the bedchamber. A thought crossed his mind. *It wasn't a thief—*

He pivoted on his left foot as he drew his sword into an awkward parry. Light glinted nearby and steel rang from striking his blade.

"Bugger," grunted the assassin. He wore a baggy doublet of plain fabric and multiple slashes, clothing which marked him as a petty nobleman, yet his speech marked him as a man of common birth and hard upbringing. "Quick on your feet, but so's a mouse when he ears the cat, and you've got no jewel to save you this time." The assassin shifted his weight forward and economically moved his forearm.

Steel rang again and Keladon retreated deeper into his bedchamber. He had no other route. The assassin blocked the way to the front room and the corridor beyond.

But voice might carry. "I raise hue and cry!" Keladon shouted. "A ruffian violates the peace of the palace!"

"No one will ear you," the assassin said. He flexed his forearm again and his sword flashed near Keladon's waist. Keladon parried clumsily and shuffled deeper into the room, further from the window and any possible witness in the gardens below. Before long he would be pressed back against the table in the corner bearing a chamberpot.

A plan hatched in Keladon's mind. At best, it would only give him a moment to strike, and if he waited until he was certain that moment had come, it would have gone. He would have to take the chance and act boldly.

The assassin pressed him. He parried more blows and edged backward. He kept his left hand behind him. Holding the left arm there to keep balance was a technique long taught to the nobility. The assassin would think him a fop with little real skill with the blade.

"You're better'n I thought you'd be," the assassin said. His eyes were hard and his grizzled brow, free of sweat. "For a man too cowardly to kill—"

Keladon's fingers closed on the rim of the chamberpot. Empty or full made no difference. He flung it overhand at the assassin's right eye and lunged forward. If the assassin reached with his free hand to catch or block the chamberpot, he would twist and expose the left side of his abdomen right *there*.

Keladon's new blade pierced cloth, skin, viscera. He drew it back as the assassin screamed. The assassin chopped weakly down with his sword, but too slow. Keladon's next blow brought his blade's edge halfway into the assassin's right forearm. The assassin's sword clattered to the floor and splashed in the blood pooling from his abdominal wound. The assassin breathed raggedly and pressed his left hand against his torn doublet. He staggered back half a step, then slipped in his blood and fell backwards. His head banged the wooden floor.

The assassin groaned, and more blood soaked the left side of his doublet. The assassin's eyelids fluttered and showed whites. Keladon watched his arms and legs for any hostile capability he might have left. Though the assassin's wounds were plainly grave, in his last moments he might feel enough pride to try completing his mission. But the assassin made no move. He gasped for breath and stared with terrified eyes as Keladon held the tip of his sword at his neck.

"I decline to kill with magic," Keladon said, "but I will defend myself with a sword. Why does Old Atem want me dead?"

"Nev'r."

"If you believe in the Divine Couple, tell me the truth. It will shorten your soul's time in exile before admittance to their hall."

"He nev'r said." The assassin grunted, and his breaths came faster and more shallow.

"Where can I find him?" Keladon said.

The assassin stared, then barely shook his head. "Reeves can't get him. You're a fool if you try. The Bawdy Priestess, near the docks. If you go there, he'll find you." Cold sweat bloomed on the assassin's pallid face. His breathing stopped. He opened his mouth and widened his eyes. With choking sounds and spasms lifting his head, his body tried to pull in more air. Keladon had seen worse at Suherabal Ford, and the assassin deserved more agonies than the Peluraki foot, but no man's death could ever be pleasant to see. The assassin managed to take in some air, but after a dozen rapid breaths, he again stopped breathing. His body tried one last time to draw breath, and for several seconds failed until it finally gave up. His clenched neck softened and his eyes stared vacantly at the ceiling.

Keladon's limbs shook, and his pity at the man's death dissipated, replaced by anger. Angry at the dead hired killer, but angrier still at the master criminal who'd hired him, and whatever powers might lie behind Old Atem. *He'll find me? What makes you certain I can't find him first? I slew you, didn't I?*

He took a breath. *It won't be as simple*, a quieter part of him mused, *as your anger wants to believe.* It would take disguise, stealth, and guile to dip into Teisoret's underworld and survive, let alone bring Old Atem to justice. But it had to be done, and he could trust no one else with the mission. He would start that night.

A SERVANT SWUNG OPEN the doors to the banquet hall. From inside the hall came King Raboros's voice. "There he is! The hero of the day!"

Chairs scraped on the hardwood floor and soon all the dozens of noblemen in the banquet hall stood at their tables. Their conversations fell silent and they turned their gazes on Keladon. Only the clop of his boots sounded through the room as he crossed five paces of bare wooden floor. The wary mix of fear and disdain he'd received in the small audience chamber last autumn was gone. The faces and postures of all present, from the dandies and sycophants to the older men held over from his father's time, now showed respect and admiration.

Keladon passed between two banquet tables. At one stood three battlemage officers in asymmetrical gray coats, a dark contrast to the ostentatious colors dominating the room, who raised their goblets to him. At the other was a man with grizzled brown hair, wearing a plain green doublet slashed only at each elbow. "Well done, Your Illustriousness."

The king had invited him to the seat of honor, but a glance showed Raboros chatting with Dobak. "Thank you, sir, but I did no better than would have any man here who chanced upon a desperate burglar."

"Nonsense! You've killed before, unlike most of these, and when the time came you acted instead of quivering in indecision." He lowered his voice. "Your father would be proud." Even lower, he murmured, "You're a true son of his."

"I am a grateful that he claimed me, sir, but his truest son is His Majesty."

The old man gave a faint nod. "I shall not keep you any longer, sir, save to invite you to a dinner I shall host tomorrow evening at my townhouse."

Another invitation? He'd inwardly cursed when a herald had entered his rooms, already crowded with palace guards, reevesmen, and Melos, and summoned him to the seat of honor at the king's banquet that evening. Every hour he spent in social obligation increased Old Atem's chance at sending another killer before Keladon could stop him. But on the other hand, if Old Atem worked with someone in the palace, being seen socializing might lull the crime master. "I should be delighted, sir. Would your servants give my valet your formal invitation?"

He parted from the other lord and wound his way through the tables to to a dais bearing a long, curved table running across the width of the room. At the center of the table sat the only man in the room not on his feet: King Raboros.

Keladon bowed, stretching his right hand toward his ankle. "I thank you for your invitation to feast with you, Your Majesty."

"Come, sit beside us, squire of Korobei, and tell us of your courage and martial prowess." The king gestured toward an empty chair at his right.

Keladon went to the far end of the dais and climbed up. He made his way behind the table, between noblemen standing at their chairs and a line of servants along the room's back wall. "The wielder of the blade that banished a thief from the Divine Couple's hall," said one nobleman with slashes like arrow fletchings on his doublet's sleeves. He glanced toward Keladon's crotch. "Perhaps I could see it—" He canted his hip and pursed his mouth. "—after the feast?"

Even if Keladon shared the other's inclination, and had no enemy to hunt for later that night, the crassness of the other's offer would have been reason enough to decline. He tried to do so politely. He had enough enemies without making more. "I have a prior engagement, sir. If you would pardon me?"

"Of course," the other said with a tone of arch sadness.

Next he passed a vaguely familiar dandy, thick red curls spilling down the sides of his face. Probably part of the crowd in the audience chamber last autumn. "Well done, sir. Many of us talk as if we could have defended ourselves as well as you, but we fool ourselves by doing so."

Keladon's opinion of the red-haired dandy warmed slightly. "Thank you." He continued on.

Soon, he passed another opulently-dressed figure, this one wearing over a red velvet cloak over a battlemage's attire. Keladon bowed, "Good evening, Your Grace."

Norobom laughed and clapped his hand on Keladon's shoulder. "Old friend, we've no need for titles between us. I'm glad you have revealed your true self once again." He smiled, exuding a serene confidence that had inspired men to stand and die. "His Majesty has you now, but have you a few minutes after the festivities for us to talk?"

"A few. Your pardons, now?"

Norobom gestured for him to pass. Keladon made his way past more men until he reached the seat of honor next to King Raboros.

Another bow, and a servant rushed forward to push in his chair as he sat next to the king.

"Wine for our honored guest," the king said to the servant behind him, "then bring out the first course." Red wine soon arrived, poured till Keladon's glass was three-quarters full. Keladon took a dry, lingering sip, and as soon as he set down his glass, King Raboros said, "Tell us all about your adventure."

"I hardly think of it as an adventure, Your Majesty."

"Don't be modest," said Dobak from the king's left. "You surprised a thief posing as one of us and had the aplomb to outduel him."

Keladon put on a wry face. "Your Lordship, a duel implies both parties are artisans, trained in the sword and the etiquette of its use. The... thief and I fought, like animals in a cage. I got inside his blade before he got inside mine."

"Would he had invaded my rooms," Dobak said, "that I might have slain him."

Servants set out delicate porcelain plates bearing sardines in fish aspic. Keladon took the distraction the servants offered to come up with a reply fitting his cover story. "I wouldn't wish such a thing on you, Lord Dobak. Even the poorest swordsman may happen to land the killing blow."

Dobak gave a look of bruised pride. "I have long trained in the art of the sword, sir."

King Raboros lifted the appetizer toward his mouth, but stopped to raise his eyebrow at Dobak. "If you had ever wielded a sword in anger, you would know our honored guest spoke wisely." He bit off half the appetizer, then set it down and reached for his wine.

The temperate words coming from the king's mouth surprised Keladon. Had the birth of the new prince given the king more wisdom? Or had Raboros been wise last autumn, and blinders Keladon had placed on himself had hidden the king's better nature?

"We have learned you had no adventure," King Raboros said to Keladon, "but we would hear more about the events."

Keladon sipped wine to give himself a moment. *The man was only a thief and you don't know why he chose your chambers*, he reminded himself, then launched into a story true in its other particulars. "I noticed the doorway of my rooms was ajar, sire. A glance in showed that someone had ransacked my bedchamber. Foolishly I assumed the thief had gone and I rushed in to see what he might have taken...."

He continued the story as King Raboros listened intently, servants brought bowls of chicken and turnip soup, and Dobak pouted. The king took no notice of his companion, and instead from time to time asked Keladon pertinent questions. "How can a thief pose as a nobleman and saunter into the palace?"

Keladon squinted for a moment, seeking something in the king's expression to show he doubted the cover story. No, the king believed it. "I do not know, sire. The palace is crowded with visitors, many of whom have never before made their way to court and would be unknown to the royal guard. A guardsman might simply have assumed him to be what he appeared."

Dobak spoke. "Or that guardsman let him in for a cut of his take."

King Raboros' jowls slumped as he looked at his empty bowl, a thoughtful look on his face. "Either possibility is intolerable. We cannot have ruffians stealing, or worse, inside our palace."

Dobak twisted in his seat to face the king more squarely. "Sire, at your word, I would call out the Master of the Royal—"

The king's raised hand cut him off. "We admire your zeal, but we have no reason to rebuke the royal guard's master. The error or the crime, whichever it might have been, happened at a level beneath his notice. When we speak to him about the matter, we will offer suggestions to prevent the same event from repeating itself."

The main course was brought out, roasted game hens stuffed with onions and basil. The hen's skin crackled as the king sliced through it, and he shut his eyes in apparent delight when he chewed his first bite.

"Your blood runs cooler than mine, sire, to treat the Master of the

Royal Guard so mildly; but what suggestions?" Dobak's tone made clear he saw none.

"We will tell him to increase the number of guards on duty, though that may not be enough." He turned his brown eyes to Keladon with a look of diligence. King Raboros cared about the problem. Perhaps only because he feared an assassin targeting him could infiltrate the palace as easily as the thief had, but still, perhaps Raboros had been finally shaken into acting like a monarch. "Think you of any other thing, sir?"

Keladon absently carved at the joint between his hen's leg and thigh. "Pair up the guardsman, and mix up the pairings every day. A lazy or corrupt guardsman would have another set of eyes on him at all times, and if he were corrupt, he would have only one day to win his partner over to his scheme."

"A wise utterance," King Raboros replied. "We will instruct the Master of the Royal Guard to do so first thing in the morning."

An unexpected, but pleasant, feeling filled Keladon's chest: respect for his half-brother. Even if the king only directed his faculties toward the need for greater security out of fear of being an assassin's target, he at least had those faculties. They had been dormant for years, blanketed by ease and rich living, but had not withered and died. The dinner continued through courses of cheese, fruit, and pastries, and though the conversation moved on, King Raboros spoke more well-thought words.

He may never be a great king, but he might at least be a good one.

After the servants cleared the last dessert plates and poured glasses of thick, sweet wine, a herald walked in from the far door, stopped in the middle of the bare area of floor, and bowed. "Your Majesty, a supplicant seeks your audience, for the purpose of diverting you and your gentlemen companions: Toreb and his troupe."

Keladon's shoulders stiffened. The king's voice sounded oblivious to Keladon's reaction. "He is admitted."

It was indeed Toreb, all broad chest and outlandish mustaches, who strode in. He wore a cloak of dull red wool, a shabbier version of Norobom's. He stopped next to the herald and doffed his hat. When he bowed, a peacock feather in his hat brushed the hardwood. "Your Majesty, great and honored lords." Even bowing, his voice filled the room. He rose to full height. "I offer you an evening of delights the likes of which you have never seen. The most skilled entertainers from across our kingdom and beyond its borders will regale you with sweet notes of voice and instrument. Others will perform feats requiring the utmost in dexterity, stamina, and strength. You will see acrobats, jugglers, a swordswallower, and an illusionist. I promise you, most high-born, that you will remember this evening for the rest of your lives." Toreb let silence hang for a moment as he looked to the king.

"You promise much," Raboros said, his tone newly bored. "Deliver, goodman Toreb, if you can."

"First, sire, I present to you Moni, the veiled dancer." Toreb flourished his arm as the dancer came in from the corridor, followed by a drummer and a guitarist. Toreb held his hand out for her and guided her last steps. All the while, he gazed at Moni's veiled face, his expression showing possessive pride. Finally he strode into the wings.

The musicians tuned their instruments as Moni stood still. Gauzy green silks draped her, and when the musicians began the tune and she began her dance, the silks slid over her body like a lover's hands. Raboros yawned, then picked up his dessert wine. He drained the glass in a few seconds, then waved to the servant behind him for more.

Moni struck her final pose. Men at the tables on the floor drummed their hands on their tables and whistled, and most of those seated on the dais gave slow, soft claps. The king finished his next glass of wine as a midget and a freakishly tall man replaced Moni at the center of attention. The midget cracked a whip and cursed the placid giant. He ended the act standing on the giant's shoulders. They received mild applause.

"Rather tedious, isn't it, sire?" Dobak asked.

"Perhaps they will end on a higher note." The sense of purpose visible earlier on the king's features had faded.

Toreb stepped up from the wings, called on the audience to applaud more, and introduced the next act, a songstress all the way from the northern plains of Rak-pawindu, named Neranaren. Keladon frowned—he had never heard of such a Rak-pawindan name—but soon remembered the singer Lar had pursued on the boat, a woman with the common Sodeleraki name of *Nera*.

She came out in a purple robe and headdress, bedecked with chains of silver bangles. Makeup lay thick on her face. She glanced after Toreb as he walked away from her. Her eyes showed a moment of disappointment. Behind her, a tall, sun-bronzed man who might actually might have been from northern Rak-pawindu entered, carrying a *doumbek*. He knelt behind the singer, tucked the drum behind his left knee, and beat rhythms directly with his hands.

Neranaren sang a plaintive song about a woman mourning a lost love. The emotion in her voice sounded genuine. Was she skilled at pretense, or did she honestly feel the pain she sang about, inflicted by Toreb, in some romantic triangle involving the veiled dancer? Keladon turned to King Raboros to discuss her artistry. The king snored lightly, chin on his chest.

The crowd's applause roused him. He turned bleary eyes toward his wine glass as Toreb returned to center stage.

This time, Neranaren avoided Toreb's gaze and haughtily lifted her chin. As she walked away, a brief frown formed on his face, but Toreb then turned with his usual showmanship to the king. "Your Majesty, by your leave, my next performer is of common birth and requires the use of drawn swords in your presence. Would you forgive him this affront, sire?"

"Will he harm anyone?" King Raboros still sounded bored.

Toreb shook his head. "The only person he might harm, sire, is himself."

"Proceed." The king reached for more wine as the next performer entered. Vos, dressed in snug tunic and hose.

King Raboros's hand stopped, and his gaze roved up and down Vos's figure. Vos stopped and flourished his right hand as another member of the troupe, flanked by two members of the royal guard, wheeled toward Vos a cart racked with drawn blades, ranging from a dagger to a curved scimitar.

Once the cart stood next to him, and the royal guards backed away a step, Vos bowed to the king. "Your Majesty, I am truly honored to show you some of my talents."

Keladon crossed his arms and watched Vos from under heavy brows. The performer started with a dagger and carried it with deference to the king and the gathered nobles, keeping it always pointed toward himself. He had skill in his art, working the dagger down his throat far enough to close his mouth over the hilt, then expelling it, both actions done by the muscles of his throat. He set the dagger aside and picked up a sword long enough that it had to enter his stomach, and then another. After the two swords, Vos reached for the scimitar, and Keladon's toes curled and teeth gritted in tense sympathy.

A glance to the left dispelled some of that feeling. King Raboros bore a look of pining lust. On the far side of the king, Dobak saw it too, pressing his lips together as he watched King Raboros's eyes. The king waved over his shoulder while keeping his gaze on Vos's performance. "We would meet this one later," he said to his manservant.

The manservant's sunken face hid any judgment he might have had on the king's request. He nodded and withdrew.

"Sire..." murmured Dobak.

"What?" Raboros said. Their conversation had the air of having be played out many a time before.

These were the men to whom he entrusted his son? These were the men for whom he'd slathered his soul with the blood of thousands of Peluraki? Keladon turned his face away from the tension between the king and his favorite. No better was the sight of Vos brazenly watching the king's face in apparent expectation of favor.

Keladon squirmed in discomfort and finally could no longer stop himself. "Sire, I have information about the swordswallower that you may wish to know."

"How could you have any such thing, Keladon?" the king asked, voice cool. Behind the king's vision, Dobak gave Keladon a look of guarded hope.

"I encountered him on the journey down the Derepar from Mitok," Keladon said.

"Encountered? We did not think you were inclined in such a way. Nor did we think that you would seek to deny us a dish you had tasted."

Keladon took a quick, shallow breath. "Your Majesty, I entered my cabin to find he had invaded it with a victim, a merchant whom he... distracted in order to pick his pocket."

After a moment, King Raboros chuckled. "We would give him a purse ten times heavier than the one he lifted from that merchant, and naïve as he looks—" The king licked his lips, seemingly without noticing. "—he's no fool, he knows we are generous. Keladon, we thank you for your advice...." He turned his eyes back to Vos and the pining look returned. "But we know what we do."

Dobak frowned, and slumped his face against his fist in defeat. Keladon said, "Of course, sire." He leaned back in his chair and reached for his wine. *Some goodman labored hard to pay the tax you'll hand over to this grifter*— Keladon took a deep gulp of the wine and pushed the thought away. A darker thought drifted into its place. *What if Vos wanted to take more from the king than a fat purse?*

"Sire, if he were to smuggle in his mouth a dagger—"

"He wouldn't." King Raboros' voice had a steely edge. "And we can defend ourself. We are younger than you and not as fat as we look."

"I stand corrected, sire." Keladon bowed his head. His heart pounded and he barely noticed the rest of the entertainers. He had offended the king, but how badly? How could he undo the damage?

As soon as the performance ended, he sought the king's leave to depart, and Raboros readily granted it.

Norobom caught up with him in the corridor outside. He led Keladon away from the main mass of departing noblemen, then into a quiet side hallway. He glanced up and down and waited for a pair of battlemages to turn a distant corner before speaking. "It was no surprised burglar you killed today."

Did Norobom know something? Keladon drew him out. "What makes you say that?"

"He could have burglarized any one of a hundred rooms, and emptied it of valuables within a minute. He happened to pick your room? And be present when you returned to it? I'd wager a thousand crowns he was sent to kill you."

"I know too much to take that bet," Keladon said.

Norobom's eyebrows flashed upward. "You figured it out. Of course, you know how this place works. Do you know who sent him?"

Keladon almost mentioned Old Atem's name, but held back. "I don't."

"Another thousand crowns says the man behind it was your dinner companion."

A blink, then Keladon frowned at Norobom. His face showed its usual confidence. Keladon whispered, "Why would the king want me dead through subterfuge?"

"Because you know the paternity of the queen's newborn son. Melos and I do too, of course, but he no doubt concluded we have too much to lose and too little to gain by announcing that fact. About you, though, I'm sure he doesn't know enough to weigh you on those scales, and his resentment of you for being the claimed bastard is so great and well-known, it tips the balance against you."

Keladon's thoughts reeled. "But I've helped him. Established him a dynasty. Freed him from Melos' harping he bed the queen."

"He should be grateful?"

"Yes."

"All the more reason he would want you dead."

"But he needn't bother with subterfuge. A countersigned warrant, and I would be imprisoned within hours and executed within days."

With an emphatic head shake, Norobom said, "He would fear you would tell the truth to your jailers, and the crowd at your scaffold. The only way to keep you quiet is to kill you before you can tell anyone."

"There's one other way. He could recognize my loyalty to the realm and him."

Norobom peered at Keladon. "You don't fully believe me. Go back to your rooms and think on it, if the servants have scrubbed away the assassin's blood enough for you to think."

"I have new rooms, here in the east wing." Larger and more luxurious than his former suite, both a reward and a guilt-offering by the Master of the Household. And closer to the king.

"Check for spy-holes, secret passages, and other traps." Norobom shook his head. "I'm disgusted to have to tell you this. The king should trust your discretion, and keep you alive for the day you rejoin me in flinging fire upon our enemies. You may tell me anything about this matter, and I will do all within my power to help you survive and gain your proper position." He clasped Keladon's forearm and stared into his eyes. "Even though it's been twenty years since you tapped a ruby, you are still my brother."

Keladon took his leave moments later. Even if Norobom were correct, he needed proof of his old comrade's suspicions. He wanted to get into the city to hunt down Old Atem, but first had to disguise himself.

He went to his new rooms, high on the north side of the east wing. Lar waited with some castoff clothes, a wool jerkin dyed black and a pair of brown workman's trousers. The open windows admitted warm night air and the sound of men's voices and women's laughter from the garden below.

"I took the liberty, Your Illustriousness, of caking your brown boots with dried mud—" Lar set the pair on the floor in front of Keladon.

"You have done well. Help me dress."

After Lar helped him untie the cords holding up his breeches, Keladon slipped on the trousers, jerkin, and boots. The trousers had a jagged, four-inch wide slit in one leg just above the top of the boot. "Very authentic," he said.

"And practical too, if I may say so, my lord." Lar pointed to a long dagger in a boiled leather sheath, lying on the dressing table. "I paid the armorer a visit and, once he remembered you, he was pleased to give a fighting knife to my master. I sized it to slip inside your boot."

Keladon went to the dressing table and picked up the knife. He wrapped his fingers around the hilt and drew it, testing its heft. With luck, he wouldn't need it tonight, but one couldn't count on luck. He returned the knife to its sheath and slipped it through the slit in his trouser leg and into his boot. He took a few steps—the sheath rubbed against his ankle—then knelt and reached his hand into his boot for a practice draw of the knife.

That done, he stood and looked at his valet. "I still need to disguise my face."

Lar reached for a rag, a tin cup of water, and black shoe polish. "We can darken your hair with this, my lord." He wetted the rag and dabbed it into the shoe polish. He moved the rag toward Keladon's forehead and Keladon shut his eyes. "It may look shiny and greasy, but among the circles you'll be traveling in tonight, the men are lucky to wash their hair five times a year." Lar worked and Keladon held still. "Would I had something to disguise the brown of your eyes."

"It's a common enough color."

"But Old Atem knows it's yours." Lar set down the black polish and wiped his hands on a dry rag. He went to a side table and returned with black tufts in his hands. "I was at least able to find false hair for your face." He checked the fit of a beard and a mustache to Keladon's face, then set them down and opened a small jar containing a pungent glue. "I hear tell it's tighter than a priest's arse-hole to remove, pardon my tongue."

"I expect it will stay on during my sojourn," Keladon said. "How did you come by this false hair?"

"Some members of the troupe when we traveled downriver from Mitok."

"I thought Nera spurned you?"

Lar's eyes glinted, but something in his demeanor seemed false. "The troupe has more than one furrow to plow. Are you ready, Your Illustriousness?"

"Yes," said Keladon.

Lar brushed glue on the back surfaces of the mustache and beard and raised them to their position. Keladon held his face as still as he could, but involuntarily winced at the stench under his nose. "The smell will fade as it dries," Lar said. He stepped back and checked his work. "That should do, especially by dim light." Lar leaned in. "Are you sure you want me stay here in the palace? You'll be entering unfamiliar territory and I might be able to assist you."

"Taking a servant with me to a seedy tavern would undo all your efforts at disguising me," Keladon said. "I will not need you tonight, but if all goes well, I may need you on the morrow. Tonight I shall be gone at least three hours, likely more. Once you've readied my attire for tomorrow, you may take the rest of the night for your leisure."

Lar smiled in honest surprise, then bowed. "Thank you, sir."

Keladon stuffed two small purses into inner pockets of his jerkin and trousers. Lar had rolled the coins tightly, and they gave no clink when the purses moved. Satisfied, Keladon made his way out of his rooms and to the palace's main gate. He ducked his head as he passed nobles and met the gaze of servants. No one questioned him. The guards at the main gate yawned and chatted between them-selves as he went out.

At this hour, the plaza outside the gate was empty. The awnings that would partially shield the viewing mirrors from the late-morning sun were in place, pulled taut between the palace wall and support poles. A clock tower rose nearby, its face too dark to be read.

An hour's walk took him steadily down through Teisoret toward the Derepar. The social strata of the neighborhoods he traversed paralleled their elevation. On the higher ground near the palace, marble columns adorned the front facades of tall townhouses, and the music and chatter of garden parties hosted by nobles or wealthy commoners drifted over tall brick walls into the street. Just inside the city's old, crumbling wall, the streets smelled of the work of skilled tradesmen. The dyers, tanners, and fullers had retired for the night to the respectable quiet of the quarters above their shops. His soles clomped on brick paving stones or thudded on packed dirt.

As he neared the Derepar, the streets grew narrower, more twisted, and all dirt. Where the better-off neighborhoods had lined, buried cesspits for body wastes, here clumps of feces sat in puddles of urine, waiting for a rain to wash them into the river. People were about, most walking quickly and furtively. From the narrow wooden houses, their windows nothing more than rough holes in the walls, and the alleys guarded by flies buzzing over mounds of horse dung, came thuds, grunts, crashes, and screams.

He easily found the Bawdy Priestess; the owners had mounted bright lamps to light up a sign painted with a curvaceous woman in a priestess' robe, lifting its hem to within an inch of her sex. He hunched his shoulders and hurried toward the front entrance.

A broad, stolid doorman stopped him. "What makes you think you can come in?"

Keladon looked in the doorman's face. He gave no hint of recognition of Keladon's high birth. Good—his disguise worked, and he had another way to enter. "Three sous."

The doorman set his hands on his hips. "Ten."

"A ha'crown? Do I look made of money? I can offer you five."

The doorman did not stir. "Let's split it down the middle, then. Eight."

Part of Keladon wanted to laugh, but he stifled it, and did his best to sound aggrieved. "That's not the middle."

"I never learned no ciphering. Eight sous, or get yourself gone."

A real streetwise man would haggle more, wouldn't he? "Eight sous? What kind of man do you take me for?"

The doorman leaned forward. "A man comes here, he knows it'll take him five crowns, give or take, to get him the drink and bawd he wants. You can spend an extra eight sous."

Keladon reached into his jerkin pocket. He uncinched the purse and counted out the coins by feel. He held them out for the doorman, who roughly snatched them. "Get inside before the price goes up."

As he pushed open the door, Keladon felt foolish. *Your first offer was too high and you haggled up too fast.* Perhaps that would turn out for the best. The doorman would signal the barkeepers and bawds that he was a man loose with money, an easy mark. In their efforts to gull him, he could turn the tables and extract information from them in return. Spending a few extra crowns to learn the whereabouts of Old Atem would be a fair exchange.

His first task, though, was to orient himself through the noise and glare inside the tavern's main room. Musicians played a lute and shawm in one far corner, and in the other, men threw dice into a box, some cheering and others cursing with each roll. Keladon found a table near the bar and close to the center of the room. Traffic should be heavy and he'd have a decent chance of overhearing stray conversations.

As he stood there, a barmaid with crow's feet and a false smile came up for his order. She cocked her hip to show she could be hired, but he kept his gaze on her face. A flicker of self-loathing crossed it, which he pretended not to notice. He ordered a beer. After she brought it, he often raised the mug to his lips to appear a typical man of the crowd, but rarely sipped.

His sidelong glances showed a mix of rough commoners with a

few slumming noblemen and wealthier commoners, such as three slender, furtive young men with smooth faces. One seemed nervous, one curious, and the last, heavily drunk.

Before long, two rough-looking men came in. From the corner of his eye, Keladon saw them share a glance and saunter to the young men. One of the new arrivals said, in a deep gruff voice, "You're at our table."

"We are?" asked the drunken one, his voice quarrelsome.

His nervous companion's voice sounded high and tight. "Sorry, didn't know, we were just moving on."

Keladon looked up as he and the other young man, curiosity gone from their face, led their drunken fellow away. "Are you a fool?" the third young man whispered harshly. "They're part of some criminal's crew. Cross them and you'll end up with a smiling neck."

Keladon angled his ear toward the two newcomers.

"The boss was mad to boiling, yeah?" said the second man. The shorter of the two, his voice was higher than his peer's and much milder.

"Yeah. Don't know about what." The first man raised his voice. "Wench, get over here. We have parched throats!" Returning to the prior conversation, he said, "Afore you got there, I heard him shout down, 'I pay through the nose for two men who couldn't drown a sackful of kittens!'"

Keladon's eyebrows rose. He studied the surface of his beer and listened even more closely.

"He wants someone dead. Who?"

"He wants a lot of people dead. He didn't shout out no names. Ah, finally, wench!"

The barmaid hurried up to them with two mugs, handles clenched in her fist. "The barkeep drew your usual."

"Faster next time," said the man with the mild voice, "or you'll serve us another way." A slap sounded, a hand against cloth, and the barmaid scurried by Keladon's table with wide, reddened eyes.

"Miss," he said mildly, "I'll have another."

The barmaid jerked her head up and gave Keladon a wary look. Regret for her lot panged him. She deserved more respect from Old Atem's men, but he saw little he could do while maintaining his disguise. He slid three sous across the gouged tabletop toward her.

She cast her gaze at the coins. "Only two sous a mug."

"I appreciate quality service."

Her face remained guarded. She reached for his old mug and her eyes widened. Evidently, the weight of a double handful of beer still inside surprised her. She soon covered her surprise and hurried to the bar.

Keladon realized Old Atem's men had talked among themselves, in low voices and criminals' cant, as he'd ordered his second drink. He listened for more but the two men said little. Their mugs thudded on the table from time to time and they discussed the merits of the different bawds for hire.

A pudgy man wearing a beer-stained apron came out a door behind the bar. Keladon assumed him to be the proprietor. The pudgy man's mouth showed a glum line as he surveyed the room, then with a weary shrug, he trudged toward Old Atem's men.

"You're slow in showing your respects, yeah?" the mild-voiced man said.

The proprietor's eyelids and mouth quivered. "I wanted to double count to show him every sou of respect."

"You did? Then show him," said the man with the gruff, deep voice.

From the corner of his eye, Keladon only saw the proprietor's back, but through a momentary lull in the noise in the room, the clink of a coin purse came clearly to his ears.

"We'll be here next week," the deep-voiced man said.

"Next week? We don't have to go yet, yeah?" asked the other man. "We have time for some of our host's bawds—"

"The boss wants his respects on time. Especially on a day like today."

After a moment, the mild-voiced man said to the proprietor,

"Next time, we'll take two bawds each, yeah?" Another moment, and empty beer mugs slammed to their table. Keladon risked a glance, and saw them heading to the front door.

Keladon raised his mug to his lips, and again did not drink. He set down the mug and worked his way through the crowd toward the door. Outside, a sliver of the moon shown above the dark buildings, but the sound of footsteps came from around the corner to his right. Heart thudding, he headed after them, walking as quietly as he could on the packed dirt. Piles of horse dung formed darker shadows on the unlit street.

All he would do tonight was follow them to Old Atem's headquarters. Tomorrow he could get a view inside the headquarters. Information he would get then he would use to infiltrate the headquarters and force information from Old Atem the night after.

Around the corner, Keladon hesitated before taking his next step. Old Atem's two men stood in the center of the street. They faced each other and argued with loud voices and exaggerated gestures. "If you'd rather plug it into Ala than Kiha," said the mild-voiced man, the shorter of the two, "you're a bigger fool than you look."

"You're the biggest fool. Why look at the bawd's face when you're plowing her furrow?"

Keladon took another step, then stopped. Their conversation was clearly false.

"What?" said the shorter of Old Atem's men. The other muttered something. The shorter man dropped his arms. "You're on to us, yeah?" He started walking toward Keladon. "Haven't lost all your common sense living uphill?"

The gruff-voiced man followed. "We apportionate good service."

"He means appreciate," said his companion. He cracked his knuckles as he walked.

"We'll grab, I mean, *have* your purse and you won't even *miss* it."

You had to disguise more than your appearance, Keladon told himself as they came closer.

"That's it, don't run, let's make it easy. You wanted to see how us lowborn live, yeah? You'll see it up close."

Old Atem's men shared a glance. Keladon realized they would not content themselves with robbery. They didn't know who he was, but they would inadvertently do their boss' work. He couldn't follow them to Old Atem's headquarters if he were dead. He raised his hands. "I'll hand over my purse. The big one. It's in my left boot."

"Do it, yeah?"

Keladon knelt and slipped his hand into the slit in his trouser leg. His fingers wrapped around the knife's hilt. His heart slammed and his breath caught for a moment. Which one first?

He sprung toward the shorter man's neck. A slash sent blood spurting, and then Keladon got behind him and stabbed him in the kidney. He yanked the knife to the side as blood spurted over his hand. He gripped the knife tighter and pushed the shorter man to the ground.

The other criminal had raised his fists. A knife jutted from one. He bent his knees and rocked his weight from side to side. The tip of his knife wavered uncertainly in the sliver of moonlight, and Keladon could make out the whites of his eyes in the dim street. The man backed away one step. "Go back uphill. My boss will make it so you'll be killed if you come down here ever again."

He'd guessed correctly—the shorter man had been the better one with a knife. Keladon glimpsed a small dark pile on the street behind and to the right of the gruff-voiced man. He brandished his blade and stepped forward and to his left. "Is that so?"

The gruff-voiced man shifted his body to face squarely to Keladon, then lurched backward and turned to run. His boot landed in the pile of horse dung and slipped out from under him. He tumbled to his back on the dusty street.

Keladon lunged forward. He stomped his left foot down on the wrist of the criminal's knife hand and knelt with the tip of his own blade at the man's neck. "Let go your knife."

Through his boot, Keladon felt muscles flex in the man's wrist.

"Now tell me where I can find your boss."

"You think I'll tell you that, reevesman? He'd give me a smiling neck."

Keladon pressed his knife's tip into the man's skin. "He's not the only one who can do that." *Could he really kill this man?* part of him wondered. Though a gutter criminal, his foe had yielded, and might give him useful information. But then another part, cold and implacable, told Keladon what he would end up doing once his foe's usefulness ended. Flashing energies and the screams of thousands of men came back to him. But this time, at the memory of Suherabal Ford, a cold smile touched the corners of his mouth.

"I'll tell you, I'll tell you!" Fear filled the man's voice.

Part of Keladon felt serenely pleased this criminal had been brought low. Another part reveled that he held a blade to the man's neck. "I'm listening."

"The warehouse where Monek Street meets the riverside! Now let me go!"

"How can I believe what you've told me?"

"You have my life on the tip of your blade! I can't lie! The warehouse on Monek Street! You have the truth, now let me go!"

The cold and implacable part flowed down his legs and arms, and into his voice. "To warn him? I can't allow that."

The criminal's voice now sounded high and small. "Reevesman, lock me up, then, until you've caught him."

The cold feeling now encased Keladon like plate armor turned inside out, to deflect, not arrows, but pangs of conscious. He spoke in a tone that showed he knew the answer to his next question would be a number greater than zero. "How many informants has Old Atem among the reeve's men?"

After stiffening for a moment, the criminal's body eased. His arm under Keladon's boot settled into the dirt. He sighed and leaned his head back to expose more of his neck to Keladon's knife.

His skin resisted the tip of Keladon's knife for a moment, then gave way. The man's blood spurted onto the street as he made a gurgling sound in his throat. He pulled his left arm up to his neck and his hand trembled as he pressed it to the wound. Blood welled through his fingers. His body jerked once, twice, and then he stopped moving and his last breath rattled in his throat.

Absently, Keladon wiped each side of his knife on the dead man's trouser leg. The implacable hold on his mind and body broke up, like ice on a pond in early spring, fractured by discordant thoughts. *Ready your blade for the next challenge*, he imagined his old swordsmanship instructor saying, followed by another voice saying *he'd yielded you didn't have to kill him—*

No, he'd had to kill the criminal. If the gruff-voiced man had lived, even in some deep dungeon, Old Atem might have found out and realized his location had been compromised. Keladon's chance to surprise Old Atem would have been lost.

Keladon returned the knife to the sheath inside his boot with a crisp motion. Even if there had been a way to spare the criminal's life, this wasn't Suherabal Ford. The dead man was not some farmer whose sole offense had been birth as a subject of the Peluraki king. The dead man and his partner had wanted to rob him, or worse, and they had chosen a life of service to a master who wanted him dead. And when he killed them, he hadn't used the energies of a magegem to destroy them like swatted flies. He'd done them enough honor to get his hands dirty with their lives' blood.

How many of those words are true, and how many lies you tell yourself?

Even if some were lies, he could make his actions a little more just. He checked the dead men's pockets until he found a small but hefty purse in an inside pocket of the smaller man's jerkin. He left bloody fingerprints on it and realized just how much of their blood he'd gotten on himself. He couldn't return to the Bawdy Priestess through the front door. Keladon went to the far side of the street and turned back the way he had come. Before rounding the corner, he slumped his posture and walked with a limp in case the doorman happened to look his way.

Once past the tavern's entrance, he crossed the street and took an alleyway leading to the building's rear. Rats scurried away from his footsteps and a drunk grunted in his sleep.

Keladon found a locked door and rapped on it with his knuckles. No answer. He tried again, louder, and the sound of cautious footsteps came from within.

Keys rattled and one scraped in a lock. The door opened a crack and the pudgy proprietor looked out with a wary eye. "Who might you be?"

Keladon held out the purse. "A returner of stolen property."

The proprietor looked from Keladon to the purse several times, his face showing puzzlement, before his eyes widened as he beheld the purse. "That's blood," he whispered.

"Old Atem's men didn't volunteer to hand it over. It's yours."

The proprietor glowered at the purse. "You think I'm stupid enough to take that."

"Your pardon?"

"He'll send twenty men, not two, and they'll search every room. They find that purse, with his men's blood on it, and I'm dead. Get out of here." The door shut and the locks snicked home before Keladon could speak.

Thoughts of what to do with the money refused by the proprietor dogged him for a few blocks, until he realized he was on Monek street, just blocks from Old Atem's hideout. The realization focused him. He found the crime master's headquarters, a warehouse looking like any other, and studied the street from the shadow of a doorway. Catercorner to Old Atem's hideout, another warehouse turned its shadowed back to Monek street. Near ground level, the wall showed darker patches, he guessed from rotted planking. That would do.

Enough work for one night.

As he worked his way up slope through the last neighborhood of the poor, he shrugged off his blood-stained jerkin and threw it down an alley. His silk undershirt, stark white in the moonlight, would mark him as an outsider in these parts of town, but those few of the stolid burghers in the next streets who happened to be awake at this hour would not try to take advantage of his status. He brushed the tops of each boot against the back of his opposite calf, and clots of Lar's dried mud fell off. He tugged at his false mustache and beard as he kept walking. Lar's language, though colorful, had been accurate: tears welled in his eyes and his face felt raw by the time he pulled off the last of his disguise.

Eventually he crossed the plaza in front of the palace. Lamps burned on the sides of the sallyport housing the front gates. He peered under the arch of the sallyport, into a passage backlit by a few distant lamps burning in the palace gardens. The gates were closed, probably locked, and a few guards milled behind them. He drew closer and noticed the guards step to the gate and hold their pikes and halberds more alertly. He stopped near enough to the gate to make out the leader of the guard detachment, the only man wearing mail instead of boiled leather.

"Good evening, Your Illustriousness," the leader said.

Keladon relaxed. "I would enter the palace grounds."

"Of course, sir, but I'll have to ask you to stay with us a time. The Master of Palace Mages would speak with you."

"So late in the night?"

The guard leader bowed his head slightly. "I can't say what might be so urgent, sir, but the Master was insistent."

He had no appointments in the morning, and the men and ladies of court would allow him to sleep late after his encounter with the thief in the palace. A clean bed could wait a little longer. "I shall be pleased to speak with Forek." His voice lacked energy.

The guard leader nodded to his men, then unlocked the gate. While the guards shuffled their places, the gate swung outward far enough to admit a man. Keladon entered and realized the guards formed a half-circle around him. The guard leader relocked the gate.

What was so important Forek wanted him detained? Keladon jittered his head, then blinked a few times to become a trifle more alert. Was this some conspiracy aimed against him? A man could easily receive a king's praise in the evening, and after midnight, find himself locked in the dungeon. He peered around the darkness, looking for clues to his fate in the guards' faces, and finding none.

After a time, Forek and some of his assistants arrived. One of them was Long Face from the team Keladon had worked with that morning. Parel was his name, wasn't it?

Forek bowed slightly. "Your Illustriousness, thank you for taking the time to speak with me at so late an hour."

"The matter must be important."

"Indeed." Forek squinted at Keladon's stark white shirt. "You were about the town without your doublet, sir?"

"I was about the town, yes."

"When did you leave the grounds, sir?"

"About eleven o'clock. Within an hour of the end of the royal banquet." What had happened in the interim?

"Sir, did a guard see you as you left?"

"I went out this gate, not five feet from a guard."

Forek turned to the leader of the detachment. "Were you on duty?"

"No, Master of Palace Mages. We relieved the prior shift at midnight."

"What report did they leave regarding His Illustriousness' departure?"

The guard leader frowned. "I don't recall one. I'll check their report again." He went to a door in the wall of the sallyport. He opened it and the glow of a single lamp made Keladon squint.

The lamplight created stark shadows on Forek's face when he looked at Keladon. "Sir, can anyone vouch for your whereabouts?"

Keladon took a deep breath. If Old Atem had suborned palace officials, then his alibi would tip off his foe as to who killed the two extortionists. "I was in the sort of place whose customers have poor memories when questioned by the reeve."

Forek looked pained. "That's unfortunate, sir. A situation arose and we wanted to rule you out as the cause of it. About two hours ago, a green magegem was tapped somewhere on the palace grounds."

Someone risked the headsman to cast a spell? "As I said, I was not on the palace grounds." Without an alibi, would they believe the truth? Keladon cleared his throat. "I trust you are investigating your own men regarding this matter."

Long-faced Parel sniffed out a breath. "We know the law, and we wouldn't defy it."

Over his shoulder, Forek scowled at Parel. "Quiet. Yes, Your Illustri-ousness, we are investigating mages visiting for the claiming ceremony, palace mages, and battlemages as well. Sir, you will understand we must investigate everyone known to be capable of tapping a gem of any color. Therefore, I must ask you to permit us to search your chambers."

Though phrased as a request, Keladon knew it to be a command. Forek had the authority to search the person and rooms of anyone except the king. "I permit it."

The semicircle of guards drew back. Forek bowed and walked beside Keladon, with the assistants following two by two. Crickets fiddled in the gardens and an owl hooted in an orchard of potted orange trees. A servant opened the way into the east wing. Lamps chuffed in their sconces and the floorboards creaked under the foot-falls of Keladon and the palace mages.

The door to his chambers was unlocked. He tensed as he pushed it open; part of him expected Old Atem to make another attempt on his life. But his chambers were neatly kept and the only person present was Lar asleep on his bedroll in the front room. The noise of their entry roused him. "Sir, did you find.... Master? Goodmen? I'm sorry, the rooms aren't ready for visitors."

Forek and the others ignored him. Parel and the other assistants opened drawers and peered under the couches and chairs. Lar's face hardened in umbrage, until he glanced at his employer. Keladon chopped the air with his hand and shook his head at his valet.

Forek's assistants soon looked through the entire sitting room.

One cranked open the windows and checked the narrow, ornamental ledge outside while his peers went into Keladon's bedchamber. Keladon gestured to one of the chairs for Forek to sit, then pushed the cushions of the most comfortable couch all the way back to their places and took it for himself.

An obvious question worked its way to the top of his tired mind. "Do you know what spell was cast, Master of Mages?"

Forek squinted at him. As he did so, he glanced at Keladon's blackened hair and the inflamed skin of his jawline and upper lip. "How could we, sir?"

"I assume your spellwatchers detected the amount of flux from the tapped magegem? That might give a clue."

"With green, sir?" Forek said. "You shouldn't need a reminder that the flux is readily variable, depending on the intensity of the desired effect."

"My thoughts run slowly at this hour," Keladon said. Forek's words reminded him of the pain in his scrotum from Father a Son. That memory soon gave way to Queen Lilera's beautiful, proud face while the conception harness bound her feet. His manhood stirred and he crossed his legs. Too late, he realized his motion showed the blood-spattered hem of his trouser's right leg to Forek.

Forek's eyes widened briefly, but he said nothing.

"Green, spells of life and health...." Keladon thought out loud. "Perhaps someone has an ailment they wish to cure in secrecy."

"Sir, a good point. I'll ask around if a woman of the court might have sought an end to a pregnancy, or a man, a cure for bawd's gift." Something moved in the corner of Keladon's eye, in the open doorway to the bedchamber, and Forek looked that way. "What have you found?"

Keladon looked too, where Parel stood with a grim expression. "Come see, Master of Mages."

Forek left his seat and Keladon followed him into the bedchamber. In the corner, the wardrobe doors had been opened wide, and the other three palace mages stared into it. They made way for Keladon and their master.

Amid a neatly folded collection of shirts sat a pale, mottled green magegem.

"Sir," Forek said, "could you tell me how that came to be there?"

Inwardly stunned, Keladon spoke as casually as he could manage. "No, I can't."

"I need to speak with your servant, sir."

Lar stood in the doorway. "I'm right here." His face showed he'd heard every word.

"Did you put that green magegem here?"

"I never saw it afore."

"When did you last open the wardrobe?"

Lar's brow crinkled. "Let me see, must have been when I helped His Illustriousness dress for his night in the city. Between ten and eleven o'clock."

"The green magegem was not there at that time?"

Lar put on a puzzled look. "Since I never saw it afore now, it must not have been there then."

"But you've been in these chambers the entire time since your employer left the palace?"

"No, not at all," Lar said as he shook his head. "I went out around midnight, locked the door behind me—I'd swear on any body part of Balar's you'd care to name that I locked it—and spent a couple of hours chatting up the girls working the overnight shift in the kitchens before coming back here."

"With a kitchen girl?" Forek asked.

"No such luck, not tonight, at any rate. I came back here, worked the key in the lock, and soon enough went to bed. Wait, not *the* key, *a* key loaned to me by the palace staff."

"But we only have your word for these events, varlet."

Lar gave him a quarrelsome look. "You find those kitchen girls, they'll remember me. Tana, she lit up to me the most. And how many dozen keys for this room ever got cut?"

"I did give him permission to leave the rooms when his tasks were complete," Keladon said.

Forek grunted, face glum. "I don't know what all happened tonight, but there's a green magegem which doesn't belong in your room, sir. We will return it to the vaults—"

Parel spoke. "Master of Mages, if I may be so bold, before we do, we can cast See the Holder upon it."

Forek rubbed his forehead with his fingertips. "Parel—"

"We need to do it now."

"Yes," Keladon said. "If you cast it, cast it now, before the traces of the people who've touched it tonight fade too far. I will gladly help you cast that spell, because I know neither my image nor Lar's will appear."

"We've never cast it in earnest," Forek said. Weariness softened his gaze and left his words dangling.

"We've tested it," Parel said.

"With results I wouldn't take to the reeve to hang a man." Forek straightened his back and breathed deeply. "We'll do it. One of you," he said to his assistants, "find a servant to bring the most freshly laundered cloth they can find, and wrap the gem up in that. Once that arrives, it's to the mage's laboratory for all of us, including His Illustriousness and his man."

So much for finally getting to bed this night. But anxiety whipped Keladon's tired mind. He took it as given the green magegem in his wardrobe was the one tapped earlier, in violation of the king's decree. Someone had placed it in his rooms to pin suspicion on him. If the same conspiracy had recruited Forek or his assistants, the conspiring mage, or mages, if left unwatched, could falsify the results of See the Holder. At that point, the only way to clear his name would be to get the tavern proprietor and the barmaid to corroborate his story, which would reveal his involvement in the killing of the two criminals to any agent Old Atem might have in the palace.

Soon, they arrived at the mages's laboratory, overlooking an inner courtyard surrounded by the south wing. The room stayed dark, lit only by glimmers of distant lamps coming through the windows, while one of Forek's assistants went to rouse two apprentices. A few minutes later the boys shuffled in and, yawning, lit lamps around the room.

The new light resolved furniture from the darkness. A set of free-standing steel cabinets ran along one wall. The cabinets had slatted, padlocked doors. Visible between the slats, blues, greens, and yellows glinted. A space between two of the cabinets held a chalked-up slate with the color names and associated numbers written in a broad, wide hand.

"Is this the start of a new day or the end of an old, Master?" one of the assistants asked Forek.

"For the magegem count? Make it both."

Two of the palace mages counted magegems through the slats, then compared the results with the numbers on the slate. "The counts agree."

"Let's get to work," Forek said. He reached into an outer pocket of his doublet and pulled out a set of keys on a long, slender chain. "Parel, remind me, which gems do we need?"

"Green and yellow."

Forek rubbed his forehead. "And paper, an inkwell, and a quill to draw the vision?"

Parel shook his head. "Those would work, but aren't necessarily what we need. Chalk on the board would be viable, as would charcoal or lead on paper—"

"I would prefer ink on paper," Keladon said.

With a squint, Parel said, "Your Illustriousness, what you might prefer is not relevant in the least."

Forek bit his lip. He glared at his assistant, yet said nothing. Keladon replied directly to Parel. "If you would ever take the results of this spell to the reeve, you would best serve justice by generating a vision that could not be edited by human hands between the end of casting and its arrival on the reeve's desk."

"An innocent man would have nothing to fear," Parel said.

"We shall use ink and paper regardless," Forek said. While he unlocked the steel cabinets and retrieved the needed magegems, assistants went to an array of wooden armoires and cabinets around the room. Soon, a sheet of foolscap, an inkwell, and a quill rested on a table, next to the green magegem found in Keladon's rooms and the two needed for the spell. An assistant untied a knot in the cloth binding the magegem, and the ends of the cloth slid down to the table.

"I assume, Master," said Parel, "that I shall cast the spell."

"You are the most adept of us at it." Forek glanced to Keladon. "Unless, Your Illustriousness, you would rather?"

"Master Forek!" Parel's nostrils flared. "You cannot suggest a prime suspect in a crime cast a spell used to investigate it?"

Forek frowned. "Parel, you know the spell well enough to tell if a caster deviated from the proper recitation. Don't you?"

With a raised hand, Keladon said, "I welcome the chance to see Parel cast it."

Lar lifted his eyebrow and murmured, "Sir, is that wise?"

"Wise enough." Keladon spoke as quietly as he could. "I will watch and listen to what he does."

Lar pressed his lips together. He shuffled forward to stand near the shortest path between Parel and Keladon. His valet wanted to interpose himself should Parel try to touch him. *That's not how the spell works* Keladon considered telling Lar, until a more important question came up. "Parel, from which portion of the magegem will you seek traces of the holder?"

"Why, the entirety of it, from handle to base. Sir."

Keladon studied the palace mage's face for some hint about the source of his animosity. Was he part of the conspiracy, or simply out to prove See the Holder had a place in administering the king's justice? "The magegem was found lying amid my clothes. Its base and sides would thus have my traces even though I have never touched it."

"And you would reduce the flux tapped from your energy source," Forek said, "if you would only seek traces from the underside of the handle. Magical energies should never be wasted, especially...."

Parel's mouth pursed. "Master. Despite our recent problems—" He blinked at Keladon a few times. "We have enough magegems."

"Yet no one, not even our guest—" Forek waved toward Keladon. "—is making any more."

"Master, we can't assume he touched the underside of the handle when, if, he cast the unknown spell. He knows the rules of magic well enough to break them."

After a moment's calculation, Keladon slapped his hand on the work table. Forek and the other palace mages started at the swift, loud motion. "Would I then leave the tapped magegem in an unlocked cabinet in my own rooms?" He let the words hang for Forek and the other assistants. "Leave that aside. I have been a mage for a quarter-century. I learned the fundamentals of our art from the first men to tap the energies of magegems since the fall of Jelor. The most secure way for a mage to grasp a magegem is with his palm under the handle and his fingers curled around it. I could no more forget that lesson than I could forget how to hold my bladder till I found a chamberpot."

Forek nodded. "The underside of the handle, Parel."

Parel put on a glum face, then reached for the yellow magegem retrieved from the cabinet. He tapped it, then touched the paper, quill, and inkwell. A few words in Jelorean and the yellow's energies stood the quill straight up above the ink. Parel then set the yellow to attend the green from the cabinet. The magegems hummed with energy.

Parel bent toward the magegem in evidence and curled up the little finger of his right hand. Keladon craned his neck to peer past Lar. Parel touched his fingertip to the underside of the handle, close to the middle, then started the spell.

The quill dipped into the ink, then swept across the paper,

leaving four lines defining a rectangle. These four strokes showed the spell had been properly cast. Keladon took a breath and looked away from the rectangle on the paper. The spell needed a few minutes to gather the information it needed from any traces left on the handle's underside, and needed a few more to determine the appearance of the person from those traces. When the quill's nib scratched a load of ink onto the paper, he could look.

Time ran on. How many minutes had it been? Shouldn't the quill be moving by now? Parel frowned, and on the other side of the work table, another palace mage whispered to one of his mates. Parel muttered a few more Jelorean words to his magegem, among them *increase flux*.

More minutes passed. "Shouldn't the spell be complete?" Forek said.

Sweat ran down Parel's face. When it hit his eye, he blinked angrily. "Any moment now, I'm sure."

A sudden blobbing sound came from the inkwell, followed by a quick tap to leave excess ink in the inkwell. The quill then hovered to the paper. With a few quick motions, it drew symbols from the Jelorean syllabary.

Not enough traces to see the holder. Recommend stop the spell.

Parel fumed at the paper for a second more, then sloughed out a breath. With slumped shoulders, he told both magegems to stop releasing flux and stop attending him. "I don't know what went wrong," he said as he straightened his back.

"A glove?" Forek said, while Keladon debated whether to say the same.

"Hmph." Parel glowered at the magegem in evidence. "The caster would have wasted a great deal of flux commanding the gem through a layer of wool or leather." He turned a challenging look to Keladon. "Have you gloves, sir?"

"Would I pack his gloves in a hot summer?" Lar said.

"If he planned something nefarious—"

Forek cut off his assistant. "If His Illustriousness wore a glove to cast a spell, I would credit him with enough meticulousness to hide the magegem somewhere other than his rooms." He bowed to Keladon. "Sir, thank you for your time so late at night. I bid you a good evening, though I must ask you speak with me before you return to Korobei."

This spell had only caused him to be viewed with less suspicion. "Gladly. Before I return to my rooms, would you share with me the records of the flux your spellwatchers picked up? In light of this new information that the caster likely wore a glove, I might be able to narrow down the number of spells he could have casted."

"I see no harm in giving you copies of those records, sir. It will be the morning before we can deliver them to you."

"That will be time enough."

"And, sir, perhaps I should remind you of our scheduled meeting at noon tomorrow to review the arrangement of mirrors at the pavilion?"

He'd forgotten that sometime in the past hour. "Thank you for the reminder. Good evening." Keladon led Lar out of the mages' laboratory. After his night of adventures, he wanted nothing more than to quickly climb into his bed.

The next morning, Lar cleared his throat near Keladon's bed. "Sir, my apologies...."

With a yawn, Keladon squinted at the daylight leaking around the heavy curtains over the windows. "What time is it?"

"Near ten."

Keladon stretched, yawned again. "You must have a sound reason for waking me."

"Yes, sir. One of the queen's ladies-in-waiting has asked you to attend Her Majesty at eleven o'clock."

The news jolted him awake. He would give up a trifle of sleep for the chance to see Lilera. Lar had ready a breakfast of bread and hard cheese, and his finest doublet. After eating and dressing, with Lar pinching puffs of his undershirt and plucking them out the slashes in his doublet, Keladon buckled on his sword belt and headed off.

Promptly at the hour, servants opened the doors to the queen's audience chamber, and a herald announced him. Keladon strode in, glancing around the room. He'd never seen it before—it had been the audience chamber of his father's wife.

Near the far wall stood the queen's throne, flanked by ornate chairs for her ladies-in-waiting. Above them, a vast painting covered most of the wall. To the left, Keladon recognized his father as a young man, Larabos's daughter in a bridal dress, and a priest standing near them. Their wedding.

The rest of the painting showed ranks of guests. From proximity to the front, he guessed which were dukes, counts, and earls. A few faces looked familiar: Norobom's mother, for one, standing next to a portly older man with narrow blue eyes. Keladon assumed him to be her husband, the late Duke. Toward the back stood a younger version of the earl who'd invited him to dine that evening, showing broad shoulders and a full head of dark brown hair.

If Keladon's mother had been a guest, the artist had been instructed to omit her.

His footsteps echoed in the room, and he returned his attention to the throne and flanking chairs. All were empty. The room held only one person, a lady in a dress of vibrant blue, with a thin white strip of widow's veil pinned to her brown hair.

Despite disappointment, Keladon bowed. "Countess Dalasa."

"Your Illustriousness. It is a joy to meet you again, after our brief meeting in the library last autumn." Her face showed amusement as she held out her hand.

He brushed dry lips against it. "I am delighted as well."

After a frowning glance at her hand, warmth returned to her features. "Her Majesty has asked me to direct you to her for a private conversation. If you would follow me, sir?"

Keladon coughed, surprised. "A private conversation?"

"In the gardens. You will be out of earshot of observers in the palace."

He took her arm and Dalasa guided him through the west wing to the gardens.

Outside, the day's heat struck him and he squinted against the sun high in a cloudless sky. Their soles crunched the gravel of the path. Keladon glanced over the flowerbeds, the rows of potted orange and lemon trees, and the bulk of the north wing. A few gardeners worked in the distance and shadows moved at open casement windows in the palace.

He kept his voice steady. "Why does Her Majesty wish an audience with me?"

"She has heard of your adventure yesterday with the thief, and would hear more."

Hope sank within him. "I see."

"You sound disappointed, sir? That a lady should pay mind to your martial prowess?"

"If I ever were a fighter, those days are long behind me. Now I only am a mage."

"I pray you, sir, forgive her. As you may have surmised, and despite His Majesty's chance interest in her delights last autumn, she lives a lonely life. A few minutes hearing tell of your exploit will fuel her dreams for months. She can only find in fantasy the companionship we lesser, freer ladies may betimes find..." Dalasa rested her hand on his forearm. "...in the flesh." She paused, then pulled her arms away from him. "Her Majesty waits ahead. Give her what she seeks, sir, and let us converse more at another time." Dalasa withdrew in the direction of the west wing.

A few more steps brought him to Lilera. She rose slowly from a bench beside the path, and the folds of her dress slid loosely over her belly. Her face looked thicker than it had the previous autumn, yet her eyes showed the same proud and wise demeanor he'd glimpsed before. She was as lovely as he remembered. He bowed deeply and extended his right hand toward his foot. "Greetings, Your Majesty."

"Rise, sir. We would walk with you a ways." She started down the path.

He followed, keeping a few inches between their arms. "First, if I may, madam, I congratulate you on bearing for His Majesty a son and h—"

"There's no need to dissemble," she murmured. "If you keep your voice low, and your lips barely move, no one will hear you, except us."

"I understand, madam." An urge welled up in him, pressing the words *I love you* against his voicebox, trying to squeeze them out. He held them back. What would he gain by speaking them? She had suffered him to plow her furrow, but hardly out of love. Their letters had helped grow nothing more than a professional friendship. *Forget your feelings for her. Move on to the next dalliance and do not look back.*

They took two more steps in silence, then she studied him sidelong. "Who tried to kill you yesterday?"

Her words jarred him out of his prior thoughts. He took a moment to respond. "As you may have heard, madam, a thief happened to be in my rooms when I returned to them...."

She lifted an eyebrow. "Do you expect us to believe that story? A perfect coincidence of place and time brings a swordsman to your chambers? Someone sent him."

"Yes. Pardon me, madam. I am putting out the story of a chance encounter to lead my foe to underestimate me."

She inhaled deeply. "And who is your foe?"

"I do not know, madam."

Her words thudded with import. "Do you work for a cause opposed by others? Remember, sir, no one can hear you."

He frowned at her words. "The only cause I work for is the study of magegems so they might better serve the kingdom." An implication came to him. "Madam, think you a foreign prince wants me dead?"

She widened the gap between them. "We do not know why the lords of Dosten or Rachpavidhu would target you."

What did it mean that she excluded her brother from consideration? King Aril had cause to seek revenge against him, and if he plotted aggression against Sodelerak and assumed Keladon would pick back up the red in time of war, he might have Keladon killed to boost the morale of his soldiers and mages. Did she not want to believe her brother was capable of harming him? No, he dare not follow that path. It led back to his secret desire she requited his love. "My foe may then be from Sodelerak."

"My husband the bugger?"

He shook his head. "A signed warrant would have me dead within a day. I welcome your interest in the matter, madam, but I am investigating a lead, and within a few days, I might know with certainty. Perhaps then we could discuss it further?"

"Perhaps," she said with a wistful tone. "We understand you have a meeting with Forek and his assistants in a few minutes. We shall not keep you longer."

Somehow he had failed to give her what she wanted. Even better, then, he'd kept his affection for her hidden. Keladon stopped, bowed. "By your leave, Your Majesty."

Keladon reached the pavilion a few minutes before noon. Parel was absent. The other palace mages wheeled the gimballed projecting mirrors into place under the canopy. Forek, puffy-eyed, hurried onto the scene a few minutes later to oversee the mounting of the sun-reflecting mirrors high under the pavilion. By one-thirty, the palace mages had all the mirrors in place to shine on the claiming table and the positions of the king, queen, and high priest. After several cycles of fine adjustments and test castings of the intended spells, Forek and Keladon went out of the palace grounds to the main viewing mirrors overlooking the plaza. A final test showed Keladon's reflectors had solved Forek's problem. Thousands of people on the plaza would be able to see the new prince's claiming ceremony.

Forek bowed. "Thank you for your help, sir. Melos will be pleased with our work."

"It is fitting for the people to have a chance to see their new crown prince." Pride bubbled in Keladon's chest before his other concerns weighed on him. "Have you had any luck tracking down yesternight's malefactor?"

Forek blew out a breath. "We know the spell was cast somewhere in the south wing of the palace, perhaps a hundred feet from our laboratory. The mage mocked us by casting so close to us. We're asking all people in the vicinity near the time of casting if they saw a known mage. So far, no luck. It was too late at night, gentles were abed, and the few servants who might have been about weren't watching the clock to know the hour. Sir, have the copies of the flux logs been helpful to you?"

"Thank you for sending them, but I have lacked time awake in my rooms for study. The queen summoned me earlier today. I shall take my leave now and give the matter my full attention. I will deliver you my conclusions by late afternoon."

Keladon spent the next hours in his sitting room, doublet unbuttoned and sleeves rolled up. A breeze rustled the curtains hanging over the open windows, but he still sweated. The flux logs showed the unknown caster had tapped the green magegem for a short, intense burst of flux. *He wore gloves, so the flux effective to drive the spell would have been a tenth part of the total*—but most green spells could be cast at various levels of flux, with less flux requiring a longer casting period to achieve the desired effect. Though in this case, the caster would likely have drawn as high a flux as the target could handle, in order to finish and leave before Forek's observers could find his location. Keladon estimated the effective flux and looked at the observing mages' notes for the duration of the spell. A hundredth of a boil for twenty seconds.

Not Father a Son. But what? He wrote down from memory as complete a list of green spells as he could, and crossed off ones requiring higher total flux. Even so, dozens remained on the list. He trailed his finger down the margin of the page and gave a thought to each spell. Grow a Plant, Preserve a Body Tissue, Induce an Abortion.... Too many fit to narrow the list any further.

In late afternoon, he sent Lar off to Forek with the list. He wished he could leave for the poor quarters of the city right away, but his dinner invitation and the late sunsets of summer tied him to the palace and its environs for a time yet. When Lar returned, expecting to help dress his master for the evening, Keladon told him to first find a small cage, two pairs of gloves, two pocket mirrors, and two small earhorns. Puzzled, the valet did as bid. Still puzzled, at Keladon's next command, he packed them in a shoulder bag and carried them out of the palace.

The dinner invitation took Keladon and Lar to the earl's townhouse a few streets from the palace's main gates. A servant guided them to an adjoining garden, surrounded on three sides by tall brick walls. Wooden tables and benches had been set up on the grass, under a temporary canopy of white canvas. Clouds of smoke and the smell of roasting pork came from an outbuilding near the carriagehouse.

Keladon sought out his host to offer his greetings. The earl started when he approached. "Greetings, sir."

"Did I surprise you, sir?"

"No, no, simply I'm struck by how much you resemble your father. He was a fine man, one well deserving of being king, and proud I was to ride with him. I could bend your ear with stories of him, sir, indeed I could."

"Perhaps later."

A twinkle touched the earl's eye. "Indeed, you have other matters to attend." He beckoned to someone standing nearby. "Have you met my niece?"

Dalasa stepped closer. "We have, uncle."

"You should tell an old man such things. Both of you."

"Your pardon, please, uncle." Dalasa's voice was full of mirth. "His Illustriousness didn't expect me." To Keladon, she added, "I trust the surprise is agreeable to you?"

Forget Lilera. He took a breath and smiled. "Of course."

The earl squinted at his pocketwatch. "We have three-fourths of an hour before the first course will be served. I'm too busy hosting to show our guest the house and grounds, would you, my dear?"

"Gladly, uncle." Dalasa gave Keladon a coy look. "My uncle's servants will be about. There's no need for your man to attend you until dinner."

Keladon dismissed Lar with a glance over his shoulder, and followed Dalasa into the house.

The ground floor hallways bustled with servants. Niches and pedestals held pieces of the earl's old armor and thin Dosotenese vases with intricate floral patterns. "Fine work," Keladon said.

"I am fortunate to have come into twelve thousand dayworks of land between Haru and Mitok towns. Not far from Korobei, in fact." She paused at a door. "Through here, sir."

She showed him into a small sitting room. Near a curtained window, a muselar occupied a stand, with a few sheets of music scattered on the lid. Dalasa shut the door behind him as Keladon said, "I would be honored to hear—"

Her hands turned his face to hers and she kissed him. "Let us play a duet of flesh," she said amid heavy breaths.

Wrongness filled him. "My lady, I—"

"You do not carry an assurance cap? No matter. I have access to sylphium should the unacceptable happen." She kissed him again and pulled up her dress's skirt till the hem was higher than his hand.

He hesitated, then broke away from her. "Your pardon, please, but I cannot." His heart pounded at the foolishness he was about to say. "I love another."

Dalasa fixed on him a frank look. "Would she ever know if we trysted here and now? It is a she, yes, or are you inclined—"

"A she. No, she would never know." He met Dalasa's gaze to heighten the impression of his next words. "But I would."

She stood for a moment, blinking once, then dropped the hem of her skirt. "She is a fortunate lady, sir. If you would excuse me, my uncle has many skills, but hostess is not among them." She left and shut the door gently behind her. He waited briefly, plucking a few idle notes from the muselar, then headed out.

The arrangements for dinner found Keladon seated far from both Dalasa and her uncle. The earl frowned, puzzled, at Keladon's seating position and her laughter at jokes told by some marquis's youngest son, but soon enough he shrugged. Relieved, and at the same time scolding himself for feeling relief, Keladon finished the last courses as lemon oil candles burned down and a houseboy turned a crank driving a waving fan.

At the earliest chance, when the western sky had just faded from indigo to black, Keladon thanked his host and left. The front doors thudded shut moments later. When they reached the plaza, Keladon turned away from the palace.

"I have an errand to run, further to my sojourn yester night. Tonight, I need your assistance."

"As you wish, sir."

Keladon laid over his plan once again. "First, we will visit the Temple of Samala in the city. Then, have you skill in catching rats?"

Lar frowned and did not answer as Keladon led the way.

They reached the temple within half an hour. Keladon climbed the worn marble steps, then hesitated outside the doors. Kala wouldn't minister to any congregants at this hour, but she would soon learn he'd visited. No help for it.

He beckoned, and Lar pulled the door open. The priestesses waiting near the rear of the chapel took note of him and conversed among themselves. Kala was not among them. One slipped down a branching corridor as another approached him.

A few minutes later, the priestess led him into the vault. As she waited in the corridor, he took the bag holding his gems from its niche and slung it over his shoulder. Soon he followed the priestess back upstairs.

In the last room before the chapel, Kala waited. "Well met, friend of Samala." The other priestess left the room.

"Greetings, Kala. It is an unexpected pleasure." He spoke forthrightly; his rebuff of Dalasa a few hours before had strengthened his resolve. His heart belonged to Lilera, despite how foolish that sounded.

She scowled and stalked forward. "You were going to come and go without asking for me?"

"I must deal with weighty matters tonight." He adjusted the sack of gems at his shoulder. The draw cord at its neck dug across his fingers.

"You're setting me aside for a fat woman? What happened to you past winter and spring at Korobei?"

"I fondly recall our hours together. But those hours are now past." He watched her expression, but her face did not waver from its cool scowl. "I love another."

The scowl turned to disgust. "Have the decency to tell the truth."

"I do not lie."

She sniffed out a breath. "If you think you tell me the truth, you lie to yourself. You have never loved. You're incapable of it. You attend to a woman's pleasure in order to disguise the truth. From her, and from yourself." A quiver crossed her face, but her voice and expression remained cool. "Go. Mayhap the goddess will bless you. I won't."

Keladon and Lar left the temple and headed toward Old Atem's hideout. Kala's words faded from his thoughts as they drew closer to Monek Street. When they left the last pavements for the dung-strewn dirt of the poor district, Keladon glanced nervously about. His fine clothing marked him as an outsider, and he wished for a disguise. But the streets were dark, and the few people walking them evidently had their own reasons for shunning notice. Eventually they came to Monek Street and turned toward the river.

A quarter-mile from Old Atem's hideout, Keladon led Lar down an alley to the street running parallel to Monek. As they approached the Derepar, the warehouses lifted dark, looming facades toward the sliver of risen moon. From the nearby wharf came the sound of the river plashing docked boats.

Keladon found the warehouse he'd seen from the rear the previous night. The planking of its front facade appeared gray in the moonlight. The warehouse had a pedestrian door, a pair of carriage doors chained shut with a six-inch gap beneath them, and unglazed windows covered by iron mesh. Steep-angled moonlight lit the windowsills, but left the depths of the warehouse in darkness. The rest of the wall was solid enough to prevent entry, unless Lar had packed a crowbar to pry the planking from the building's frame.

He turned to Lar and raised his finger to his lips, then angled his ear to the warehouse. Silent. Keladon handed Lar a pair of gloves and put on his own as he went to the pedestrian door. He tried turning the doorknob. Locked.

"Have you ever picked a lock?" he whispered to Lar.

"Never, sir. Don't you have magic to do so?"

Keladon pointed his chin toward one of the bags slung over Lar's shoulder. "Greens and blues are deaf to Pick a Lock. We'll have to force it."

Lar stepped forward. "Allow me, sir." He glanced up and down the street, then lifted his foot and reared back. With a swift jab of his leg, his sole struck the door just above the lock. Metal groaned against wood and the door swung a foot and a half open. Lar set his hand on it and pushed it wider, then gestured for Keladon to enter.

The warehouse's dark interior was the coolest place he'd found since he'd arrived in the city. He stopped again to listen. Though he still heard no voices or the movement of people, the squeak and skitter of vermin now reached his ears.

Lar's voice came from the vicinity of the broken lock. "I can shut the door, but it won't hold, sir. Passersby might notice and alert the reeve."

Keladon stepped closer. His foot came down on something small and rigid. He bent, and his fingers confirmed his guess: the strike plate from the door jamb, torn loose by Lar's kick. He touched the extended bolt jutting from the edge of the door, and the splintered wood in the jamb. The bolt needed an intact hole in the wood to hold the door shut.

He could make one by tapping a green and bidding the wood of the jamb to fill the splintered wood on the interior side of the door. But he had more important tasks for his greens. "Find something to prop the door closed. From the street, the door should look enough like properly locked to fool most passers-by."

"A fine idea, sir." Lar scrounged for a few moments, then pushed a small crate across the dirt floor. Keladon shut the door and Lar maneuvered the crate against it. When they pulled their hands away, the door remained closed.

That done, Keladon focused on his mission. He had the gems and all the spells' components, save one: a small animal to carry, under the command of a blue, a magical eye and ear into Old Atem's hide-out. "Now I need a rat."

"I'll get you one, sir." Lar cupped his hand to his ear and peered into the warehouse's dim interior in the direction of soft skittering. He slid his bag off his shoulder and pulled out a hand-sized cage trap and a paper-wrapped morsel of cheese. "I'd meant to sample something from the old earl's kitchen, sir, but I guess it wasn't meant to be."

Keladon's eyes had adjusted to the darkness enough to see racks sagging under crates and barrels, and the faint outline of rafters under the peaked ceiling. "Meet me in the back corner when you've caught our rat," he said, and pointed.

"Of course, sir." Lar started off.

Keladon took his bag of gems to the appointed corner. A diffuse glimmer of moonlight revealed a cat-sized hole under a plank. He set down the bag, took off his gloves, and pulled out a green gem and a blue. Next to them, he set his pocket watch. The gems had been fresh when he'd left Korobei, and he quickly subtracted the energies he'd spent in his encounter with the assassin in Harumal Wood. Given the flux needed to control a rat at—he reflected on the size of Old Atem's hideout and the distance across the street—up to forty paces' distance, plus that needed to Pass Light and Pass Sound, the blue magegem would be fully drained in eight thousand drops of time, about an hour and a quarter.

You could tap the second blue if need be, and then he reflected how much charge he would need to Compel Truthful Answers the next night. Better to leave the second blue untouched.

Unless you could buy another blue? He remembered what Forek and Parel had let slip the night before. Were magegems disappearing from the palace's vault? An unscrupulous palace mage could earn a pretty purse stealing and selling magegems one by one to Teisoret's criminal underworld. Perhaps Old Atem himself trafficked in them. How fitting it would be to use one that passed through Old Atem's hands to bring the criminal his comeuppance.

How long would it take to find a man who could sell you a blue? Without Old Atem finding out?

Footsteps sounded nearby. Keladon's heart sped up. As the falling steps grew closer, accompanying sounds became audible: the scratch of tiny claws on metal and a high-pitched, anxious squeaking. "Hope you weren't waiting long, sir," Lar said.

"Not at all." In the deep gloom, the black iron rods of the cage striped the gray rat. Keladon sat cross-legged on the dirt floor with his left hand near the two gems. "Set down the rat and, from your pack, lay on the ground near me the earhorns and the mirrors."

Once the objects were dim but distinct shapes on the dark floor, Keladon said, "While I work, remove the rat from his cage. Turn his flank toward me." He tapped the green as the cage door clanked and the rat squealed.

"You're a squirmer, little beast, aren't you?" Lar muttered to the rat.

"I'll need you to hold him a few minutes." Keladon picked up the earhorn, cradling it between his thumb and the last joints of his first two fingers. He pressed it against the rat's flank. The rat squirmed under the pressure of the earhorn. Through his fingertips, he felt its heart race.

He started casting Graft Onto a Body. The rat writhed and its heart sped even faster as the green's energies flowed into its body, inducing skin, muscle, and bone to grow around the edges of the earhorn. Could its heart beat so fast it stopped? Lar swore as the rat struggled against his hands. Grafting the pocket mirror onto the rat's flank next to the earhorn proved no easier.

After the earhorn and mirror were grafted, Keladon ordered the green to withdraw its attention from him. "Hold him yet. I'll cast three more spells, though they should be quick." With his right hand, he reached for the blue. He touched the earhorns together and did the same with the mirrors' edges. He lay the ungrafted mirror on the dirt and pushed the point of the ungrafted earhorn in beside it. The rat's heart still raced, but its struggles had eased. Had its body spent its energies on resistance? He might have to find it food and water along the way through Old Atem's hideout.

Time to send it on its way. He moved his head closer to the creature, close enough to hear the rustle of its fur against Lar's gloves, and he touched its back. *"Command a Creature,"* Keladon said in Jelorean, *"this rat, flux nineteen-hundredths of a boil per drop of time, begin."*

The rat grew still. Its heart slowed drastically within a few beats, in counterpoint to Keladon's. He'd cast this spell a few times over the years, on frogs in the laboratory. Never something with a brain even as large as a rat's, and never when his commands to the creature could make the difference in whether he lived or died....

"Set it down," Keladon told Lar.

"It won't run off, sir?" Lar sounded dubious, then shook his head. "If you say it won't, sir, I reckon I ought believe you." He squatted and laid his cupped hands on the dirt between his feet. He drew his hands apart and the rat slid down to the ground. It stood in place and slowly turned its head toward the blue.

Keladon listened to the street outside. No traffic. He shut his eyes to aid his memory of the area. *"Send this rat, speed one forearm per drop of time, out this hole and ahead twelve forearms."* That should get it to the far side of the street.

The rat scampered out the hole under the siding. The mirror on the dark dirt floor suddenly glowed, revealing the moonlit street. Old Atem's hideout showed a washed-out gray wall against the deep black of the river. No way of seeing what lay on the rat's other side, toward the higher elevations of Teisoret. The earhorn picked up the same sounds Keladon had heard before they broke into the warehouse. The lapping river, distant shouts, the quiet thud of small feet—

"Aggressive posture full! Rotate quarter turn right."

The image in the mirror shifted to a sideways view of a wall. The earhorn sounded with a cat's hiss, angry but confused. A moment later, the hiss faded, and the dim sound of footsteps followed, growing dimmer as they went on. Keladon told the gem to rotate the rat another quarter turn to the right. Seen in the mirror, a white-patched black cat loped up the street and clawed its way up a wooden fence. From the top, it turned reflective eyes toward the rat, then jumped down to the other side.

Keladon let out a breath and ordered the rat back to its original path.

Being unable to see the rat, and only getting a view to its side, forced Keladon to send it more slowly than he liked. Frequent pauses and turns checked the rat's position against the mental map of the area he'd made the night before. Every second drained more of the blue's energy.

Soon, the rat waited at a corner of a building. Only an alley lay between it and Old Atem's hideout. Keladon took a few seconds to check the view in the glass. Did it drift slightly from the direction it should be showing, or did he see things? The magegem's energies dissipated the further the rat traveled from it, and if the effective flux reached too low a level, the spell would lose its hold on the rat's mind. If the flux faded to a level where the rat could struggle against the spell, the image would drift with the rat's chosen movements in the few feet before the rat would break free entirely.

"Sir, is all well?"

Even if the flux remained high enough where the rat now stood, would it remain high enough across the alley? Keladon raised his hand to bid Lar be silent. *"Increase flux, twenty-two-hundredths of a boil per drop of time. Rotate quarter turn right."*

The rat's turn shifted the view in the mirror to the wall of Old Atem's hideout. Keladon peered along the line where the warehouse's wall met the ground. There, that gap under a board should do. He spoke the instructions in Jelorean and the rat crossed the alley.

The rat slipped through the gap into a dirt-floored storeroom. Barrels stood in three-high stacks nearly reaching the ceiling. The only light came from the bright glow of lamps from the next room, visible under a wide, rolling door in the middle of the far wall. A mix of gruff male voices burst through the earhorn. From the next room? Probably, but all the sounds he heard came from the same place, the single earhorn below him. *Next time, put two artificial ears on an animal spy...*

The rat's progress remained slow. He had to find a crack for it to slip into the next room, keep it there long enough for him to see what it found, then send it back to avoid detection while he planned its next steps. As he sent the rat toward the wall to find a crack, the image drifted, and Keladon quickly increased the flux to thirty. His left hand couldn't feel the higher flux leaving the magegem, but he knew it drained faster. He sent the rat slowly along the wall and solid construction showed in the mirror. No passage yet.

Send it under the rolling door? Another gruff burst of voices, louder this time, came from the men in the next room. They were probably a few paces away. Even if they played dice or told tall tales over a bottle, one might still notice a rat with a pocket mirror and an earhorn grafted onto its side. So much better if there was a crevice in the corner of the room, but how much time could he spend looking for something that might not be there....

Long seconds later, he saw a crevice in the wall's right hand corner. After a moment's relief, he gave a preparatory blink, then widened his eyes. He spoke the commands to send the rat through. He ordered it back to the storeroom, then shut his eyes to better recollect what he'd glimpsed in the mirror.

Half a dozen men on benches. A large table held two lamps, some tin cups, and a pair of bottles. The men were in the main room of the warehouse, with rows of crates behind them. A side wall bore a few doors, all shut, half-visible behind stacked crates. At the far end of the main room, thick beams held a walled, windowed loft near the peak of the roof, accessible by a nearly-vertical ladder.

Was Old Atem part of the company on the benches? Probably not. His position and his secretive reputation suggested he shut himself behind a door. To the side of the room or in the loft? One more look, then Keladon would send the rat that out of the storeroom for good.

The men shouted again as he ordered the rat back through the crevice into the main room. The sounds came more clearly now. Empty cups slammed to the table, punctuating shouts of "For Kor! For Bilem!"

One drunken voice called out, "When I find the men what waylaid them...."

"Bloody vermin!" shouted another. "Hey. What?"

As Keladon ordered the rat back through the crevice, a thought chilled him: The last man to speak didn't refer to the killer of the two criminals the night before.

"Balar's balls, what sort of rat was that? It had something shiny on its side. Balar's balls, yes, and don't tell me not to swear by His Holy Nutsack, d'you think Kor and Bilem are feasting in the Divine Couple's hall this night?"

Keladon held his ear closer to the horn. The men argued with loud and alert voices. His awareness of the ever-draining gem weighed on him. The longer the men were vigilant, the longer he would keep the rat out of their sight, and the greater the likelihood the gem's energies would run out before he found what he needed.

An older voice told the man who'd seen the rat, "Go outside, have a breath of air, clear your head."

An inaudible protest later, the older voice said, "We're all ready to stab someone, but save it for the gang what waylaid Kor and Bilem. Word'll come down from on high who we'll go after. Till then, all of you, save your anger for when we'll need it."

A chair pushed back and heavy feet stomped out of the room. After a moment, quiet conversations picked back up and bottles and cups clinked and thudded.

Word from on high. Old Atem was in the loft. Keladon had to get the rat moving that direction. Following the shortest path, along the right-hand wall of the main room, would expose the rat's left flank to the men around the table, and anyone else in the room who might glance its way. He would have to send the rat around the room the long way, its left side a few inches from a wall the entire time.

Time was wasting. He ordered the rat through the crevice.

Judging by their voices, the men at the table gave the rat no heed. The rat pressed on, beyond the area fully illuminated by the lamps on the table, into the dimmer reaches of the main room. After it crossed a pair of closed carriage doors, Keladon listened for footsteps, turned the rat to see its surroundings, and increased the flux. He glimpsed rows of stacked crates in the darkness, then sent the rat on. By the time the ambient light in the warehouse grew brighter again, the gem spent fifty boils per drop. Keladon glanced at his pocket watch and did the mental arithmetic. Perhaps fifteen minutes left.

The brighter light came from a lamp hanging from a hook mounted on a pillar supporting the loft. Between the rat's location and the lamp stood the ladder. Near the ladder's foot, a guard had folded arms and an unsettled look on his face. He angled his head, presumably to listen to the conversation at the front of the room.

Keladon sent the rat along the wall, past the guard. A quick check showed it had drawn nearly even with one of the pillars holding up the loft. He increased the flux to fifty-three, then sent the rat across the open floor. A few moments later, he sent it climbing up the pillar.

It soon reached the top. A set of parallel joists, supporting the loft's floor, ran from a beam bridging the pillars to the outer wall of the warehouse. Keladon listened for activity in the loft. Nothing. He sent the rat along the beam to a central joist, then carefully along a narrow space atop a warped joist and under uneven decking. Progress slowed further. If the rat fell, even the dullest criminal would notice the glass and earhorn magically grafted to its broken body, and Old Atem would realize someone had spied on him.

Two-thirds of the way to the outer wall of the warehouse, muffled voices came to him. Old Atem? Probably. But he needed to be certain. He had a few minutes to try, didn't he? He ordered the rat forward along the joists to the outer wall, then toward the back corner of the warehouse. The floor below held stacks of crates thick with dust. If the rat fell here, it might avoid notice for a few days, but that would be a slender reed to rely on. Keladon sent the rat back along the underside of the loft's rear edge, toward the voices. Was there an opening somewhere between the wall's studs and sheeting?

There. He sent the rat through a fallen-out knot in a board. He needed a moment to orient himself to the view transmitted from inside the loft's wall. A sliver of light came from a crack. Keladon stopped the rat near the crack and listened.

What had to be an open window let in the sound of the river lapping just outside. An old man spoke, his voice assured despite being barnacled with age. "I haven't heard of any other gang trying to horn in on our protection racket."

"It's not a gang, father." A cold, youthful voice, with a sound of streetwise intellect in it.

The older man spoke. "The city reeve swears none of his men killed Kor and Bilem. Maybe the palace is all eager to clean up Teisoret with the high and mighty coming to town."

"I shouldn't think it's the palace." The younger man's tone grew amused. "It's our rabbit."

Keladon's heart pounded. He leaned his ear closer to the horn.

"D'you want me to take back my title, boy?" The voice sounded gruff, yet affectionate. "He's a country bumpkin who's lucky to be alive."

"You think he's some country squire who lucked into some emeralds and sapphires? He earned those off his father, and for good cause. He's killed more men then you and I could in ten lifetimes."

The old man took a moment to reply. "True, but he did all that twenty years ago. Using rubies, and he swore off them right after."

In the mirror on the floor near Keladon, the image shook. The rat's squeak sounded through the earhorn.

"Increase flux, fifty-eight-hundredths of a boil per drop." Keladon whispered, even though he and Lar were alone, dozens of paces away from Old Atem.

"Another rat up here?" Old Atem said. "Where is that damned cat when you need it?"

How much energy remained in the magegem? Keladon checked his watch. Five minutes, at most. Not enough time to get the rat back to him to remove the pocket mirror and earhorn. He couldn't leave it in its hiding place in the wall—if the spell ran out, it might end up walking into Old Atem's office, its spy equipment visible for the master criminal and his semi-retired father to see.

Keladon sent the rat back out of the crack and onto the joists holding up the loft. He sent it back toward the corner of the warehouse, then down the inside of the corner. Very little time left, he had to get it out—

The mirror showed a cat-scratched gap in a rotted siding plank. He sent the rat to it, then outside. The view turned gray-white with moonlight. He glimpsed a narrow stone ledge with crumbling mortar, and beyond, the choppy dark murk of the Derepar.

"Descend," Keladon commanded. The image showed more ware-

houses downriver, then drifted again. A hair more flux, just for a second.

Only one thing could guarantee Old Atem would never find the spying rat.

A few more words and the rat jumped into the water. Keladon commanded it toward the river bottom. The image grew murky. Distant smears of light, one of them Old Atem's window, bobbed as the power of the river jostled the rat's body. Bobbing turned to thrashing as the rat's survival instinct fought the spell. Keladon kept the rat underwater until the thrashing ceased.

He stepped the flux back to fifty. The view in the glass drifted along and bobbed with the river current. Were the rat swimming for its life, the image would be thrashing. Keladon stopped the flux from the blue and let the river carry the rat's corpse toward the sea.

Keladon took a moment to refocus himself on his surroundings. He couldn't see the gem in the dim light inside their hiding place, but he knew it held only a few dregs of energy. He would need the second blue the next day. And a yellow.

"We've found our quarry's lair," Keladon said to Lar.

"We have, sir? That's wonderful news. What shall we do next?"

Keladon smiled. Even his face felt tired. "We shall return to the palace and have a deep night's sleep."

MAYBE IT WAS because his employer was an old man of forty, or perhaps working with magic wore a man out, but when they returned to the palace, Lar had no desire to sleep. Teisoret! The palace! He could sleep on a boat to Mitok town when they journeyed home. So, once His Illustriousness snored under silk sheets, Lar tiptoed out the door out of their rooms and quietly locked it behind him.

Lar made his way to the kitchen in the basement of the east wing. The corridors were mostly empty. Three hard-eyed battlemages passed him, and the shouts of nobleman gambling over dice came from some locked room. But in the kitchen, despite the hour, cooks and junior servants were at work, feeding nobles's late night revels or preparing meals for the next day. One set of work tables held large, shallow porcelain vessels. Their contents were red with wine and dotted with shiny discs of oil. Spices flecked the liquid.

"Tana, what are they marinating?" he asked a baker's assistant as she kneaded dough. He leaned against her workbench.

Flour covered her arms to the elbows, and dusted her tied-back blond hair. "Hundreds of sausages." Her expression grew a little more open. "It's for the king's next feast."

"I see." He'd chatted her up the previous night and had put some thought into what words might impress her. If they happened to be true, so much the better. "My employer will be in attendance. Perhaps he'll have a chance to eat the bread you're baking."

She lifted the ball of dough and smacked it onto the kneading board. "What I'm baking won't last past breakfast."

A male servant came their way with a flat tray of sausages. He peered at Lar and set the tray down across three of the marinating vessels. "Is this knave bothering you, Tana?"

"I'm fine, Los."

"Are you? I want my friends to have things go their way. You deserve better than some bumpkin working for a bumpkin lord wasting your time."

Lar pushed his elbow off the workbench and stood tall. "If Tana wants me to leave, she'll tell me."

Tana smiled weakly. "Thank you, Los, but he's not bothering me."

"Whatever you say." Los gave Lar a cold look of warning as he dropped sausages into the marinade.

Go ahead, watch me all you want. Lar put the other man out of a mind and turned a dreamy, attentive face to Tana. "Of course your bread will get quickly eaten. Your loaves must be the most delicious to come out of the kitchen."

She yawned, then shook her head. "You say the same things to the girls working here by daylight, don't you?"

Lar put on a wounded expression. "I only have words for you."

With a grunt, Los picked up his now-empty tray. Tana's gaze never left Lar's face. "Pfah. You come here at all hours, don't you?"

"To pick up my employer's meals, yes. But even if the girls here then were as lovely as you, I wouldn't have time to say how-d'you-do to them. And they're nowhere near as lovely as you—"

"Because I'm the only one here when your master's sleeping off his drinking and dicing?"

"Tana...." An angle occurred to him. "My master hasn't time for that. He has serious tasks for the good of the kingdom."

"That keep him up well past midnight?"

"Yes. That's when the bad men are about. Criminals. Foes of all that's good and pure."

Tana retrieved a stack of bread pans from a cabinet and clanked them on the workbench next to the dough. "A highborn works for the city reeve, then?" Her tone held disbelief.

"No, no. The reeve can't be trusted to know what my employer does. Why that look? I'm telling the truth and you don't believe me?" Lar smiled lazily to show he took no offense at her doubts. "You've heard of Old Atem?"

Tana's brow crinkled, but her hands still kept working dough into the pans. "I've heard of him. How have you? Does he ply his trade in the provinces?"

"I'd never heard of him before my employer started after him. We found Old Atem's hideout tonight."

"Pfah," she said, but her tone was less dismissive than before.

At a doorway to an adjoining part of the kitchen Lar glimpsed Los. He put the sausage handler out of mind and smiled at Tana. "He lurks in a warehouse down by the riverside."

"Where?" The way she said it told Lar she'd warmed to him.

"I can't say that. I have to protect you. He'd kill you if he knew you knew his whereabouts."

Los left Lar's sight as Tana said, "But not you?"

He resolutely shook his head. "I chose to take the risk with my employer. I'm brave like that."

Tana's eyebrow rose, and her gaze met Lar's for a long moment. "Tell me more while I get the dough in the oven."

THE NEXT NIGHT, Keladon returned to the king's banquet hall for yet another feast. With the dead thief two days behind him, he had lost the seat of honor at King Raboros' right hand. Keladon relaxed when he realized the attention of the dandies and sycophants had moved away from him. He took a seat at a lower table, with noblemen he didn't know, and engaged in small talk over dishes of garlic cream soup, salted greens with vinegar, roasted onion, and smoked sausages still warm from the kitchens.

"His Majesty is stuffing us with food," said a marquis with grizzled hair and heavy-lidded eyes. The cut of his purple velvet doublet showed him a few years behind the current style.

A wide-eared youth, a duke's son, said, "With everything the king has served so far, I wonder how he can top himself tomorrow night."

"His cooks have something exquisite planned for the claiming-day feast," said a battlemage officer, one of ten or twelve recently arrived from the provinces and scattered around the hall. "Wouldn't you think so, Your Illustriousness?"

"Custom would suggest it."

"Speaking of the claiming day," the duke's son said, "What think you of your nephew, sir?"

The other nobles at the table paused the orbit of their utensils and glanced sidelong at the duke's son. Either the young man didn't know the king's desire to keep Keladon at arm's length, or thought it a desire he could frustrate. Perhaps the king's distance, halfway across the room, made the duke's son reckless.

Keladon hesitated as well. A moment of panic burned his throat, *does he suspect?* No, how could he? "I should think he has brought joy to both His Majesty and Queen Lilera. As he grows, may he bring joy to the kingdom as well."

The marquis was the first to raise a glass. "Hear, hear."

Once the glasses returned to the table, the conversation shifted, to Keladon's quiet relief. The noblemen discussed hunts, military service, and the charms of various ladies of court. Keladon replied as the others expected. The servants brought out the further courses, ending with orange wedges and sugar-crusted pastries.

After dessert, the herald announced the evening's entertainment: a return engagement of Toreb and his troupe. Keladon glanced at the king and Dobak, where they sat in profile at the middle of the royal table. Dobak pouted and stared sullenly at his dessert wine. King Raboros lifted an eyebrow to his companion, then turned away to face the entertainers.

As Toreb introduced the evening's show, his fingers twitched and sweat beaded on his forehead. Had he or his troupe displeased the king during their previous performance? Keladon wondered. If so, they wouldn't have been granted another. Perhaps his players had been given new numbers to perform, and not enough time to rehearse them.

Moni the dancer snared the gazes of the marquis and the duke's son. After she finished her performance, the noblemen's murmured compliments hung around the table. The midget and giant worked their same routine, competently as before, drawing as much laughter. Toreb remained nervous, stumbling over the false Rak-pawindun of his patter when he introduced Neranaren.

A smatter of applause sent the singer and the *doumbek* player to the wings when Toreb returned to the forefront. It took him a noticeable effort of will for him to act the confident impresario. "Next, for your delectation, I present to you, Suhelum the juggler."

A frown tightened around Keladon's eyes. Where was Vos? Not that he lamented the swordswallower's absence, but the rest of the troupe had performed in the same order as two nights earlier.

Keladon sipped his port and used the motion to cover a glance at the king. Raboros frowned as the juggler, a middle-aged man wearing a long, baggy tunic of Peluraki style, cycled four balls through the air.

Did Toreb save the swordswallower for last to hold the king's attention all the way through the show? No intervening performer could want the king's attention now. Raboros's frown deepened and he slumped back in his chair. He dropped his face against his right fist and his mouth buckled. Next to him, Dobak squinted at the king, the juggler, and the side doorway where Toreb waited. His face showed puzzlement that soon turned hopeful.

After Suhelum, more performers came and went. Eventually Toreb led out the entire troupe for final bows. The impresario hurried through his patter, bungling words. "....Our alluring juggler! Our amusing dancer! Thank you, sire, honored sirs, and gentlemen, we bid you goodnight!" Toreb hurried his performers out of the banquet hall as best he could. Their numbers confounded his effort.

King Raboros spoke over his shoulder to his manservant. The king brooded over folded arms. The manservant bowed and backed away, and his sunken face looked even more solemn than usual. Behind the king, Dobak's face showed quiet delight. He quickly masked it when King Raboros straightened his body and glowered at the departing entertainers.

Vos's absence explained Toreb's nervousness. The king clearly wanted to tryst with Vos again.

So why was Vos absent?

Flighty though the swordswallower might be, Vos clearly had a venal streak. Raboros likely had given him more coins that earlier evening than he made in a hundred nights picking the pockets of wife-bored merchants. The prospect of another evening would have brought the swordswallower in front of the audience. On top of that, Toreb no doubt took a cut of Vos' earnings, and would have used whatever leverage he had on Vos to ensure he performed.

Toreb must have known the king's interest in Vos. If the swordswallower had taken sick, or injured himself in a rehearsal,

Toreb would simply have said as much to placate King Raboros. So Toreb didn't know the reason for Vos' absence or was unwilling to say.

The noblemen began filing out of the banquet hall. Keladon walked with them, distractedly answering when others spoke to him. Vos' absence dogged his thoughts. The swordswallower would have performed, had he been allowed to....

Had Dobak done away with Vos? He had a motive. But a glance at Dobak fit with the evolution of his facial expressions since the moment Vos had failed to perform. Dobak had been as surprised as anyone. Pleasantly surprised, but surprised nonetheless.

The king's manservant, repeatedly bowing, moved against the main current of the room, toward the king. Toreb, sweating and worrying his lower lip with his teeth, followed.

Most of the crowd showed Toreb and the manservant a moment's annoyance at their passage, then returned to their conversations. "An excellent meal," Keladon overheard the curly redheaded dandy tell another.

"The chef chose boldly, making sausages the main course, and fortune favored him."

The dandy said, "That sausage maker, Yoret, is a man of high skill."

An eddy in the crowd took the noblemen out of Keladon's earshot. He took another step and an intuition erupted in his mind, like energies suddenly released by a gem. Gooseflesh stippled his neck and jawline. He shuffled along with the crowd, while he studied the intuition in hope of finding something wrong with it. The hope proved vain.

Scald the Cuckoo's Egg. The spell required a sample of the putative father's semen to test the paternity of the child in question. The Jelorean commentators on the spell had only written about putative fathers voluntarily yielding semen in the moments before the spell would be cast, to provide the freshest possible samples and enhance the disfigurement and pain the spell would inflict, should the child in question prove to not be theirs.

Clearly, King Raboros would not authorize the spell be cast on his putative son and heir. If the new prince were proven a cuckoo's egg, he could not claim the throne; Raboros would become a king in name only, mocked by all from the highest nobles to the basest peasants; Queen Lilera would be fortunate to escape with her life; the Peluraki would take the opportunity to strike in Sodelerak's confusion. Despite his flaws, Raboros would not set the kingdom on fire by volunteering a sample for the spell.

But if a third party, such as Vos, could extract the putative father's semen by his arts and store it, such as in a tied-off sausage casing stolen from Yoret, then a mage with a green could, late at night, cast Preserve a Body Tissue, and keep the sample fresh for days.

The ideal time for an enemy of the kingdom to cast Scald the Cuckoo's Egg against the newborn prince would be during a claiming ceremony. Especially this claiming ceremony. Many more than a few hundred highborn would see it. Forek's work in preparing to Pass Light and Pass Sound would demonstrate to thousands of people in the plaza that the prince was not the son of the man whose semen contacted him.

The plot failed there. The king would deny he was the source of the semen. *Some interloper provided it to disfigure our rightful son....*

The enemy needed Vos. Producing the swordswallower and casting Compel Truthful Answers would prove that the semen scalding the new prince belonged to King Raboros, and remove the last chance to explain away the spell's results.

Lost in thought, Keladon wandered into the central courtyard. He was alone except for a trio of battlemages strolling through the far corner. Lamps on posts spaced along the paths flickered and a slight, cool breeze rippled the pavilion's canopy. The golden glow of lights diffused by curtains filled the windows of the palace's new wings and the tower of the old castle in the distance. If the enemy worked his dark scheme on the morrow, this evening would be the last peaceful one the kingdom would know for months. Years.

He should tell someone—wait, in truth? He had no evidence, just suppositions. Even if he had evidence, who could he trust with it? He might confide in an agent of the enemy. Even if he warned a person who truly sided with the kingdom, the enemy or his agents might overhear and work to neutralize them. He would have to rely on himself to find evidence of the supposed conspiracy and the enemy's identity.

He had one clear angle to start with. If his intuition was correct, the enemy kept Vos captive. Toreb might have some inkling as to who abducted the swordswallower. Or he might have more than an inkling—he might have handed Vos over.

Keladon took one last look at the cool, quiet courtyard. He wished he could stay. Perhaps Queen Lilera would go for a stroll in the cool night air.... He shook his head to dispel the daydream and hurried to find the impresario.

THE TROUPE CAMPED in the mustering field north of the palace walls. Torches flickered on poles and performers called to one another. Keladon entered the encampment unchallenged, but as he walked down a grassy sward between two rows of tents, the performers stopped talking and watched him with narrowed eyes.

The *doumbek* player, shirtless in the warm night, rose from a stool under the rolled-up flap of a tent. He dried his pale arms with a long cloth tinged brown with washed-off pigment, then whipped the cloth to rest over his left shoulder. He folded his arms and stopped astride Keladon's path. "What do you want from us, high-born?" His accent reminded Keladon of the Teisoret slums. "Our women aren't for hire. Our boys neither."

"I would speak with Toreb. If you would show me his tent—"

"Why would he want to speak with you? Sir."

The other's tone stoked Keladon to anger. He kept it off his face and out of his voice. "I intend to start a fair at Korobei, and I want the finest troupe in the kingdom to perform at it. I needn't talk to Toreb if he gave you authority to reject such requests—"

The *doumbek* player hastily stepped aside and bowed. "Your pardons, please, Your Most Gracious Excellency. He's in the third tent ahead on the right."

Toreb's tent looked comparable to the others. Patches dotted the canvas and a simple slit marked the only entrance. Keladon stopped and lifted a flap. A candle somewhere inside cast long shadows across the floor toward the entrance, and a woman's voice murmured within.

Into the dim interior, Keladon said, "I would speak with Toreb."

"Who wouldn't?" The impresario's voice sounded inebriated and testy. "Who are you?"

"Keladon, squire of Korobei, son of the late king."

Toreb's tone shifted. "Come—come in, Your High—Grace—my lord." Sounds came of a man's weight shifting in a seat, a flask thudding onto a tabletop, low cursing.

Keladon entered the tent. Toreb stooped over a low table bearing a bottle on its side and a puddle of red wine. Two chairs made of thin pine faced one another across the table. Moni stood with arms folded over her torso near a flap in an interior wall of the tent. The candle gave the room a restful glow at odds with Toreb's nervousness. The impresario bowed and gestured at one of the chairs. "My lord, if it please you, you may sit here."

"It would please me," Keladon said.

After he sat, Toreb said, "Girl, our guest."

With a rustle of frayed skirts, Moni hunched forward and lifted the spilled bottle. A double handful of liquid filled the bottom. "Wine, my lord?"

"Thank you, no." Keladon kept his gaze on the impresario.

"What have I done to earn the honor of your visit, sir?" Toreb asked.

Keladon decided to approach his real inquiry indirectly. Perhaps he could lull Toreb into revealing something about Vos' absence and the conspiracy that might be behind it. He built on his lie to the *doumbek* player. "I intend to start a fair at Korobei. An annual event, to be held in late summer, with a focus on the magical arts, and an ample need for diversions. Your troupe is known throughout the kingdom, and I have seen your excellent performances with my own eyes. For those reasons, I want your troupe to perform at Korobei."

Toreb blinked a few times. "I... Thank you, sir." His usual bluster seeped into his expression. "We are delighted a gentleman of fine taste would be interested in our entertainments."

"Fine taste is rarer than one might think," Keladon said. "There are a number of your performers who I particularly wish to see. For one, Moni." He turned his hand palm up to indicate her.

She shrank back, and gave Toreb a questioning look before speaking. "Thank you, my lord."

"The juggler with the Peluraki name, I forget—"

"Suhelum." Toreb cleared his throat. "Sir, I assure you, and my pardons if it may have seemed I intended to trick anyone, but he is no Peluraki. I know the Peluraki stand low in my lord's regard. His name in truth is Sorem, and he hails from the tradesmen's streets of Teisoret."

Keladon forced himself to chuckle. "Is that the most grievous lie you have told your audiences? I had expected far more, and far worse." He waved his hand to shoo the thought away. "The midget and the giant. Nera and her *doumbek* player. And Vos."

"Vos?" Toreb drew out the syllable.

"I understand your hesitance. I will speak plainly. Yes, I still detest his invasion of my cabin in the boat we took here from Mitok town. However, his behavior, at least as I hear of it, has been prudent around the palace. I trust your management of him has something to do with it? And above all, his performance two nights ago was the highlight of the evening. I would gladly put aside my disdain for his past actions to present my guests with his artistry."

Toreb sat straighter. "Thank you again, sir, for your leniency and stern advice on the boat. I have taken it to heart in dealing with him."

"I must confess to great surprise when he was absent tonight. Is he well?"

Toreb blanked his face. For the next moments, he only blinked. Then a sad expression came to his face. "He had a minor training accident yesterday. He coughed up blood from somewhere in his chest. I rested him tonight to speed his healing."

"Did he sit out willingly?" Keladon asked.

"No, no. Eager to perform, he is."

Then why didn't you tell the king why he was absent? Keladon gave a tight, wry smile. "My fellow mages and I have done poorly explaining our abilities to the goodmen of Sodelerak."

"Sir?"

"I spoke obtusely. I mean to say, any mage with a few years of training in the handling of green magegems for medicine could have healed him in a few minutes. I assume you did not know that?"

Face blank again, Toreb said, "I did not."

"Now that you do, I am certain we can find a palace mage able and willing to heal him." Keladon quirked his mouth and angled his head at the impresario. "We all know the king's interest in Vos from two nights back, and his disappointment in your man's absence tonight. The king would reward all of us—you, me, and the palace mage casting the healing spell—if Vos were healed and able to perform for him, ah, privately."

Moni's eyebrows rose at *reward*. She angled her head toward Toreb, but he didn't notice. With wide eyes, he leaned away from Keladon. "I don't know about that, sir."

"The king inherited full coffers from my—old Radobom—and is generous with his wealth. You won't even have to work for your share. Point me to Vos' tent and I'll be back within the hour with a palace mage, if not Forek, Master of Mages, himself."

Toreb shook his head. "I wouldn't impose. Not on Your Lordship, not on a mage from the palace—"

"It's no imposition. None of us would turn down a purse of gold, and I always wish to learn b watching a fellow mage work. I also want Vos healed so he can perform at the Korobei fair. Now, point me to his tent—"

"Well, sir, I don't know if he'd be in it. We have a healer, a crone with all sorts of herbal witchery, shoddy stuff compared to what a mage can do." Toreb took a breath. After a flicker of a frown, Moni kept her face rigidly expressionless. Toreb's next words came slowly. "He might be in her tent or his own. I would need some time to find him. Sir, you said you could be back in an hour. Please, go, find a palace mage trained in physic, and when you return, I will have learned where he is and I'll lead you straight to him."

Keladon gave Moni another glance. Her face, still expressionless, projected an air of feigned ignorance. The troupe lacked a healing crone. Or was it that questioning by a highborn, no matter how innocent he might be, made him nervous? Keladon had seen it happen often enough. Though Toreb had been confident in the encounter on the boat, hadn't he?

So Toreb lied. What would he do in the next hour? Run? That seemed most likely. He wouldn't be fool enough to fight a king's son, even if his troupe had the advantage of numbers.

Keladon let his right hand drift toward the hilt of his sword. "If there are only two places to search for Vos, take me to both of them, now."

Toreb's mouth froze half-open. After a moment, he said, "Of course, sir. If you'll follow me?"

The impresario led Keladon outside. The night had grown windless, the air, thick and close. Crickets sounded in the tall grass, and a campfire's glow suffused around a half-dozen intervening tents. No one stirred between Toreb's tent and the campfire.

Toreb shuffled his feet. "It's a touch cool, sir, wouldn't you agree?"

"Cool? Your blood must run colder than mine, goodman Toreb."

"I can't know about that, sir, but if you'll pardon me?" Toreb asked. Keladon nodded and the other slipped into his tent. It took a minute, longer than Keladon had expected, with the muffled voices of Toreb and Moni coming a few times to his ears, before Toreb returned wearing a long, baggy jerkin. He stopped, bowed, gestured. "Sir, if you would?"

"Lead the way, goodman."

Toreb clamped his lips together. "Of course, sir." His jerkin's lower panels swung with his steps as he started toward the campfire. Keladon followed two steps behind, wondering what heavy things the other carried in his pockets.

Toreb whistled two bars of some tune. Keladon didn't recognize it. Toreb whistled it again, louder and with staccato, and again.

Curiosity got to Keladon. "Tell me more about that song," he said as they approached the last tent before the campfire. The fire flung shadows against the reddened canvas walls of nearby tents. The shadows moved into ready poses of exaggerated limbs and peering heads—

Toreb ran forward, past the campfire and into the darkness beyond. An angry grunt came from someone else between Keladon and the fire. He looked up. The *doumbek* player charged him, swinging a four-inch-wide log.

Keladon jumped backward. He drew his sword as the *doumbek* player rebalanced himself into a fighting posture. "Who dares attack a king's claimed son?" Keladon said. He held his blade at the ready and stole a glance at the members of the troupe around the campfire. All watched with stunned expressions.

"Kiseb!" called a woman's voice. Nera. "He's a nobleman! Don't you remember seeing him in our performances before the king?"

Kiseb held the log in front of him. He kept his gaze on the tip of Keladon's sword. "You heard Toreb call us to fight." He swung the log at Keladon's sword. Keladon whipped the blade out of the way and danced a step back.

"Against a nobleman?" Nera said. "Don't be a fool!"

"We outnumber him." Kiseb kept the log's end moving. Keladon feinted toward Kiseb's left. The *doumbek* player moved the log to parry. Keladon jabbed his sword tip toward Kiseb's face.

Kiseb staggered back two steps, avoiding the blade and keeping his balance. "Come on, you, help me! By our oaths to one another! We're all brothers against outsiders!"

Sorem said, "If Toreb wants us to risk the hangman, he should damn well stay to fight."

Kiseb looked around, and Keladon stole a glance as well. Toreb had not returned from the shadows behind the fire. Kiseb's face grew haggard, and his gaze went from Keladon's slashed doublet to Keladon's sword to the log in his own hand. The haggard look shifted toward one both resigned and galvanizing himself to action—

"Tell me where Vos is," Keladon said, "and I'll let you run off."

"Vos? How should I know?" The muscles in Kiseb's club arm bunched and flexed.

Nera spoke. "Kiseb, no!" She lowered her voice and said to Keladon, "Vos, my lord?"

The log in Kiseb's arm kept Keladon's gaze as he replied to her. "Is he with the healing crone?"

After a moment, she said with a puzzled tone, "Healing crone, my lord?"

"I thought as much," Keladon said. To Kiseb, he said, "My offer to you stands. I have no quarrel with you. You followed Toreb's command without knowing whom you targeted. If I am told everything you and your fellows know about Vos' whereabouts, I can overlook your affront, provided I never see you again."

Kiseb kept the log-club in front of his chest, but his shoulders slumped and his eyes were downcast.

"Sir, sir," said Nera, "I praise your mercy, but, sir, do you have to banish him?"

"He sought to harm a king's claimed son. Regardless of circumstances, that must be punished."

Kiseb let his arms fall to his sides. He dropped the club. It landed on one end, teetered, then clattered to the ground. "Your punishment is more than fair, sir."

Keladon kept his stare on Kiseb's eyes, until the latter bowed his head in defeat. Keladon then turned his head to Nera. "Tell me what you know of Vos."

Her shadowed face looked uneasy. "I don't know where he is now, sir."

"That is not my demand," Keladon said. "When did you last see him?"

"Two nights back. Perhaps two hours after our performance. I—happened to see him approach Toreb's tent."

Keladon suspected she had been spying on Toreb and Moni at the time. He thought of confronting her with that, but what good would it do him, never mind her? Even if all her fellow performers knew she was the receding vertex of a love triangle, better to leave it unspoken. *The heart drives each of us to things we would not choose.* "Continue."

"He stood at the flap while they spoke in low tones, and he handed Toreb something small. A tiny purse, I guessed. Toreb grimaced in distaste as he took it. I assumed Vos gave Toreb a cut of some grift he had worked on a highborn of the palace."

"You may well be right. What happened then?"

"Toreb went off with him. Not like that. Out in the open, toward the palace."

"Toreb carried the tiny purse as he went with Vos?" Keladon asked.

"I assume so."

"But you do not know for certain." Keladon thought over all she had just told him. "This happened two hours after your performance that night?"

Nera cringed. "I can't swear to that, sir, I don't have a timepiece. None of us save Toreb do. But I know the moon was up—" She shut her eyes for a moment, then opened them and jutted her finger at the sky. "—about there." She pointed to where Keladon remembered the moon hanging when he left the tavern to follow Old Atem's henchmen.

"Thank you." Keladon's gaze took in all the gathered performers. "Does anyone else have something to say about Vos' whereabouts?"

A few members of the trope muttered "No, sir," while others shook their heads.

Keladon thought further. Toreb had taken the distasteful object —assume it to be an assurance cap filled with the king's semen— and Vos away shortly before someone had cast Preserve a Body Tissue somewhere on the palace grounds. Who had cast the spell? Where?

Presumably, a guard had seen Toreb and Vos enter the grounds. Why not go to the Master of the Royal Guard and ask?

Because that guard, or the Master himself, might be in league with the enemy.

Until he identified the man behind the conspiracy, Keladon could not trust anyone. His best lead, Toreb, had vanished into the night. Though he knew in his bones the impresario wasn't coming back, Keladon said, "Should Toreb return, someone here must inform me immediately."

"We certainly will, sir," Sorem said.

"You mean he's gone?" asked the midget from the midst of the crowd. "He hasn't paid us for tonight's performance."

"He put on a long jerkin just before he ran off," Keladon said.

Another performer said, "That's right, I saw him wear it." A few others nodded.

Sorem set his fists on his hips. "His long jerkin with deep pockets. That thieving bastard. Time to check his tent in case he left a few sous behind in his escape." He stalked into the darkness, and most of the other performers streamed after him.

Soon, only Kiseb and Nera remained. Kiseb bowed, showing his balding scalp and dropping his knee to the dirt. "I'll run off, my lord, just as you said, but may I beg of you something? A few minutes, sir, to pack up some clothes and my drum."

"I will not deprive a man of his livelihood," Keladon said. "But you must leave the camp and the city for your crime against me to be pardoned."

Kiseb backed toward the darkness between tents. "Wait," Nera said.

"I will not relent," Keladon said.

"Sir, I do not ask that. Kiseb, wait for me, and I shall journey with you."

He looked wounded. "Please, don't say that. Earn your living with the troupe—"

"If Toreb is gone, the troupe will scatter to the winds," she said. "I have no one else to rely on. In all that has happened lately, you alone have stood by me, and I want to stand by you now."

His face showed disbelief. Nera turned to Keladon. "Thank you again for your clemency, sir." She hurried to Kiseb and led him into the darkness between the tents. From the other direction, Toreb's tent, came angry shouts.

Keladon sheathed his sword and returned to the palace. His thoughts raced ahead. With Toreb flown, Old Atem had become his best lead. All the more reason to invade the master criminal's hideout and compel the truth from him as soon as possible.

Two hours later, Keladon carefully made his way along the ledge between Old Atem's warehouse and the river. Water slicked the stones under his boots. A sack with three gems hung over his shoulder, ready to tip him off balance. His legs trembled with the fine effort demanded of muscles unaccustomed to it.

A few paces away, Lar nervously sucked in a breath. Keladon steadied himself and gave his valet a chiding look. He needed silence more than anything. He returned his gaze to the damp stones and took his next step, avoiding a spat plug of chewed tabac.

Finally he stood beneath Old Atem's window. A lamp glowed within. Keladon breathed deeply and thought through the steps of his plan one final time. *You're as ready as you can be, and the clock continues to run.* He reached his left hand in front of his body and over his right shoulder, then pulled the yellow from the sack. He gripped it and murmured in Jelorean. The released energy tingled his hand. Slowly, quietly, his right hand drew his sword. He held the tip straight up and gave the yellow a few commands.

He drifted up into the air. The joints between the warehouse's siding planks ticked down his field of vision. Crevices gave glimpses of the dimly lit interior. He glanced at the river and the ledge below. Instinctive unease made him shiver, but then a grin lifted the corners of his mouth. Not quite birdlike, but he flew.

Above him, the open window grew closer. A gust set papers rustling inside. Keladon touched his sword's basket hilt to the wall to steady himself. His grin dried up. He was about to turn the tables on the man trying to kill him.

He's just a higher ranked pawn than the two henchmen you knifed. You're here to get him to identify the man pushing the pieces. You need him alive.

Until he gives you that man's name.

He murmured more Jelorean, and the yellow's energies moved him to the side of the window. He bent his torso sideways for a glance inside. It showed a tall oaken chair back and the top of a head of black hair above it. Keladon still had the advantage of surprise. He dropped his chest toward his knees and pulled back his right arm, to pounce through the window and thrust the sword. Another murmur to the yellow slid him to the window. He set his left foot on the sill and jumped into the room.

Two steps and a cocking of his elbow brought the tip of Keladon's sword to the side of Old Atem's neck. "Don't move," he said, voice low and tight. He shuffled to the side, watching Old Atem's profile for any movement and glancing about for his father. Flies buzzed nearby, and a metallic smell came from the floor under Old Atem's chair.

He had been slashed across the neck. A look of surprise and

indignation showed on Old Atem's chiseled face. Across the room, an older man, the former Old Atem and the current one's father, had been stabbed in the chest. A closer look showed his killer had sent the blade between ribs and into his heart. An expert move.

He stopped the flux from the yellow. The metallic smell of fresh blood finally hit him. He grimaced and forced himself to focus. Fresh? How fresh? At the periphery of the blood pools under the dead men, individual drops had turned into reddish-brown stains. In the main, though, their blood was thickening but still liquid. They had been killed within a half-hour, Keladon guessed.

Was the killer still in the warehouse? The door to the room was ajar, and a faint blood track in the partial outline of a boot heel led outside it. Keladon carefully followed it, stepping over the track and bringing his feet down as lightly as he could.

A square hole, about two feet on each side, opened from the loft to the ladder he'd seen the night before. Blood pooled on the dirt floor below. Keladon knelt and stuck his head out the hole. The guard, same one as the previous night, lay with contorted limbs and unseeing eyes. He had a dagger in a sheath on his belt.

Racks of barrels and crates hid the front of the warehouse from Keladon's view. A sudden intuition told him the men there were also dead.

He descended the ladder. His gaze darted around this end of the warehouse as he went. Any dark corner could hide the killer.... Keladon felt foolish, knowing he jumped at shadows. If the killer hadn't been in Old Atem's office, rifling through papers for some incriminating evidence, he had long departed.

At the foot of the ladder, Keladon swung and jumped as clear of the guard's blood as he could reach. His left boot landed a few inches from the edge of the blood spill. He stepped clear and scraped his sole back and forth on the dirt floor to scrub off the blood. Keladon drew his sword and looked for any blood track left by the killer's boots. There. Was that it? He looked further and saw another footstep marked by blood. He looked for more steps. The next lay closer

than he expected, product of a shortened stride. Perhaps the killer
had injured his leg coming off the ladder. Keladon filed the observa-
tion away, then started toward the front of the warehouse.

In the gloom between two rows of barrels, another intuition told
Keladon the killer's true purpose. He had come to kill Old Atem. Any
other dead were necessary to silence witnesses, but irrelevant for his
purpose. No evidence in Old Atem's office had needed disposing. Old
Atem had been the target and it was no coincidence he'd been killed
as Keladon closed in on him. The killer, or the man who'd
commanded him, feared Old Atem might share too much of the
truth. Who had hired him to kill Keladon, and why? Keladon now
would never know.

And how had the killer known Keladon had closed in on Old
Atem? Had he given that name to Dalasa or her uncle? To Lilera?
No....

At the front of the warehouse, a single lamp, turned low, stood
on the table and cast long shadows of the tabletop across the floor.
Slumped forward from their chairs onto the table, or collapsed in its
shadow, lay dead men. The two nearest the rear of the warehouse,
who had sat with their backs to the killer, had died in their chairs.
One had a slit in the side of his neck, the other, a slash across his
kidneys. Their weapons, a curved dagger and a short sword,
remained in their sheaths.

The men on the other side of the table had reacted, but slowly.
Toppled bottles and the cloying smell of cheap wine showed part of
the reason why. Two died near the pair of carriage doors at the side
of the room, to Keladon's right as he approached. Behind them,
another dead man slumped face-first against the left-hand carriage
door, stabbed in the back. The right-hand door stood slightly ajar. A
puff of wind set its hinges creaking.

How many men had sat at this table the previous night? He had
accounted for five.

In the shadow of table, a man stirred.

Keladon went closer, sword ready. The man lay on his back and pushed his right foot against the dirt. Keladon guessed he tried to get his back against the wall six feet away. Blood stained his shirt over his abdomen, and the floor under him. Sweaty pallor filled his face, and a glazed look, his eyes. He held a short sword in a wavering grip. "You're not him." His eyes widened in a moment of shock. He pushed the sword away and thrashed his head. "Oh angel, I swear by your Divine Master, I mean you and Him no insult with my blade." He groaned, though whether from the pain of his wounds, or his remorse at offending someone he took to be an angel of Balar, Keladon couldn't tell.

"I, and He, take no insult."

The dying man feebly waved his hand toward Keladon's right shoulder. "You have come to carry my soul to the Divine Couple in your sack? You know what sort of man I am. How could I deserve to be taken there straight away?"

Keladon knelt by the man's side and tore his shirt away. Two deep slashes crossed his abdomen and the stink of feces reached Keladon's nose. Deep red blood welled through the lowermost wound.

Keladon set down his pack and reached for the green. "It is not a man's place to know whether he deserves entry into the Divine Couple's hall or not. *Attend me.* But I can say you ride the knife edge between entering directly and being sent through the purging fire." Keladon spread the fingers of his right hand to touch both wounds at once. The thick, greasy texture of blood against his fingertips told him he had found them. "*Target your energies on the wounds I touch.* It will help you if you tell us about the man who did this. When his time comes, we must know him by sight, to prevent him from deceiving us."

The dying man appeared to take it as given that Balar and his angels could be fooled into given an evil man entrance into the Divine Couple's hall. Guilt panged Keladon. If the spell were too late and the man were to die, stories about Balar and Samala were the only comfort he would have in his last moments. If those stories turned out to be lies, he would never know. *"Flux two-fifths of a boil per drop of time...."*

"I don't know his name," the dying man said. His mouth opened in a rictus of pain. He slid his hand toward his wounds, but shied away from touching them. Through gritted teeth, he said, "It burns, angel."

A response came quickly to Keladon. "If you felt no pain, I would know you lied." He could pray after the claiming ceremony, if he still felt guilty then.

"How much we men lie, you must test us so. The boss gave word to let him in months back. We hadn't seen him a while. Then we hear someone coming from the back of the warehouse and he's swinging his sword before we can react."

"How did he get in?"

He looked anguished. "I don't know, angel. I swear I'd tell you if I knew. But I can tell you what he looks like." The dying man took a long, shallow breath. "He had a nose broke once or more." The man's eyes rolled back for a moment. "A scar on his chin. Smells of chewed tabac." His eyes glazed and he stared past Keladon's shoulder.

Had he lost him? *"Flux one-half of a boil—"*

"He limped." The man's eyes turned lucid for a moment. He cast an imploring look at Keladon, plainly wanting his words to be heeded. "I'd never seen him limp before, angel." His eyes glazed and his chest sank as his final breath rattled in his throat.

Keladon moved his blood-stained right hand to the man's neck and pressed the backs of his fingers under the jaw, seeking the man's pulse. All he felt was the cool slick sheen of the blood he'd carried from the man's wounds. Dead.

"Flux zero boils per drop of time."

Keladon squatted in the bloody dirt and returned the green to its quiescent state. Flies buzzed and the tang of blood filled his nose. His shoulders slumped and he sloughed out a breath. Somehow the man behind all this had decided he was too close, and had decided to cover his tracks. The killer had climbed the rear wall of the warehouse, after spitting out spent tabac, and killed the men Keladon had needed to divulge their secrets.

At least Keladon had a description. Misshapen nose, chin scar, tabac chewer, new limp. How many hours, days, weeks would he need to spend in the slums of Teisoret to find the man? Impossible. He had till morning. He would have to go to the king. The kingdom's fate relied on it.

So, too, did the fate of his son.

He widened the gap between the carriage doors with his elbow, then slipped out of the warehouse into an alley. To his right, the Derepar splashed against the stone wall at the riverside. Lar waited there. Keladon's face hardened. He reached into his pack for the blue, then stalked toward the riverside, muttering in Jelorean as he went.

Lar emerged from the shadows behind the building. "Sir, did you find—"

Keladon clamped his hand on Lar's upper arm and cast Compel Truthful Answers. Lar grunted. "Who is your master?" Keladon asked.

"Who—ah—" Lar grimaced. "You, sir."

"Whom did you tell we had found Old Atem?"

A confused frown. "Sir? No one—" Lar's face paled and sweat beaded on his brow. "Oh, no, did she—" He groaned. "Tana, in the east wing kitchens."

Anger distorted Keladon's face. "Where did she lift her skirts for you? In a storeroom or in the laundry? Were two minutes plowing her furrow worth wrecking your master's plans?"

"Sir..." Lar cried. "Wrecking your plans?"

"Old Atem and his men are dead. The mastermind trying to kill me had Old Atem killed to keep him from being compelled to reveal the mastermind's identity."

Lar's head swayed side to side, disbelief on his features. "I can't believe she could have been a spy for anyone. She's too innocent, sir. Maybe it was the jealous fellow, what was his name? He might have overheard." His head slumped further. "Sir, I have done you a grievous wrong. I'll find new employment when we return to Korobei...."

Keladon loosed his grip on the valet's arm. *"No flux. Release your attention from me.* We'll discuss your error and its punishment later. I must keep you now. You are the one man in Teisoret loyal to me."

With a sober expression, Lar lifted his head. "How may I serve you, sir?"

Keladon set down the sack of gems from his shoulder and returned the quiet blue to it. "To begin, carry these to the Temple of Samala, on our way back to the palace."

"Your Illustriousness, certainly you must realize, and today of all days, His Majesty cannot grant an audience at this horrid hour despite all your importunity." The clerk had a thin fringe of fair hair, and a nose narrow and straight. He straightened his back where he sat behind a wide desk, and fixed Keladon with an impassive look. The one lamp in the room burned low on a corner of the desk. It shadowed his eyes and the far side of his face. "We have a scant seven hours till the claiming ceremony."

Three o'clock, according to a clock ticking in the corner of the room. The sound, combined with the color palate of greens, light wallpaper and dark curtains, made Keladon's eyelids droop. He snorted in a breath and forced his eyes wide. The last three late nights caught up with him, but sleep had to wait until after Raboros claimed the newborn prince. "It is because today is so momentous that I must deliver my news now, and only to the king."

"Most men would claim their news is momentous," the clerk said. "whether it were or not, sir." He crossed his arms.

"Fair enough. Consider this, if you please. If you were to relay my request to the king, and it were momentous, he and Melos would applaud your initiative—"

"Applaud?"

Keladon angled his head. "The Master of Offices would barely smile. Regardless, he would think well of you. And if my news were trivial, would your employment grow any worse than it is now?" He let his words hang. The clock ticked away a few more seconds of the night.

The clerk looked thoughtful. "Wait here, sir." He went to a side door. Boards creaked under his feet. While the clerk's back was turned, Keladon yawned. Seven more hours till the ceremony. He could sleep after that.

Low voices at the door roused Keladon slightly. The clerk slipped out and two palace guards entered the room and took places on either side of the door. They talked among themselves in low tones and from time to time studied Keladon with narrow eyes.

He returned them a haughty look and found a seat along the wall across the room from the guards. Sitting proved a mistake. His eyelids drooped more and his chin sank toward his chest. He woke with a start. One of the guards watched him, his face impassive. Could he trust these men to not be servants of the unknown enemy...? and Keladon dozed again.

The creak of hinges and the pad of footsteps roused him more fully. The clerk had brought a higher-ranked official, gray-haired and wrinkled. The official's unslashed doublet sat unevenly on his shoulders, and at his hip, one of the cords for holding up his breeches flopped, undone. Called away from sleep, or his mistress? The official scowled and blinked heavily. He stalked across the room and Keladon rose to face him.

"An audience with the King, Your Illustriousness? What asinine joke are you playing?"

"Would a man of my station joke?"

The official blinked, paused. "I would wish to believe one could not, sir. However, were you more familiar with the palace, you would know many of comparable station to you would want to rouse the king as a joke on His Majesty's loyal servants."

Shameful, and not surprising. *The nobles he talks about will be the men seen by your son and next king.* "Sadly, I know you have the truth of it. But as you recognize, I am not a gentleman of the palace."

"True, sir." The official's tone made the words the slenderest of clefts in the armor of his regard.

"It may be that my reputation proceeds me. Is it known that I have loyally and effectively served Sodelerak's past and present sovereigns for two decades?"

The official bowed his head. "All who love our kingdom, sir, know of the prowess you showed in the campaign against Pelurak."

The fingers of Keladon's right hand twitched. A tic born of high activity and little sleep, he told himself, but sudden memories belied that: his fingers flinging scalding balls of crimson energy against the massed Peluraki foot. "Did you serve as well?"

The official looked wistful. "I was only a clerk working for your father's councilors, sir."

"Even a clerk may be a hero." Keladon took a deep breath. "Then or now." He gestured toward the door.

"His Majesty cannot be woken on such a slender word, sir, even one spoken by a man of your deeds and reputation." The official sighed and rubbed his eyes with a slow adduction of his thumb and forefinger. "Let us ask Melos. If you would wait here, sir."

The official and the clerk went out. The two guards remained. His partial victory over the official appeared to have reminded them of his station: they bowed their heads when he looked at them, and thereafter, their gazes avoided his. *If they serve our enemy, they won't act now....* he soon dozed again.

Creaking hinges and the shuffling of the guards's feet woke him. He shook his head to become a little more alert, then looked into the next room. There, the official flourished his arms toward the open doorway, and the clerk bowed his head and chest and made the same gestures to someone yet unseen.

Keladon rose as Melos entered the room. "Greetings, Master of Offices. I am pleased...."

Behind Melos came a man favoring his right leg. His nose was crooked, and a shiny spot, a mix of off-white and purple taut with scar tissue, stood on his chin, near a wad of tabac distending his lower lip.

Keladon's heart pounded as he forced himself to finish speaking. "...you have woken to attend to my request."

Melos and the killer didn't know what he'd seen and heard. Even if the killer had lurked around Old Atem's hideout and seen Keladon leave, he must have assumed all Old Atem's men were dead. He wouldn't have left the last man alive otherwise.

"Your Illustriousness," Melos said, "when you are an old man, sleep is an uncommon gift at the best of times. Preparations for the claiming ceremony and its following events have required my attention the entire night."

Kelason would have to make Melos and the killer believe he was ignorant of their conspiracy. Once dismissed by them, he could find a way to foil their plot. "I'll be brief and let you return to your tasks." Keladon stopped for breath and moved his head to show he'd just noticed the killer. "I don't believe I've made your acquaintance."

"Patot. Your Illustriousness." He bowed minimally. His sheathed sword bobbed against his hip.

Keladon raised an eyebrow to Melos.

"Patot is assisting me in preparations for the day's events, sir," Melos said. "Tell me what news you have that you wish to share with the king."

Best to lie as little as possible; one doesn't need to remember the truth. "Do you know the basics of the geometer's art? Two points are enough to draw a line."

Melos frowned. Keladon went on. "It struck me a few days ago that one attempt on my life could be happenstance, but two suggests something willful is at work. So I investigated—"

"You?" said Patot. He worked the wad of tabac to the other side of his mouth.

"Yes. I've spent the last few nights making inquiries in the slums of Teisoret. My suspicions were confirmed. Someone did plot my murder." He watched Melos's face for any reaction, but the old man gave none.

Keladon glanced past Melos and Patot to the official, the clerk, and the guards. "But before I say more, I would suggest we speak privately. Even if magic were not to block all sound from this room, its walls would block some."

Patot gave a brief, slight shrug. Melos lifted his chin and turned to the others. "Leave us." The official and the others quickly left. After the door shut behind them, Melos softly asked Keladon, "Who?"

"A Peluraki spy."

Melos' eyes briefly widened. He masked the reaction. "I see why this news matters to you, sir, but why should we wake the king with it?"

"Because I have evidence the Peluraki spy ring plans to disrupt the claiming ceremony tomorrow."

"You may give that evidence to me."

Keladon shook his head. "Master of Offices, I know your loyalty to the king is unquestionable. But sound seeps through the palace's walls, and the ears that pick it up may not be as loyal as yours."

After a thoughtful moment, Melos said, "Then you shall have the chance to tell him. We must keep this very quiet, for the reasons you set forth. Patot, we will guide Keladon through the tunnels to the king's apartments, to ensure no one might happen upon us and wonder what has us about."

His heart slamming, Keladon said, "Let us go."

They went into a wide corridor. Nearby, a plain door opened onto a storeroom for bed linens. They stopped in the back of the storeroom and Patot pushed a panel on the wall. It swung open to reveal steps leading down into darkness.

Patot pulled a lantern from a niche just inside the opening and lit it on his second twist of its flint wheel. He handed it to Melos and reached into the niche for another, for himself.

"Hand me one as well," Keladon said.

Patot squinted into the niche. "Sorry. Sir. The only lantern left is out of oil." He slammed shut the niche's door, then waved at the darkness below. "After you. Sir."

Keladon kept his feet planted. "Lead the way, if you please."

Melos and Patot shared a glance. "As you wish. Sir. Do shut the panel behind you."

The wooden steps creaked under Patot and Keladon's feet. Between them, Melos trod lightly. By the time Patot neared the bottom, he grunted each time his right foot landed. At the foot of the steps, the tunnel's cool, damp air enveloped Keladon, and its dank, musty smell filled his nose.

Patot led the party through the tunnels. Rats scurried away from their lanterns. Keladon kept his attention on the twists and turns and mapped them against his knowledge of the palace's above-ground spaces. From the green room, the king's apartments were to the east. Now, if his sense of direction worked accurately, they headed southwest.

They stopped below a set of stairs leading up into darkness, and Melos and Patot shared another glance. "His Majesty's apartments are at the head of the stairs," Melos said. "Knock twice, pause, then twice more. A servant will unlock the door and allow you to wait while he wakes the king."

Keladon's heart thudded so strongly he felt sure they could see his torso rock with its beats. He kept his voice confident. "The servant will answer to me?"

"He will answer the pattern of knocks, I assure you."

"Yet we should all go together. The king is more likely to listen to you and me than to me alone."

Melos shook his head. "By entering that door, His Majesty will know I approve your visit to him, and that it is a matter of grave import."

The fingers of Keladon's right hand curled toward the hilt of his sword. "I bow to your judgment, Master of Offices." He faced the darkness dominating the stairs, turning his back to Patot as he did, and listened for the faint sound of a blade being drawn behind him. There—

He drew his sword while he pivoted to his right. Steel clanged, and the blow knocked Patot's blade low and to Keladon's right. Shadows jumped across the walls as the lantern in Patot's left hand twisted with his body. Keladon thrusted, aiming the tip of his sword above Patot's right arm, toward his heart. He slashed the killer's arm.

Patot staggered backward and brought his blade up. They traded parries. The lantern bobbing in Patot's hand brought out a stark relief of pain and anger on his face.

Behind Keladon, more light danced across the tunnel walls and dimmed. Melos fled. How soon before he sent a troop of palace guards through the tunnel to help Patot? Too soon. Keladon would have to quickly finish the killer.

Patot weakly swung his sword. Keladon parried. A trickle of blood dampened Patot's sleeve. *Is that all he has?*

"Not very trusting of you," Patot said, "drawing your sword on me like that."

"Pardon me for making your task difficult," Keladon said as he feinted. Patot parried and shuffled backward, putting most of his weight on his left foot.

Patot had more strength remaining in his right arm than he wanted to let on. Keladon slid to his left and let his sword's tip droop. Patot's right arm visibly tensed. Keladon knew his next attack would come a fraction of a second before it did. Patot slowly swung his blade. Keladon knocked it away with a sharp parry, but it remained firmly in Patot's grip. The killer pulled his sword back to guard before Keladon could counter.

The killer knew time was on his side. He need only fight defensively until the royal guard arrived. Keladon had to lure him into the path of his blade.

A plan came to him. He moved further to his left, near the tunnel wall, then sent a strong stroke toward Patot. The killer moved his lantern to block and moved backward, waving his arms slightly as if his balance was weak; but Patot quickly settled his feet.

Keladon let his sword's tip droop even further, inviting an attack. It came, a lunge aimed at his heart. But as Patot lunged, Keladon shuffled to his right and lifted his sword. When Patot's right foot landed to complete the lunge, his ankle buckled.

Keladon slashed his sword over Patot's left shoulder to the side of the man's neck. He jumped back as Patot swung the lantern at his head. The swinging light showed the killer's wide eyes and a glossy reflection on the blood spurting from his neck.

The lantern sailed past Keladon, and a moment later, glass crunched a few paces down the corridor. The light suddenly flared from spilled, burning oil, imparting a ruddy cast to Patot's face. His blade clanged on the floor and he fell. His left arm shook as he reached for his neck.

Keladon eyed him warily. "Why does Melos want to disrupt the claiming ceremony?"

"Go—" Blood gurgled from Patot's mouth. "Go to the purging fires."

"That's where you're bound if you don't tell me."

"Where I'm bound if I do...." Patot gave Keladon a contemptuous look as life left his eyes.

The flaring light from the broken lantern shone well past Patot's corpse, onto the far wall of the stairs where he'd meant to kill Keladon, and a dozen paces up the corridor where the palace guard would soon come.

Where to next?

From far up the corridor, the creak of leather armor, the clomp of boots, and the mutter of voices answered him. Keladon set off the other direction and stepped over the dying flames rising from the sheen of spilled lantern oil. The darkness ahead grew even more black as the fire behind him burned itself out.

Keladon quietly sheathed his sword, then felt his way with the fingertips of his right hand on the wall's cool, rough stone. He held his left hand in front of his face to protect himself from possible low ceilings invisible in the dark. He stepped quietly and cocked his ear in the direction of the dying fire and Patot's corpse. Though the guards' distance rendered the words indistinct, one voice's timbre of authority carried to Keladon's ears. The tromp of footfalls sounded soon after the voice.

The wall beyond his right hand fell away. Keladon's balance wavered. After he regained it, he paced a circle and reached out to check the walls around him. He was in an intersection, with two tunnels leading away to his right, one to his left, and the current tunnel heading straight on. The guards would have trouble following him from here. But which path? Didn't matter. He picked the tunnel to his left and kept moving.

Within a few minutes, the sounds of jostled equipment and low voices faded, then fell silent. The steady rasp of the stone under Keladon's fingers became familiar, and his growing ease in the dark tunnel allowed him to walk more confidently.

Another thing sped him along. His watch weighed down his pocket. Only six hours remained until the claiming ceremony.

He took a deep breath to calm himself. Before long, he would find an exit from the tunnels. Once out, he could reconnoiter his surroundings and figure out how to reach the king while avoiding Melos. There had to be an exit somewhere. Only a matter of time before he found it.

Time he could not spend frivolously. He hurried on. The floor sloped downward. His fingertips traced the wall's rough striations. There had to be a crossing tunnel or a set of stairs somewhere—

His fingertips touched air. Finally, a crossing tunnel. He groped for the far side of the tunnel and his face twisted in puzzlement. Too narrow... and, more groping revealed, too small. A circular hole no more than a pace in diameter, chest high in the wall. He reached in as far as he could and felt nothing but air.

A crawlspace? Leading where?

If out of the tunnel, where didn't matter.

He climbed in and crawled forward. His hair brushed the crawl-space's ceiling and he lowered his head. The stone floor felt rough through his undershirt and doublet. He reached ahead, still nothing but air. He pulled his feet into the tunnel and his boot's hard soles clomped against the stone.

A mournful sound came from somewhere. Keladon froze, listened. A human voice? Deeper than a rat, certainly, but wordless. The sound did not repeat. A draft in some cross tunnel, perhaps.

Or you're hearing things. He crawled forward a few more feet, and his hand touched something. Smooth, wooden, cylindrical. Another one a few inches to the right. He reached between them and felt more rough stone. A dead end?

No. The sound of his breaths had changed. He waved his left hand above his head. The tunnel angled up.

The tunnel smelled oily. A hunch came to him. He sat in the angle of the tunnel and felt for the smooth wooden cylinders. He ran his hand up the top and found an oily rag. More groping found a flint wheel on the tunnel floor. He struck the wheel near the rag and the torch lit up the space around him.

The vertical portion of the tunnel went up three paces. Rectangular depressions had been roughly hacked into one wall. Overhead, a stone hatch blocked the tunnel, with a thick, foot long rope hanging from it.

Keladon climbed. Where did the hatch lead? It was still ten or twelve paces below ground level, he guessed. He angled his ear to the hatch and waited. No sound. Only one way to find out.

He pulled the rope. The stone hatch opened toward him and stopped a few inches from the tunnel wall. He ducked his head and looked up. On the other side of the hatchway, a wooden surface covered the entire hole. He reached up. The wooden surface slid easily as he pushed. A moment later, the hatchway was clear, and he crawled out.

He stood next to an empty wooden crate in a corner of a spacious room, ten paces by fifteen, with rows of shelves running along the short axis of the room. The shelves held hundreds of gems, of all the colors. A shiver ran over him. He had found his way into Forek's magegem vault.

The vault had only two exits. The one behind him led back into the deep tunnels. The other would debouch in a basement or a ground floor room of the palace, with watchmen posted there.

Men watching for intrusion from outside, not from within. He had a chance to surprise them and escape.

More thoughts occurred to him. Forek and Parel had both let slip that gems were going missing from the vaults. Had the gem thieves dug the tunnel behind him and stocked it with torches to aid their work?

Keladon cleared the questions from his mind. Gem thieves were the least of the kingdom's problems. He looked down the aisles for a passageway or a door. He found the latter, a thick slab of wood with horizontal bars of riveted iron. Gripping the handle, he pressed his ear to the wood. No sound from beyond. No light from underneath. He slowly pushed the door, and it opened on silent hinges.

In the next chamber he stood more gem racks, and a faint glow from under a door in the far corner. Keladon set his torch down on the stone and crossed the new room to the door. He stepped cautiously and held his scabbard tightly against his left hip. Where light shone, vault employees likely worked. The sound of a rack bearing dozens of gems toppling against the stone walls or floor would summon all the palace mages and their clerks at work at this hour. Even a faint click of his scabbard against a rack might alert them.

He reached the door. Kneeling, he cupped his ear toward the gap under the door. The stone floor set his bony, middle-aged knees to aching. Only a few moments, just to hear who was out there....

From twenty or thirty paces away, an imperious male voice echoed down the stone walls. "Then where have those gems gone?"

A second voice stammered. "I don't know—"

"Do you think we are fools? A score of rubies, and sundry others, go missing over the course of two months. We know from audits done immediately before and after your watches that at least three gems went missing while you two sat here."

"Audits?" said a third voice.

"We know how to count gems. We didn't even need to train under Forek. Yes, we audited the vaults."

"If there was a theft, your auditors must be lying to pin it on us," the second voice said. "Are you part of the scheme along with them?"

The imperious voice grew cold. "*You* accuse *me?*"

"If there's been thieving, I have to accuse someone, because we're innocent!"

Keladon stood. An interrogator and two palace mages watching the vault. A few armed men would have accompanied the interrogator, to intimidate the palace mages. He would have to neutralize at least five men to escape the vault and try to stop Melos.

How hard would it be? Around him waited how many reds—?

No. He had vowed to never again tap a red.

But these weren't Peluraki foot, ignorant of the power to soon be turned on them. The mages, the palace official, and the armed men backing him knew what reds could do.

A clammy feeling stole down Keladon's sides. Whatever their faults, at least some of those men were loyal subjects of King Raboros. He would not kill them with his sword, let alone a red.

So he would go back into the deeper tunnels. He at least would have a torch to show his way to an exit. The aboveground levels of the palace would be filled with both guardsmen and Melos' spies, all of whom would be on alert for him. He would need a green, then, to cast Dye Hair, Color Eyes, or Shift a Face. Or all three. And whatever he cast, he would have to do it quickly, before Forek's spellwatchers noticed a green had been tapped. Strike Shift a Face from the list. It would need too much flux for too long. Change the color of his hair and eyes, and hope it would be enough.

So, disguised, once he found his way out of the tunnels, he would find and warn the king. Resolve filled his chest. All he needed was a green.

He went back to the first room he'd entered. He picked up the torch, then paused a moment, staring at his sword. Above ground, it would mark him as a nobleman. With only his hair and eyes disguised, someone from a distance might identify him from his height, body carriage, and the accessories of high birth. He would leave the sword here.

With the torch lighting his way, he found a rack of greens. He lifted a richly colored one and something troubled him. What?

Greens. Melos had to have stolen one to preserve the king's semen. But the interrogator had mentioned scores of reds had also been stolen. What did Melos need them for? Did he sell them on the black market? Did he arm a cadre of battlemages for the aftermath of the disrupted claiming ceremony?

Melos had no need to steal a single magegem. He must have palace mages, perhaps of high rank, in his conspiracy to cast the needed spells. Helpers of that rank could carry magegems out the front door of the vault in full view of their underlings. They wouldn't need to sneak through the tunnels and use the hidden hatchway. Despite the cool air, a trickle of sweat ran down Keladon's neck. Even though Melos wanted to kill him, was the Master of Offices innocent of the crime being plotted against the kingdom, the crown, its heir?

If he were guilty of theft, why would Melos or his helpers investigate missing gems?

Keladon thought for a few moments. He wasn't done here. He set down the green and returned to the shelves in search of a well-charged blue.

DAWN TOUCHED the windows when Keladon entered the anteroom of Melos' office. At a high desk, three clerks conversed over stacks of paper. Behind the desk, next to Melos' door, a guardsman leaned his weight on a halberd and rubbed his upper lip with the back of his free hand.

The clerks looked over with bleary eyes but didn't move. "Who are you?" asked the one nearest Keladon.

"Lonak. Servant of Balar and high priest Rolabok." Keladon spoke with higher pitch than usual, and affected an accent from the southern provinces. He lifted a thick bundle of fabric hanging from, and partially bunched in, his left hand. "The high priest sends me to converse with your master about the claimed child's swaddling cloth."

The clerk squinted. Did he wonder why a junior priest wore a white silk shirt without a cloak? Did he suspect the fabric bundle was a slashed doublet, turned inside out, and folded into a bag for two gems? Worst of all, did he see through Keladon's black hair and blue eyes to his true identity? Yet the clerk only waved his hand. "Our master approves."

"The high priest insisted your master approve it himself."

The clerks muttered among themselves. Their spokesman finally said, "I'll announce you, but be brief, priest. Our master is busy preparing for the ceremony." The clerk went to the door and Keladon hurried around the desk after him. The guard straightened his halberd and looked at the far wall as Keladon passed.

The clerk knocked and waited. When Melos' muffled voice sound within, the clerk held out his hand to Keladon, *wait here*, and opened the door. "Your pardons, Master, but a priest on an errand from Rolabok needs a few minutes.... The swaddling cloth.... I don't know why the high priest seeks your input, Master...." Eventually, the clerk nodded. "Very well."

The clerk stepped back. "Five minutes, priest."

Keladon nodded and went past the clerk. Would the clerk keep the door open? From the corner of his eye, he saw the clerk reach for the handle and shut the door with the air of long habit. The old man's tight grip on his secrets would give Keladon the privacy he needed. Fitting that a villain should be snared in his own trap.

Or fitting that a loyal servant of the king would have the chance to explain himself in private.

Melos stood at a broad desk. Twenty sheaves of paper, bundled with twine, sat in neat rows near the front right corner, and a set of loose papers lay arrayed on the desk closer to him. An unlit lamp stood on the front left corner, and the end of a bell rope hung within arm's reach of the old man. The door thudded shut and Keladon ran around the desk while Melos said, looking up, "What does the high priest—"

Keladon's right hand clamped Melos' mouth and pushed the old man against the bundle of gems held by his left. *"Attend me,"* he whispered to the green, *"target your energies upon the man I touch, Paralyze Four Limbs, flux three-tenths of a boil, now."*

Melos' limbs went limp. He glared while Keladon pressed his slack body between his arms. He worked his jaw, trying to bite Keladon's hand or cry out.

Keladon pressed harder and wriggled his hand, jamming Melos' jaw shut with the heel. He laid the old man on the floor, with the bundled gems as a rigid, misshapen pillow, then slid his left hand from the green to the blue. He whispered in Jelorean. Melos winced and drew in a jagged breath.

"I have cast Compel Truthful Answers on you," Keladon said. "If you call for help, I will slit your throat before the guard enters the room."

Melos' eyes glinted. "You have no sword," he muttered through his forcibly clenched mouth.

"Are you certain I lack a dagger in my boot?"

The glint faded. Keladon eased the pressure on Melos' mouth and jaw. "Where is the king's semen?"

Through clenched teeth, Melos said, "In His Majesty's body, or the body of one of his companions."

"I'll ask again, with better words. Where is the sample of the king's semen to be used in casting Scald the Cuckold's Egg against the new prince?"

"What are you going on about?" Melos' eyes slammed shut and he groaned. "I don't know."

"Who has the sample of the king's semen?"

The signs of pain further ebbed from Melos' face. "I don't know."

Had he rigged up an intricate pattern of ignorance to protect himself against the chance a mage would suspect him of the conspiracy? Or was Melos truly innocent? "Who took the sample of the king's semen?"

"I don't know.... You think there is a plot to reveal the new prince's relationship to the king? You think I am involved in it?

Keladon's suspicions of Melos' innocence, growing since his musings in the vault, were being validated. Though if anyone could sail against the wind of Compel Truthful Answers, it would be Melos. "In what material was the semen stored?"

"I don't know." Melos' eyes showed ongoing calculation.

"Did you order the procurement of Vos to capture the king's fancy?"

"No."

"Did you order the provision of Vos with the assurance cap and instructions to collect the king's semen?"

"No."

"Who cast Preserve a Body Tissue on the sample of the king's semen?"

"I don't know."

"Who burgled my chambers to leave the green used in preserving the king's semen?"

"I will keep telling you—" Melos winced. "—'I don't know' until you realize I have nothing to do with any conspiracy to cast Scald the Cuckoo's Egg. But you have thought this through. A conspiracy must exist."

Keladon had only a few more minutes before palace mages would arrive outside the door. His heart thudded while he asked the next question. "Why did you order me killed?"

Melos drew a tight breath, a sign he considered a lie. Then he relaxed. "Because you know a secret that, if revealed, could destroy the kingdom."

Incredulous anger pooled in Keladon's gut. He moved his face within inches of the old man's, and whispered, "You wanted me dead to prevent me from ever telling anyone of my role in the new prince's conception?"

Melos whispered back. "Yes."

"Did you think I would be forced to tell it, I would reveal it voluntarily, or both?"

"Both were possible. Aril's spies no doubt know you visited the palace at the time the queen was gotten with child. I am certain they know of King Raboros' inclinations. If Aril suspected the king recruited another man to get the queen with child, he would put you on the list of suspects to interrogate, and his agents could overwhelm you as you have just done me."

"You've addressed one of the possibilities." Keladon shifted his hips to relieve the pressure of the floor against his rump. His arm clamping Melos' mouth began to ache. "Under what circumstances did you think I might choose to reveal it?"

"Your father left you a single rich estate, a title of mild nobility, and the third largest vault of magegems in Sodelerak. If you decided you wanted more, you hold the threat of blackmail over the king and queen."

Keladon's anger flared up, like a thick seam of grease dripping onto hot coals. He shoved his hand against Melos' mouth and chin. "All I want is a life of quiet study at Korobei. You thought I might put the kingdom's security at risk for the sake of a few baubles?"

"Yes." Melos' eyes showed self-reproach.

Keladon's anger eased. "Do you think it now?"

"No. You risked much coming into my office to find the truth about a conspiracy to disrupt the claiming ceremony, when your safer course would have been to go straight to the king and condemn me."

"If I let you go, will you try to have me killed, now or ever?" He peered into the old man's eyes.

"No—" He winced. "Only if I hear you breathed a word about the prince's paternity to anyone. Until then, you have proven to me your loyalty."

Melos had said what Keladon had wanted to hear. Time to forgive. Yet forgiveness did not come easily. The old man's cold calculations had nearly cost him his life.

Are you so weak you can forgive that?

No. I am strong enough to forgive because I serve the kingdom. His anger at Melos faded, and another thought swept its last dregs away. In terms of whom they served, he and Melos were alike. Keladon took a breath. "Will you work with me to find the plotter and foil his plot?"

Melos' breath sighed in around Keladon's hand. "Yes."

Keladon spoke a few words of Jelorean and moved his hand from Melos' mouth. "We start right away. I'll help you up." He pushed himself to a crouch, then reached for the old man's hand.

The sounds of footsteps and muffled conversations came from the anteroom. Soon came a knock on the door. "Master?" said the clerk through the door. "Some palace mages have come because they believe magegems have been tapped in your office."

Melos spoke up. "Their belief is clearly erroneous. The priest and I have been discussing matters for today's ceremony."

"I will dismiss them." Footsteps shuffled away from the door.

As the anteroom fell silent, Melos said, "I gleaned some facts from your questions, but tell me all you know about the plot to cast Scald the Cuckoo's Egg."

Keladon summed up what he knew, and worked in questions of his own for Melos. The second assassin had been ready when the gardener's dropped tool had alerted him to wait in Keladon's rooms. A kitchen boy had overheard Lar mention Old Atem when chatting up a baker's girl, and that news had flowed upward to Melos' ear.

Once his curiosity about the attempts on his life was sated, Keladon turned all his attention to the conspiracy.

"Have you any idea who is its mastermind?" Melos asked.

"I had so strongly assumed it to be you," Keladon said, "I haven't thought of another. It must be someone who knows the king did not visit Her Majesty on the evening in question. A servant might have noticed sound or motion from the king's private chambers during the time he was supposedly with the queen. That servant could then have alerted someone else." Keladon thought more. "Or the king himself let slip the truth of that night to one or another of his paramours."

"There is one other explanation," Melos said. "A person who knows as a fact who bedded the queen that night."

Keladon's shoulders slumped. "Norobom."

"The facts fit."

With a slow shake of his head, Keladon said, "Can that be? He's served the kingdom for twenty years."

With a squint, Melos said, "I have kept my position, and my head, by trusting no one. I cannot rule him out as a suspect. Twenty years of service, you said? Twenty years when the king had no heir. Had the king died a year ago, and a civil war ensued, Norobom would have had command of the battlemage corps and a rich duchy from which to muster lancers, archers, and pikemen. Were it not for the new prince, he could well be the next king."

Melos's voice lacked resoluteness. Keladon said, "You doubt his guilt."

"If it exists, we lack the evidence to conclusively show it." He glanced at a clock in the corner of the room. "And less than two hours to find any."

Keladon tapped his fingers against his stubbled chin. "I know the last whereabouts of both the king's semen and Vos. Toreb, the leader of the troupe, brought both of them into the palace two nights ago."

Melos mirrored Keladon's gesture of hard thought, then winced and dropped his hand. "You needn't have been so forceful when you Compelled Truthful Answers."

"Would you have treated me softly, had our roles been reversed?"

Melos bowed, conceding the point. "Let us return to our task. Brought into the palace, you said? What time?"

"Between ten and midnight, give or take."

Melos pulled the bell cord. The clerk soon opened the door. "I need every gate guard who was on duty at midnight two nights ago," Melos said. "Bring them here within thirty minutes."

The clerk showed no surprise. No doubt Melos gave odd commands from time to time. "To the anteroom, Master?"

"That will do." The clerk bowed and reached for the doorknob. "And before they arrive, deliver us here a blue magegem, deep and rich." The clerk nodded and shut the door behind him. "Now we shall wait."

Keladon rocked from side to side and looked around the room. His soles ached from consecutive nights of unaccustomed walking, and his mind felt grimed over with the residue of too much excitement and not enough sleep. Melos' office lacked chairs.

Melos gave him a dismissive look. "When I am in here, I work, and any guests I have work with me."

"Then let's work," Keladon said. He could sleep after Raboros claimed the new prince. "Can we postpone the ceremony until after the conspirators are found?"

"No."

"You didn't even think about it."

"I know without needing to think, even if we could postpone the ceremony at this late hour, doing so would be a gross blunder. We would imply, to those perceptive enough, or those with their ear to rumors and gossip, that the king has doubts about the prince's paternity."

Keladon bobbed his head in acquiescence, then said, "We could at least shut down Forek's projection of the ceremony to the crowd on the plaza outside. Even were the conspirators to succeed in disfiguring the new prince, better to let only a thousand nobles see the event, rather than ten thousand people from all estates. A thousand nobles could be sworn to secrecy, or encouraged to hold ranks, and that might hold." His last words dried up, like a stream flowing into the deserts of far northern Rak-pawindu.

Melos peered at Keladon. "You do know not even ten nobles could be sworn to secrecy, let alone ten hundred."

"I know. But we ought to have a plan in case the conspirators succeed."

"We shall instead discuss how to prevent the spell from being cast," Melos said. "The spell can be foiled if we find the assurance cap containing the king's semen. Turning up Vos would also be useful. If we can find and arrest the conspirators, we well should find those items."

Melos paused for a knock on the door. The clerk led in two palace mages to places on the other side of the desk. The younger of the mages set down a bundle he carried and untied it. The blue reminded Keladon of the dowager duchess's eyes. For a moment, Keladon wished he were back at Korobei, with researches on his schedule and affairs of state off his shoulders. The older palace mage extended his hand toward the blue and said, "As you requested, Master of Offices."

Keladon recognized the interrogator's voice. "Well chosen," Keladon said. "Before you leave, I should tell you, two more magegems are missing from the vault, and the men you questioned earlier may well be innocent of theft. There's a narrow passage from the tunnels into one of the vault's lower chambers. Look under a crate in a corner of that chamber."

The interrogator's eyes widened. His gaze fixed for a moment on Keladon.

"And have a man bring me my sword from that lower chamber, if you would."

The interrogator looked to Melos.

"Why do you make eyes at us?" the old man said. "You doubt the word of the greatest mage in the kingdom?"

"Certainly not, Master of Offices." The interrogator and the younger mage hurried out.

After the clerk shut the door and left Melos and Keladon alone, the old man said, "The theft of magegems, primarily red ones, and the conspiracy's need to cast spells also point to Norobom."

"Reds would have value on the black market, and the conspirators could suborn a palace mage to cast their needed spells." Keladon's alternative explanation sounded weak. Still, Norobom could be innocent. Perhaps a set of junior mages, some from the battlemage corps and some from the palace, had rankled at both Melos and Norobom's positions and worked up a conspiracy to rise with King Aril's help.

"The guards may tell us the truth," Melos said.

And if they didn't?

Before Keladon could pursue that line of thought, from the anteroom came the sound of tramping boots. The clerk knocked. "Master, the guards are ready to be questioned."

Keladon nodded to Melos. The old man said, "Bring them in, one at a time."

The first guard came in as Keladon bent his left arm and held the blue against his chest. The guard shrank back. "Mage, Master, I—"

With his free hand, Keladon gripped the guard's upper arm. "If you speak the truth, you need fear nothing." He spoke to the magegem in Jelorean. The guard's arm trembled under his grip. "Two nights ago, when you stood your watch at the gate, did either Toreb or Vos enter the palace grounds?"

"Who, your mageship?" The guard's eyes darted, as if he wanted to look behind himself for the answer but dared not turn his head. The only discomfort he suffered was self-inflicted, out of fear of the gem, and not an effect of the spell.

A few more questions confirmed the guard had not been

involved. Melos and Keladon quickly dismissed him. The next three guards had the same things to say.

The fourth guard, a short fellow with broad ears, answered Keladon's first question with "Torev? Bos?" His teeth began to gnash.

Keladon leaned closer. "Toreb is stout and mustachioed. Vos is slender. Vos's usual air is insouciant—brazen—but he might have been under duress."

"I don't—know—" He winced and sweat beaded on his fore-head. "—no—" His lips curled back and he groaned. He curled forward as if gut-punched and his hands groped for the tabletop.

"Who told you to admit them to the palace?"

"Gray. Gray tunic. Brown hair in a bowl cut. Someone's servant."

Melos reached for a stack of papers and pulled a bundle from the middle. He set it before him and untied it with bony fingers. Keladon caught a glimpse of the board atop the bundle, where some clerk had written with a precise hand *Duke Norobom, household, and associates.*

"What was the man's name?" Keladon asked. He tightened his grip on the guard's arm. "His master's?"

The guard sucked in breaths. "I don't know. The man had offered me a purse that afternoon, ten crowns, and promised me twenty more if I would admit the two men."

"Did he pay?"

"Yes, yes, straight away. He must have been waiting in the gardens near the gate. Came to pay me as some of his mates led Toreb and Vos to the north wing." He thrashed his head from side to side and his lips worked until he managed to speak. "I swear to the Divine Couple I had no idea who he was or who he worked for or what he wanted with those two men."

Melos raised an eyebrow and gave the guard a jaundiced look. "He doubled your month's pay and you thought his purpose innocent?"

The guard trembled. "Master, there's crimes and then there's things that someone would rather keep hidden. I swear to the Divine Couple I felt sure it could only be the latter."

Melos flipped another page and his gaze ran halfway down. "Did the man have a knick near the top of his left ear?" His fingertip rested on the paper under a line of text.

"What? Yeah. But I had no idea who he was—"

"Quiet," Keladon said. He took a closer look at the words Melos pointed at. Clearly, the man who'd paid the guard was a servant of Norobom's. Still, the conspiracy might not have involved his old comrade. A servant could conspire against a master. "Can you describe any of his mates?"

"Sir, not really. They were amid the trees and I only caught a color when they happened to pass a lamp. Perhaps from a jerkin."

"Or a doublet," Melos said.

The guard's face grew more alarmed. "I couldn't say any goodman or highborn would be mixed up in these bad deeds."

"Commoner or nobleman, the man involved is plotting high treason against His Majesty," Keladon said. A stern presence filled his face. "Which color did you see?" A sinking feeling answered him before the guard replied.

"Red, sir. A glimpse of red."

Norobom sat on a bench in one of the palace's gardens. His crimson cloak nearly brushed the lilac shrubs behind him. Birds wheeled in the blue sky above. The sun hung above the north wing of the palace, but the morning still kept a faint touch of cool.

A glorious day to fulfill his destiny.

The assurance cap of preserved semen lay bundled in a cloth in an inner pocket of his doublet, and Vos remained, moaning through his gag, in a cell near the secret tunnel his men had dug into the magegem vault. In less than two hours, the mincing sham king would become an object of ridicule, and Norobom would rise, if not to the title of king, to the power of one. His father would be proud. Delight curled up the corners of his mouth and energized his limbs.

He took a deep breath. Victory had not yet crowned him with

laurels. He needed his energies for the claiming ceremony and its aftermath.

His servant came closer, and as usual, a wonder how the man had long ago caught a knife to the ear fleeted past Norobom's attention. "She said...?"

"Her Majesty would walk with you, sir, if you wait here."

"You are dismissed."

The servant headed down the gravel path. Only his crunching feet and birds' sporadic calls interrupted the still morning.

Norobom stood as Lilera approached. He would pretend to respect her. In his memory, he saw lines from King Aril's last message to him. *The clearer the* casus belli *Sodlerach gives us, the greater your reward. Ideally, the mob tears her limb from limb on grounds of infidelity. Because our sister would never break her vows to her husband, the mob would have lied and insulted her honor. Our armies will avenge her.*

We would miss our sister, but we know she would be pleased to die for Plurach.

The fool thought Norobom would order his battlemages to support the invader. Instead, an invasion by Aril would confirm Norobom as savior of Sodelerak and master of its king. He smiled to himself as Queen Lilera came his way.

Norobom glimpsed a flounce of skirts as he dropped his knee to the gravel. "Your Majesty, grateful I am that you would walk with me, given how soon you will be called to the pavilion."

"The old women would inundate me with their superstitious tutting if I did not take the air. Arise, Your Grace."

Norobom rose to his full height, barely taller than hers. She still bore signs of her recent pregnancy. Her makeup could not hide a thickness of her face, and her dress bulged over her midsection.

"Let us set off," she said.

He held his arm out for her to take it. She dropped hers to her side and took the first step down the path. He hurriedly followed until he reached her side and matched her pace. She walked at a largo tempo and her skirts muffled her footfalls.

Norobom glanced around. Her servants and his stood well out of earshot, keeping pace with him and the queen with measured steps. "Madam," he murmured, "your brother sends his greetings."

To her credit, she kept her pace while her features showed a few seconds of thoughtfulness. In a very low but still firm voice, she said, "Thank you for finally revealing yourself."

"I want you to be prepared, madam. During the claiming ceremony, ensure your son's head is clear of his swaddling, then remain still. Allow me to do what I must."

She angled her head and lifted her eyebrow. "You will prevent my husband from claiming my son."

"Yes, madam."

"How? Will Keladon reveal his role?"

Norobom studied her face. Had she taken a fancy to his former comrade? Negligible as he was, Keladon had balls enough to fill her womb. Plus, he'd been the only man to plow her furrow in two decades. "Madam, I believe you know he too will do what he must."

She took two steps while fear clouded her features. "The spectators will not take kindly to me or my son."

He put on an assured expression. "I—we—will see to it care is taken, madam, of you both." He remembered a line from Aril's messages. "'Certain steps at certain times.'"

A dull, placid expression stole over her face. Norobom relaxed. Thirty-five years old and she still stupidly trusted her elder brother. Another step, and she asked, "Can I do anything to help you?"

"You need only remain still, madam," Norobom said. Her shoulders slumped. "You must remain still for the spectators to think nothing of you or your son. If you remain still, I will have the best chance to protect you. You want me to take care of you and your boy, don't you?"

"I desire nothing more." Her voice sounded too small for her height and status.

"Then do as I have asked, madam." They neared a fork in the path. She would veer left, to loop back to the old tower. The right-hand path led toward his offices in the north wing. He stopped and bowed. "By your leave?"

She gestured with her fingers toward the right-hand path. "Till the ceremony, Your Grace." She looked away from him and resumed walking toward the old tower.

Norobom watched until she rounded a bend in the path and the corner of a tall hedge obscured her. He then headed toward the north wing, past a fountain featuring a statue of a nymph, between two rows of potted orange trees, then straight toward a pair of double doors giving admittance to the building.

His servant waited outside. His arms were crossed and, when Norobom neared, it became plain that something serious troubled him. "What?"

"Your Grace, a clerk in your office pulled the hidden signal cord. One of Melos' officials has come to arrest you."

Surprise shifted the muscles of his face. *How*—?

—did not matter. The old man's spies had unearthed enough. Even if Melos lacked the evidence to send him to the headsman, an arrest would disrupt his plans for the claiming ceremony.

Norobom spoke with assurance. "Instruct Doret to fog the glass." Doret would lead a cadre of battlemages to shut down Melos' spell-watchers. "He will protest it is ahead of schedule and tell him I am well aware of that and he will do it anyway. He will send a message to me after he completes his assignment. I shall wait in the tunnel under the inner courtyard of the north wing. Tell Lusak to square up his deck and meet me there for a game." Lusak had command of the main squad of battlemages who would secure the claiming ceremony against interference from outside the pavilion. He would use Lusak's battlemages to surprise Melos' henchman, after Doret had blinded the old man to spells being cast around the palace.

The servant bowed and held the door open. Norobom hurried to the nearest tunnel entrance as quickly as his ducal dignity allowed.

His mood remained high. The old man had placed a minor inconvenience before him, one he would easily step over. If anything, he welcomed the challenge. Overcoming it would further prove his superiority over Raboros and Melos; it would further prove he was his father's true son.

KELADON SAT across from the clerk's desk in the Master of Battlemages's office. The clerk had taken with aplomb the arrival of a nobleman and half a dozen members of the palace guard. He had invited Keladon to sit, then asked for permission to continue his duties. Keladon had granted it. Two guards had shadowed him continuously as he carried papers to and from a bank of file drawers in a small side chamber.

All six guards now stood in ready positions around the room. Two waited behind Keladon and two held places on the right-hand wall, across the room from and facing the door. The last two flanked the door, in case their quarry came in, saw the trap, and tried to bolt.

The clerk dipped his quill, tapped off excess ink against the inside of the jar, and wrote. The quill scratched over the paper. The festive mood of the rest of the palace did not penetrate this office. Small wonder, the clerk must be smart enough to know what the presence of Keladon and the guards augured for his master.

Norobom's a duke and the Master of Battlemages. Why could he want more?

A giant map of the kingdom caught Keladon's gaze. Tiny Korobei beckoned him, and called up memories of his assistants, his researches, his books. Soon enough he would be home. Beyond Korobei lay the vast swath of Vonen-Kiget, Norobom's duchy. He had rich lands and a position of high honor. What more could he want? A crown his father had failed to win?

Clanks came from the doorknob. Keladon turned his head and the guards shifted their weight, readying for action. The clerk kept his head down.

"Strike, lads!" shouted Norobom as the door flew open. Battlemages burst in, gray blurs streaked with red. Crimson balls of hot energy crackled from their gloved right hands and the red light flashed off the walls.

The two guards flanking the door fell first, screaming as they tumbled to the floor.

"Down, men!" Keladon shouted. He sprang from the chair and huddled with his back to the clerk's desk. A vibration from the other side told him the clerk had taken cover as well. The first battlemages through the door flung killing jolts to the fallen guards' heads, while two more flung fiery swirls of energy at the guards behind Keladon. The guards' confused looks contorted with pain and the men tumbled to the floor. The air felt like a kitchen's, hot and stinking of burnt flesh.

Alone, with only a sword for defense. Norobom's battlemages would burn him down before he could scratch them. Panic writhed in his gut and he squirmed more tightly against the desk. This is what the Peluraki foot had felt.

More battlemages rushed in. From the far side of the room came the clatter of a halberd against the floor. "I yield—"

A battlemage flung another bolt of energy at the surrendering guard. The flying ball left a streak across Keladon's vision. It lifted the guard off his feet and crashed him into the wall. He screamed in pain, a wrenching sound, and more memories of Suherabal Ford came back.

The last surviving guard screamed too, but in anger. "Vile treachers!" He swung his halberd in a wild arc at the nearest battlemages. They scrambled backward, but some of their comrades were ready. Two more bolts of energy sparked across the room. The last guard groaned and collapsed. His halberd slid from his hands. The stench of burnt flesh heightened.

The battlemages moved into a semicircle around Keladon. Some smirked and others looked at him with affectless eyes. "What have we here?" one said.

If you're going to die, do it on your feet. Keladon stood. "You have a king's claimed son," he said, and drew his sword. A battlemage laughed, but his laugh subsided when Keladon pointed the sword in his direction.

"We'll burn you down before you can stick all of us," another battlemage said.

Keladon moved the sword point. "But before I'll stick you?"

"Wait," said Norobom. Boots clomped on the wooden floor behind the semicircle of battlemages facing Keladon. Between the battlemages's gray-clad limbs and torsos, a long red cloak compelled his eye. The battlemages parted for their master.

"Keladon? Why the disguise? Black hair and blue eyes don't become you." Under his blond hair, and through eyes as brown as oak, Norobom exuded supreme certitude.

Keladon had forgotten about the spells he'd cast on himself in the tunnel. "I didn't want to look like you," Keladon said. Blue eyes. Where had he seen blue eyes recently? Why did it matter?

"When did you hire on with the old man?" Norobom asked.

"I work with Melos, not for him, in an effort to protect the kingdom from treason."

"Treason?" Norobom said. "I am the only man who can deliver the kingdom from the treason of Balar that put a mincing cuckold on its throne."

Two of the battlemages blanched at the blasphemy, but the rest remained resolute, more loyal to their Master than their god. Keladon barely heeded them, as he realized where he'd seen blue eyes and what they meant. "You believe the Divine Couple should have put you on the throne... brother?"

Norobom's face paled for a moment, but then his lips curled in an awkward smile. "What makes you call me that?"

"In Her Majesty's audience chamber, there's a painting of King Radobom's wedding to Larabos's daughter. Your parents attended. Rather, your mother and her husband the duke. Both of them blue eyed. Never have I seen a child of blue eyed parents with brown eyes. But my father, King Radobom, had brown eyes."

"A clever surmise," Norobom said. He inhaled deeply despite the room's stench, and a smile tightened his cheeks and eyes. "It is true you are as a brother to me, though our father's seed has nothing to do with it." Did the battlemages hear his words as *our fathers*? Or did they know the truth, but their loyalty to him overwhelmed Sodeleraki disdain for bastards and cuckoo's eggs? Norobom gestured at the fallen guards. "Keladon, we were brothers-in-arms, fighting for the glory of our king, Radobom. We felled his enemies by the thousands and won him a victorious peace and an enemy princess for a daughter-in-law."

"I tapped reds for the glory of our kingdom," Keladon said.

Norobom suddenly looked solemn. "So much the better. Keladon, I know your triumph in the Peluraki War was so great you vowed never again to tap rubies, but I know you are like me. You could still cast Burn at Distance, and you would revel in it. When I Scald the Cuckoo's Egg today, and reveal that some base knave sired the Queen's bastard—" He raised his eyebrow and a smile, directed only at Keladon, tightened his cheekbones. "—all the monsters of ambition will turn out their armies and all the rubies they can scrape together."

He thinks I could join him. Part of Keladon felt aghast at Norobom's deluded zeal. *I am no traitor. Raboros is both a pathetic buffoon and our rightful king.*

Another part of him remembered the sword in his hand. He let it droop.

"You want a civil war," Keladon said.

"I do not *want* it," Norobom said, and his tone was almost believable. "But it is inevitable that some gentlemen fools and foreign sovereigns will misjudge their chances and think me defeatable."

"Foreign sovereigns? You expect King Aril to attack?"

"You wouldn't, old friend? Our kingdom would appear leaderless, he has long nursed revenge against us, and his sister will be dead at the hands of patriotic Sodeleraki lords. But let him try. The Corps of Battlemages is loyal to me alone." He gestured at the men behind him while his gaze remained locked on Keladon. "With my battlemages, I will triumph, but at some cost of blood, treasure, and the peace of mind of the kingdom. You can lower that cost if you join me."

"I did not serve our father's glory. I won't serve yours."

"Glory? I will take on no glory. A cuckolded king keeps the majesty of a king, even though he loses the authority of one. I will merely be a protector of the kingdom and the king."

Behind Norobom, one of the battlemages looked aggrieved. "You will earn the crown, master."

Norobom flicked his wrist at the battlemage. "Nay, nay. Raboros is our king for the rest of his life. Only if he would die without issue, and first should happen to adopt me as his son, have I any chance of kingship. But enough of me. Keladon, set aside your distaste for rubies and your misguided loyalty to the mincing king and the old man, and join us. Soon enough, you would return to Korobei and your peaceful studies."

Keladon's sword arm fell toward his side, the tip aimed at the floor. "Your words are sensible."

Norobom eased forward and spread his arms wide. "So they are."

"But still treason!" Keladon cried as he lunged forward, raising his sword and thrusting toward Norobom's chest.

A crack thundered through the air near Keladon's head. Burning pain flared through his right palm and needles of heat pricked his face. His body went rigid and he released his sword. More pain lashed the back of his hand where the outer loops of the basket hilt struck skin. His left hand clenched his right forearm to stifle the burning pain from his hand.

He grimaced and bent at the waist. His fallen sword lay in two main pieces, with slivers of steel, glowing with heat, scattered over a couple of paces.

Norobom had leaped away from Keladon's sword. The

battlemages balled up their gloved right hands, ready to fling burning energy at Keladon. Norobom called out, "No, men!" as he returned to the front of the formation.

Did he offer clemency? Keladon immediately felt foolish for even thinking that. Norobom's expression confirmed his feeling. Under Norobom's supreme confidence lay a thick undercurrent of cold-blooded cruelty.

"Keladon's deceitful and cowardly attempt on my life has denied him a quick death. We shall give him a slow and painful one after I have come into my rightful station. Lock him in one of the cells near Vos."

Two battlemages stilled and pocketed their gems. They grabbed Keladon's upper arms and pulled him toward the door. He struggled against their grips and kicked at them. His boot struck one battlemage's shin and elicited curses.

A third battlemage took hold of his feet and yanked on them. A moment later, Norobom's hard backhand slapped Keladon's cheek. "The more you struggle, the slower and more painful your death."

Keladon went limp. He would not help them. The three battlemages grunted at his weight. Two more fell into place behind him, and one of them leaned forward with a two-foot cloth tightly rolled up. "We can't have you telling tales to people in the halls." He held the ends of the rolled-up cloth and moved it to Keladon's mouth.

Keladon tightly pressed his lips together. The battlemage tugged on the cloth's ends, trying to force it into Keladon's mouth, then nodded to one of his comrades. Someone's gloved hand, fingers still hot from the recent spellcasting, pulled on Keladon's chin, prying his jaw open enough for the battlemage behind him to work the cloth into his mouth. The heel of the gloved hand clacked shut his jaw. The battlemage behind him pulled off his glove with the sound of thick wool sliding over skin. Even with both hands bare, the battlemage took long seconds to tie a rough knot.

"Check his pockets," one of the others said. Someone took

Keladon's watch while the mage at his feet rearranged himself. He now faced away and gripped Keladon's ankles, pressing them tightly against his sides. Keladon and his captors set out for the door. Norobom gave him a last cold look. Keladon glared back, then slumped again after the door shut behind him.

He had failed. Failed his king and his land.

Failed his son.

Failed the woman he loved.

Hanging limply from the battlemages's arms, Keladon's pains thundered into his awareness. His cheek still stung, but the greater hurt came from his burnt right hand. Jostling by the battlemages brushed together scorched skin. He winced and drew in harsh, tight breaths.

The battlemages carried him through corridors and down stairwells. With the claiming ceremony scant minutes away, the palace bustled. The battlemages strode brusquely forward past servants and petty officials, who pressed themselves closer to the walls. Keladon writhed and grunted to get the others's attention. One minor official glanced at Keladon without any flicker of recognition, then paced on. The servants and the other officials would not even look at him.

The knot binding his gag loosened with the jostling he received. The battlemage at his feet relaxed his grip. Perhaps he had a chance.

Outnumbered five to one?

Worse, his only viable chance required him to wrest a weapon from one of the battlemages and turn it against them. The only weapons anywhere nearby were the reds in their pockets. He would have to throw away a vow kept for twenty years. Couldn't there be another way?

They stopped near a door for one of the battlemages walking guard behind him to come forward and open it. Beyond, the ceiling sloped sharply downward toward darkness. Just inside the door, a wall held a cabinet. The few hours since Patot had led the way down a similar tunnel felt like a few years.

The battlemage standing alone at the door shuffled across the threshold to the stairwell's landing. He reached for the handle to the cabinet's door. The captor holding Keladon's ankles shifted from side to side and relaxed his grip on Keladon's left foot—

Keladon pulled his knees toward his chest. His left foot slipped free of his boot and he kicked the battlemage in the small of the back. The battlemage lost his grip on Keladon's right foot and tumbled forward, crashing into his comrade at the lantern cabinet.

The two battlemages fell down the stairs while, in continuous motion, Keladon planted his feet on the floor and twisted to his right. The loose gag fell from his mouth as he slipped his left arm free from his captor on that side. He plunged his left hand into the coat of the captor to his right. "*Attend me*," he said as soon as his fingers brushed the surface of the red in its pocket. He hurriedly spoke the readying words while he bent his right elbow to fling a fiery ball at his captor's face. "*...Burn at Distance one boil now!*"

Energy crackled. Heat singed Keladon's face and already-burnt right hand. His captor screamed, an inarticulate sound that burbled into silence. He lost his grip on Keladon's upper arm and started falling.

Keladon pulled the red from the inside of the man's jacket and pivoted on his left, stockinged foot. He moved his right arm as he spun until his forefinger lined up on the next battlemage's chest. He loosed a bolt of red energy. The battlemage stumbled backward but held his feet, and his face showed surprise as blood gushed from the smoking hole in his coat.

One more. Keladon crouched and ran two uneven steps, one boot on and the other down the stairs, keeping the just-wounded man as a shield between him and the last battlemage.

The last battlemage snarled in Jelorean. Another ball of energy crackled, striking his comrade in the back. The now doubly-wounded battlemage crumpled forward.

Keladon, still moving in a crouch, came clear of the doubly-wounded man and flung a fiery ball across his body at the last battlemage. The crimson bolt smashed into the last battlemage's chest so forcefully it knocked him off his feet. He groaned on the floor and reached trembling hands for the wound in his chest.

Keladon caught his breath and almost gagged. The burnt-meat stench filled the corridor. Sound came from somewhere on the flight of stairs leading into the tunnel. He had to silence the two he'd kicked out of the way. He crept forward and blindly sent two bolts down the stairwell. He held his breath and peeped past the edge of the top step. The two battlemages lay unmoving.

He turned away, only to see the three dead men around him. His gut churned, and not at the smell of roasted meat. A vow kept for twenty years, cast aside within a few seconds....

Keladon squatted on the floor. Elbows on knees, head in hands, he gulped deep breaths. The air was slightly fresher down here.

He had killed these men, with vicious and unnatural energies. But they weren't innocents unlucky to be born subjects of another king. They were traitors, loyal to the greatest traitor of all, a monster of ambition who sought a station even higher than his rightful one. A monster about to plunge the kingdom into chaos. The peace of the kingdom had demanded Keladon break his vow. To keep it would have inflicted pain, plunder, rapine, and death upon tens of thousands of the rightful king's subjects. Even if the Divine Couple had no hall and he, no next life, he would have judged himself in this one as harshly as Balar and Samala could.

And of those thousands, one would die pilloried by the crowd, then forced by custom to be sent to the headsmen by her husband. The kingdom had to be saved, and Lilera had to live, else the rest of his days would taste of ashes.

He reached for his watch, then remembered one of the dead battlemages had stolen it before he left Norobom's offices. It didn't matter. The ceremony could only be minutes away.

A glance showed the gem in his hand to be a medium-deep red, just beginning to mottle to lighter shades. He stilled its energies. Decades-old training, and his assistant pulling fresh reds from a handcart at Suherabal Ford, flooded back. From the red's appearance, it had twenty-five or thirty killing bolts left.

From the southeast corner of the palace grounds, the clock's bells began to ring ten o'clock.

LILERA'S MAIDS lifted the front hem of her dress just enough for her to climb the steps to the pavilion. Despite pregnancy's changes to her body's shape and size, and the trickles of sweat running down her torso, she strode in measured steps and held her head with dignity. The claiming ceremony was a ludicrous Sodlerachan custom, but a queen's job was to comport herself to the ways of her husband's land. Aril had told her that, one summer afternoon when they were both children, playing in one of the great halls with mote-speckled sunlight slanting through the mullioned windows. Remembering her brother calmed some anxious part deep within her mind.

Why be anxious? She knew who would help her. Norobom was a fine man, even if he wasn't Keladon.

Calming, too, was the wet-nurse behind her, carrying the swaddled boy. Lilera's son slept now. Her maids and the wet-nurse had chattered in low Sodlerachan the entire morning, speaking in idioms she hadn't followed. Lilera had picked up the gist: attempts, based in folklore, to augur her son's future in his every cry and burp and soiling. Did sleeping on his way to the claiming table mean he would lead a safe life in his uncle's house?

Once under the pavilion's canopy, she glanced behind her, careful to avert her eyes from the dazzle reflected toward her by the gimballed mirrors on the ground. The wet-nurse took the last two steps to join her on the pavilion. As soon as she did, a line of men tromped along the lawn, across the path Lilera and her son had taken. The men stopped and wheeled to face the pavilion. Well-dressed, pretty young men, squinting against the sun and carrying ornate swords.

Raboros had recruited his paramours for the cuckold's guard. It fit her husband in a manner too truthful to be put into words. She sniffed out the barest breath she could and turned to the crowd waiting under the pavilion's canopy.

The assembled faces represented most of the highest born in the realm. Her husband stood closest, on the other side of the claiming table. His doublet was finely slashed, and puffs of his undershirt had been teased through the slashes to look like a score of white silken flowers. A golden clasp at his neck bound a purple cape, and his circlet sat properly level across his forehead. He glanced at her and the sleeping boy, then looked away, to the table glowing in reflected light, the statue of the Divine Couple, high priest Rolabok with eyebrows like gray vines sending out tendrils. Raboros didn't insult her by ogling his paramours in the cuckold's guard. *Thank Plur.*

Behind the king stood Melos and Forek. Near Forek, on a small stand with a padded top, stood a blue magegem. Around Melos and Forek stood the array of mirrors and horns collecting light and sound to pass to the crowd in the plaza. The mirrors showed an indistinct mass of people, and the noise of a crowd came faintly from the horns. The spells had been cast, then.

Lilera stood taller and reviewed the people behind Melos and the palace mage. She saw dukes and duchesses, among them Norobom's mother; but Norobom himself was not present. Lilera's shoulders slumped. Readying himself for what he must do. That had to explain his absence. She looked beyond, to marquises and earls. Dalasa stood next to her uncle and cast appraising glances at nearby men. A few days prior, Dalasa had revealed her interest in Keladon to Lilera. After a pang of jealousy, Lilera had agreed he was a well-formed man. What had changed that set Dalasa to appraising other men?

Keladon, with his obscure and minor title, would be at the back of the crowd were he present, but through the press of bodies she couldn't see him. If he wasn't there, he likely helped Norobom.

Finally, along the pavilion's outer railing, battlemages, distinctive in their oddly-cut gray coats, watched the crowded nobles with narrow, cautious eyes.

Her attention returned to the blue magegem on its stand. She'd read about the spells, and the words came to her mind. *Target your energies upon the glass I touch and the horn I touch. Pass Light, Pass Sound....* At three hundred yards from the pavilion to the plaza, the flux would be twenty-hundredths of a boil per drop of time, or twenty-five? She would ask Keladon later, when they both were safe, but felt confident in her estimate.

A warm feeling filled her, but then a part of her mind pushed the feeling down. *What does it matter? You'll never have a chance to cast anything.*

At a signal from Melos, Rolabok shuffled forward under his heavy blue robe, and bowed to king, then queen. "Your Majesties, all is ready."

"Proceed," Raboros said.

The old priest raised his voice. "The claiming of a child as his own is one of the highest responsibilities a man may make. That the men of Sodelerak do so is the custom that most separates our way of life from that of barbarous nations...." The homily continued for a time. Raboros looked bored, as usual. The dukes and duchesses behind him shifted their weight. When the old priest pronounced that men who refused to claim their children sinned against the Divine Couple, a few of the male nobles looked at the floor while guilty expressions flashed over their faces. No doubt many others should as well, but repressed their guilt with arrogance.

Norobom's mother gazed flatly at the far wing of the palace. How many bastards had her husband sired?

Was Raboros the only man in the pavilion to have no such stain on his record?

The old priest concluded the homily, then turned to Lilera. "Where is the child not yet claimed by any man?"

"With me, Holy One." Melos had drilled her in the scripted formalities for hours. The wet-nurse lifted Lilera's son with both hands and hid her face behind him.

"Place him on the table."

Lilera barely turned her gaze toward the wet-nurse, and the woman laid him down under the hot glow of twice-reflected sunlight. Her thick hands moved gently out from under him, then she scuttled back a few steps. The boy squirmed, yet remained asleep.

The old priest said, "Who is his mother?"

"We are, Holy One." She reached forward and loosened the swaddling around his neck.

"And who, his father?"

The gods had cursed kings and queens with the need to sometimes lie for reasons of state. Aril had told her that too. "Raboros, first of that name, King of—" She enunciated, "—So-del-er-ak."

The old priest turned to the king. "Have you reason to doubt your wife's word, sire—"

"No."

The old priest's eyes briefly widened. Tension shivered through Lilera, then dissipated as she studied him more closely. Reading from his face, the old priest lacked any suspicion of the truth; he had instead been mildly affronted when Raboros' rapid answer cut in on his words.

To the crowd, the old priest asked, "Does anyone here assembled, in the sight and hearing of Balar and Samala, have any reason to doubt the mother's word?"

A silence answered him, as expected, but then came a motion in the higher ranks of the marquises, followed by a deep, masculine voice. "I do, Holy One."

Murmurs erupted in the crowd as the man who spoke pushed forward. Lilera's heart pounded in her chest, and Melos's old face paled. The approaching man bunched his fists at the back of his neck, then released a long red cloak which he clasped at his throat.

Lilera relaxed. Norobom had come. All would be well. It had to be. He had promised it, and through him, her brother had promised it as well. Behind Norobom came two battlemages, frog-marching someone whose drooping head was concealed by a black woolen sack. *Keladon?* No, someone with slender arms and narrow waist.

Who? Why?

She didn't need to know. Aril would explain in time. She relaxed again.

Raboros turned to the newcomers. His face suddenly looked more regal than Lilera had ever seen. "Norobom, your jest is an affront to our person and our royal dignity. Cease it now and you may keep your head upon your neck."

Norobom bowed. "I do not jest, Your Majesty. I am instead the one man who seeks to protect you from the passing off of a bastard to inherit Sodelerak's throne." Norobom nodded to the battlemages frog-marching the masked man. One jerked back the mask, to reveal the delicate eyes and fine bones of a young man. Lilera knew before looking at her husband that the young man had caught Raboros' fancy sometime ago.

Raboros shrank back a step. Norobom lifted his left arm. "Men, it is time." His voice carried under the canopy. "Let no one interfere."

From their jackets, all the battlemages drew out their red magegems.

BAREFOOTED AND BREATHING HARD, Keladon ran out of a stairwell and into a long corridor. A quick glance helped him find his bearings. *There, that door should lead to a room overlooking the central courtyard—*

He entered a sitting room. Settees and armchairs in the tall, curved Larabosian style faced a fireplace. The far wall held a portrait of Larabos' daughter in the bloom of her youth. Like an honor guard, two open casement windows, knee-to-head height, flanked her portrait. A dozen servants crowded the windows, craning their necks and jostling each other for better views. Some showed furrowed brows.

After four steps into the room, Keladon asked, "Is something amiss at the ceremony?"

Startled, the servants whirled to face him and bowed. "My lord," said a stocky footman, "perhaps you—" His eyes widened at the sight of the red in Keladon's left hand. "—could tell us?"

The servants drew back. Keladon went to the window and peered out. "How many battlemages?"

"Ten graycoats around the outside of the courtyard, sir," said a kitchen girl, "and at least four at the back of the pavilion."

"Probably more at the front, where we can't see," the stocky footman added. "And someone with a booming voice says the new prince is a bastard."

"Sir," the kitchen girl said, "are you Lar's master? Is Old Atem behind this?"

Keladon craned his neck to corroborate her count of battlemages and the footman's guess about others unseen. Accurate enough. About twenty battlemages in the courtyard and the pavilion. One red would be enough, provided he surprised them as much as possible. "Old Atem has no hand in this, and the man denouncing the new prince is a liar."

Norobom's voice echoed off the palace walls fronting on the courtyard. "In what did you store the semen you retrieved from His Majesty?"

After a pause, a groaning voice barely carried the silence reigning over the gathered guests. "An assurance cap." The attitude was unfamiliar, but by the timbre of the voice, Keladon recognized Vos.

"To whom did you give the assurance cap?"

"Toreb. The impresario who hired me to his band of entertainers."

"Who then gave it—what, old man?"

Melos' voice sounded quiet but firm. "You expect us to believe this villain's story, merely because you wave a blue magegem at us and claim you Compel Truthful Answers from him?"

"I *claim* it? Who here can speak Jelorean? You, old man?"

"You can only compel the subject of that spell to say what he believes true. Plainly, you have worked another spell on this villain to make him believe his story."

Melos must have assumed Keladon had been killed or captured. With the battlemages in control of the central courtyard, Melos's only option was to lead the assembled nobles to question whether the semen that would scald the infant truly came from the king. No spell existed to make a man believe a falsity was truth, but with luck, none of the assembled nobles knew that.

Except for Norobom.

"Stand back," Keladon told the servants. To the red, he said, "*Attend me.*" It warmed slightly as it prepared its energies for his commands. He took a breath to settle himself, then readied his right hand. He leaned out of the window and turned toward a pavement where he'd earlier glimpsed a battlemage.

Keladon spoke and gestured to release a bolt of energy. Its flash reflected off the near wall and its crackle echoed through the courtyard. The battlemage cried out and startled sounds came from the nobles crowded around him.

The battlemage collapsed to the pavement as Keladon turned his attention to the four battlemages at the back of the pavilion. Another bolt, another, a third. Battlemages groaned and fell. Screams of surprise and fear filled the courtyard, and the gathered nobles crouched down in confusion.

Keladon climbed onto the windowsill, bent his knees, and jumped. *Keep them bent*, he thought as a bed of roses rushed toward him. From twenty paces to his right, a bolt of energy from one of the battlemages struck the window frame above him. The servants in the sitting room shouted in fear.

He landed. Thorns ripped his stockings and pierced his soles. Pain twinged his knees. More thorns scratched at his doublet. "*One boil,*" he said, and flung crimson fire at the battlemage. The bolt of energy pocked the marble wall near his target.

The battlemage froze in a half-crouch. Trained in red spells, perhaps, but not in keeping his wits in battle. Keladon's second bolt caught the man in the chest and toppled him backward.

Keladon crouched and hurried to a hedge nearer the back of the pavilion. He glanced around him. Most nobles crouched, faces ashen with confusion. Scores of nobles lay prone, and a few crawled toward the wings of the palace. Gray smudges in his vision along the palace walls to his right showed some battlemages had taken cover—

He collided with someone and tumbled to the ground. "Get out of here, idiot!" shouted a nobleman picking himself off the ground. "The graycoats are trying to massacre us! Get to the buildings!" Fiery balls crackled through the air. Nearby, someone shouted in pain.

"Coward!" Keladon shouted back. "There's a thousand of us and they can't kill more than three hundred. Fight them! You have seven chances in ten of surviving if you do! And if you don't, they'll hunt you down and kill you at their leisure!"

The nobleman looked chastened. Keladon crouched even lower and duckwalked a jagged route to the hedge. Bolts from the pavilion flashed overhead. He fell prone and glanced through a rose bush's thick stems.

In the pavilion, two battlemages lurked, each behind a pole holding up the canopy, only occasionally peeping around the poles to look for him. He would need luck to hit them. Charging the pavilion, a red dangling from his hand, would make him too clear a target—

A bolt of energy crackled from the battlemage on his left and gouged the lawn a few paces from the rose bush.

He was a target here too. Every second brought Norobom a second closer to marking the newborn prince a bastard. Keladon swallowed dryly and tensed the muscles in his legs, ready to charge despite the odds, when he saw movement at the rear of the pavilion.

A group of noblemen, among them Dalasa's uncle, converged with drawn swords on the battlemage to Keladon's right. The old earl himself stabbed the battlemage through the back. The battlemage's face contorted and his eyes bulged when he looked down at the tip of a sword piercing his chest. The old earl pulled his sword out and blood poured from the battlemage's wound. He slumped toward the railing and his red slipped from his hand to the lawn.

To the left, a trio of noblemen, led by the curly redhaired dandy, arrayed themselves around the battlemage on that side. Something tipped the battlemage to their presence. He whirled to face them and flung a bolt at one of the noblemen. His target fell, but the redheaded dandy and his peer hacked the battlemage until he collapsed at their feet.

Keladon rose to a crouch and ran the last steps to the pavilion. Fear of exposure to the battlemages gripped his chest, compounded with further fear the noblemen might misidentify him. "I am Keladon, squire of Korobei, son of our late king Radobom!" A better call came to him. "I am Keladon, victor of Suherabal Ford!"

"Welcome, sir!" shouted the old earl around panted breaths. He had his hands on his knees but pushed himself upright when Keladon climbed over the railing.

"Let us bring down the traitor!" Keladon said, and headed forward. The other nobles who'd fought the two battlemages fell in behind him. The cowering crowd made room. Some of the highborn put on steely looks and joined him. Swords shished as their owners drew them.

Through the crowd of guests under the pavilion, Keladon looked for battlemages. Some lurked in corners of the courtyard, backed against the walls by highborn with drawn swords. They would not to interfere.

The crowd in front of Keladon thinned out. Keladon slowed his steps and dropped his right hand to his side. Six battlemages remained in the pavilion and resolute in their cause. Five stood in an arc, bowed out around the claiming table. They held high their right hands. Their magegems were near as red as Norobom's cloak. Another stood close to the claiming table, ready to fling burning energies at Melos, Forek, and Rolabok. From time to time, he glanced over his shoulder at the king.

Raboros gave the battlemage a cautious look and kept his right hand two feet from his sword's hilt. Vos lay in a crumple, moaning, bruises livid on his cheeks. Atop the table, the swaddled newborn slept, unaware of the tumult around him.

Norobom stood at the claiming table, a green in his hand. Behind the table, Keladon barely recognized Queen Lilera. Gone was the spirit she had shown in her letters, in the gardens, or even with her legs in the conception harness. She looked passive, like a ceramic doll whose wrappings covered a broken body, until her gaze lit on Keladon. Her face showed relief, confusion, doubt, and hope, all within moments. He could not guess her thoughts.

Though Norobom's back faced Keladon, his arc of battlemages screened him. He set the assurance cap on the claiming table near the newborn, then drew a knife from a pocket of his doublet. Norobom made a small slit in the assurance cap, then picked up a green magegem.

Keladon's right arm flexed—

"Stop there, Your Illustriousness," said the battlemage in the center of the line of five. "Let go the ruby."

The five battlemages all watched him. Keladon looked past them, trying for a clean view of Norobom's back. He would have only one chance to save the kingdom, and his son.

Norobom turned abruptly. "Keladon? You're the one trying to disrupt me as I save the kingdom from a cuckoo's egg?" He chuckled, then set the green down on the claiming table. "Of course you would. The boy is your son."

Someone in the crowd gasped. Keladon gauged the line between his right hand and Norobom's chest. He slid his right foot out two inches to give Burn at Distance a slightly clearer line between battlemages, and as he did so he spoke. "Scalding the boy will prove nothing. All we have is some man's semen and the testimony of a gunsel ensorcelled to believe a lie to be truth."

Norobom straightened his shoulders to fully face Keladon. He smirked. "Would you name the spell I could have used to befuddle that one's mind?" He flicked his wrist toward Vos, as if he flung dirt off his hand. The smirk remained.

"The boy on the table belongs to His Majesty." Keladon shifted his weight further to his right. Not much of a sight-line to fling burning energy at Norobom, but it would have to do.

Norobom kept smirking. "His Majesty will make that decision after I prove the bastard behind me is not his son."

The battlemage spoke again. "Your Illustriousness. Drop the ruby."

Keladon drew in a breath. The time had come to—*wait, what is she doing?* Seen from the corner of his eye, Lilera padded around the claiming table toward Norobom. Her face was solemn, vibrant. *I can't risk burning her—*

With her right hand, Lilera picked up the assurance cap, and her left shot out to the green resting on the claiming table. She muttered something, and Keladon read Jelorean words on her lips.

"Your Grace," she said.

Norobom turned toward her as she swung the slit assurance cap toward Norobom's face.

His right hand shot out, but he had too far to reach across his body. The assurance cap smacked his face. Norobom screamed, a high shriek, and collapsed to his knees. He shrieked again, his lips pulled back in pain, and clawed at his face. Burnt skin sloughed off his face, revealing shreds of scorched muscle and glimpses of death-white bone.

The battlemages covering him looked around in confusion. Noblemen standing with Keladon rushed forward and held the tips of their swords at the battlemages' necks. "Drop your magegems," the old earl said, "or die."

Five gems clunked to the floor. The sixth battlemage, covering Melos and the others near the table, set down his red.

"Face on the floor, all of you," the old earl said. "Arms out. Don't move." The battlemages did as he ordered. Keladon stepped around them.

Norobom writhed on the floor, still clawing at the ruined left side of his face. "Whore!" he shouted between groans of pain. "Repugnant to Balar and Samala! You conspire with me and then betray me!"

Lilera lifted her shoulders. She drew in a pinched breath, then said, "We serve our husband and king."

"Lying whore!"

Raboros stepped forward and Keladon blinked in surprise. The king's face, though still fleshy, held an expression of resolve that tempered the scorn with which he regarded Norobom. "You began this day, traitor, by impugning our wife's honor. You continue it by your attempt to besmirch her good name."

From the right side of Norobom's face, Keladon read that he readied a rejoinder, but a wave of pain washed the expression away and wrenched from him another groan.

King Raboros looked with lofty sadness at the dead nobleman killed by the battlemages. "You are guilty of treason and armed rebellion against your rightful king." He raised his voice to the crowd. "Do three highborn witnesses agree?"

"Yes," said the old earl. A chorus of others followed.

Raboros drew his sword. "By the laws of our forefathers, your properties, your titles, and your life are forfeit. Your time in the purging fires will be long."

"You are an accursed mince," Norobom said through clenched teeth. "Your wife is a lying whore."

"Would someone silence this traitor, till his cell door locks him inside to wait for his execution?" Raboros said.

"I will," Keladon said. He went to the claiming table. Lilera had set down the green. "Your Majesty, if I may?"

She pressed her lips tightly together. "You may." Her gaze avoided his, and instead, she brooded at Norobom, writhing and moaning on the floor.

Not only had she set down the green, but Keladon realized at a touch she had stopped its flux and released its attention. "Well cast, madam."

Lilera glanced at him then. "Was half a boil sufficient?"

"More than enough, madam."

Keladon took the green and knelt near Norobom. The spell had turned his face into a red, raw mass of scorched skin and muscle, and collapsed one eye. He had been fortunate to suffer so little from half a boil. Blood streaked his fingernails from where he'd clawed at his burns.

Norobom moaned and gave Keladon a cold stare with his surviving eye. "You complacent gelding—"

A few words of Jelorean, and Keladon sent enough flux to his vocal cords to silence him for an hour. Time enough for the Royal Guard and loyal noblemen to shut him in deepest dungeon.

As Keladon rose to his full height, Lilera spoke to Raboros. "Thank you for upholding our honor, our husband." With a wince, she balled her right hand into a fist and pressed it against her hip.

"Are you injured, our wife?"

She grimaced. "The spell we cast has splashed back upon us."

Raboros faced Keladon. "Your Illustriousness, attend Her Majesty."

"Yes, sire." He went to Lilera. "Your hand, please, madam."

She slowly unfolded her fist. The tips and inner faces of her middle and ring fingers had lost skin, exposing damaged muscle and, in a few spots, eroded bone. An amount of damage he expected from half a boil.

"I will do what I can, madam, but the effects of the spell resist healing, even with magic."

"We have saved our son from more suffering than this," she said. "We will revel in any scar you cannot heal."

"I must touch your hand to heal it, madam. My touch will cause pain."

She set her left hand on her belly. "Scant weeks ago, we felt worse pain than this."

Keladon's heart swelled. He loved her. Even though he could never tell anyone that fact, it warmed him. He took her hand. She winced and sucked in a breath through gritted teeth as he started casting the healing spell. "You bear it well, madam." His heart swelled again, and words he could say came to his mind. With luck she would know what he meant. "I am proud you are my queen."

"As are we," said Raboros. The king then went to the claiming table and rested the fingertips of his right hand on the newborn's chest. After glancing at the high priest, he turned his face to the looking mirrors showing the crowd on the plaza, and raised his voice to fill the horns waiting to carry it to them. "I claim this boy as my son."

TWO DAYS LATER, Keladon rose early, to ready himself for a royal audience under the pavilion at ten o'clock. His decision proved wise when just before nine came a rap on the door of his rooms. Lar answered, spoke with the person without, then hurriedly went to Keladon. "His Majesty wishes a few private words with you in the northeast garden thirty minutes before the scheduled audience."

"Of course I will meet him there and then."

Lar relayed the message, while Keladon mused over the king's request as Lar finished tying his doublet and pulling on his boots, tutting over every knot.

At the appointed time, he entered the garden. A morning rain had passed, leaving beads of water on the leaves and cooler air over-watched by off-white clouds. Summer loosened its hot grip. Soon it would be harvest time in Korobei.

Someone moved near a clump of potted orange trees, and Keladon set his longing for home aside. Raboros walked down one of the gravel paths, alone, his entourage twenty paces behind him. Lar held back and Keladon hurried to the king. Raboros stopped and waited as Keladon approached and bowed. "Your Majesty, I am your servant."

"Walk with us. We have things to tell you, and things to ask of you."

Keladon had guessed the latter. There was no need to ask privately if a man would take rewards from his sovereign. "I shall listen to your every word, sire."

Raboros briefly smiled, then continued down the path. Keladon walked abreast of him to his right.

The king's expression grew sober. "We are truly grateful to you for all your services to our realm over the past ten months. You have assured the continuance of our father's line upon the throne and preserved our kingdom from domination by a traitor. Though there is a limit to what boons we may grant you, be assured there is no limit to our gratitude."

"Your words honor me, sire." They went a few more steps in silence. "Sire, if I may, you spoke of the traitor's attempt to dominate the kingdom. I put together some of it, but if it please you, I would know a fuller story."

"It would indeed please us. Your service has shown us you are worthy of our confidences. Melos and his mages compelled truthful answers from the traitor prior to his execution yesterday. Likewise have they worked the same spell on every battlemage in the palace and in Teisoret. From those few who are guilty of conspiracy, Melos has gleaned enough facts to construct the mosaic. The traitor sought to prove us a cuckold, to cause all our subjects, highborn or low, to hold us in contempt. He would then offer the Corps of Battlemages to support our reign, provided we raised him to an extraordinary position as my regent and heir." Raboros shook his head. "Would we knew what drove him to such a goal."

"Sire, I have some insight. I realized it when I attempted to arrest him. I challenged him with it before his men led me toward the dungeons, and he believed it to be true." Keladon measured his next words before speaking. "He was my bastard half-brother."

The king stopped walking. "You are certain?"

"I have two evidences, sire. First, his eyes were brown, like my father's, and both his mother and the old duke's were blue, according to the portrait of your parents' wedding in Her Majesty's audience chamber."

"The second evidence?"

"Her Majesty scalded him with half a boil of energy. From my recollections of Scald the Cuckoo's Egg, supplemented by my readings in the royal library yesterday, so much energy should have carved away bone from his skull and exposed some facet of his brain. It did not injure him so intensely, but it injured Her Majesty's hand to the extent one would have expected."

Raboros' boots crunched on the gravel. "We do not follow."

"The charged semen came from someone not at all related to Her Majesty—"

"—but a half-brother to the traitor," Raboros said. "The greater relatedness of the source and the target weakened the spell's effect?"

"Precisely, sire."

They walked a few steps in silence. Raboros breathed deeply. "We have been a fool. We are a man, with urges as strong as any man's, though we may differ from most in our urges' objects." His face grew abashed. "But we have satisfied those urges with so much indiscretion, we gave the traitor all he needed to attempt the destruction of the kingdom entrusted to our rule."

Perhaps Balar works in the world of men after all, to get you to see that. Keladon kept his thoughts away from his face.

Raboros sniffed in a breath, and pulled back his emotions from his voice. "We are fortunate you serve us despite our past follies. We assure you, we shall satisfy our urges with more circumspection in days and years to come. We will do so to honor all your services to us, both those given in the past and those yet to come."

More steps crunched by without words. Keladon broke the silence. "Sire, how may I serve you in the future?"

"We invite you to stay here at the palace for a time, to work as Master of Battlemages, before you retire again to Korobei."

Though he'd expected the offer, Keladon still felt pinned from breastbone to shoulder blades. "Sire?" he asked weakly. "I know the Corps of Battlemages had a treacherous leader, but am I the best replacement?"

"Yes," Raboros said with a regal tone. "Although we are confident that all the conspirators among the battlemages have been found and punished, the Corps' trustworthiness among both highborn and low has fallen greatly by the traitor's actions. It needs to restore its reputation, starting from the top. You have been seen by thousands of our subjects as a paragon of loyalty and the traitor's greatest foe. If you become Master of Battlemages, you will rebuild much of the Corps' trustworthiness in an instant. Also, you are an outsider, and thus have no clique within the Corps to favor at the expense of the Corps as a whole. Third, the poor performance by the traitor's men in the courtyard suggests most of our battlemages are ill-trained for combat, whereas you have proven yourself, both with sword and magegem. Lastly, though decades have passed, you remain reputed as one of the greatest battlemages since our father's scholars rediscovered the use of magegems from the Jeloreans' lost vaults. Your appointment would give our foreign foes pause before going to war with us."

A wave of inevitability flowed down the inside of Keladon's chest. He would say yes. He'd known he would say yes from the moment he realized Raboros would ask this of him. "How long do you wish me to serve, sire?"

"How much time do you need to reform the Corps and appoint a worthy successor?"

Keladon glanced at the gravel. "I should think a year or two, sire."

"Do you assent to spend that year or two in these tasks, squire of Korobei?"

Keladon had no reason to expect Raboros to recognize Keladon as his half-brother, even in private. But the needs of Sodelerak mattered more than a few hurt feelings. "I assent, Your Majesty."

Raboros nodded in acknowledgment. "We and our kingdom thank you." He took a few more steps without talking.

"Sire, if I may, no doubt you have more important matters than my—"

"How find you Her Majesty?"

Keladon managed to keep his step steady, but his breath caught and words eluded him for a time. "She could be a good mage, sire."

"She could? Yes, she cast a spell, and we recognize your ability to judge prospective mages. However, that's not what we mean."

"Sire...."

"Tell us the truth, squire of Korobei."

An odd feeling welled up inside Keladon. Whether loosed by Raboros' recent words or born elsewhere, all the parts of himself that usually worked together to keep a tight rein on his words buckled under the pressure of this feeling, like a castle wall of olden days struck by a battering ram. Keladon breathed deeply and looked Raboros in the face. "I love her and no other woman, sire."

After another step, Raboros said, "We see."

No, he didn't. No one could. No one had ever felt what Keladon felt. "Sire, above all, I serve you and your realm, and second, I serve the cause of learning all that can be known about magegems and their uses. But after that, I would do anything to share Her Majesty's presence, even for a moment. When I am apart from her, I think back on my times with her, and long for more such times to come." Keladon's heart thudded. He drew a breath to steady himself. If he would be exiled, or worse, so be it. He had spoken the truth.

"We admire your candor, though we did not expect such an answer."

"Sire?"

"Our intent in asking the question lay elsewhere. As we stated, we compelled truthful answers from the traitor. We learned he spoke with Her Majesty early in the morning before the claiming ceremony and alerted her to his plans."

Keladon bowed his head. They kept walking, now at half the speed of his pounding heart. A sour expression came to Raboros' mouth. "Her failure to report his words to her is, by one measure, an abettance of treason, and hence, treason itself. Yet were we to send her to the headsman, we would give King Aril a cause for war, and our subjects would conclude she had been involved in the traitor's conspiracy. That there was truth to his accusation. How find you her now, squire of Korobei?"

Keladon stopped and bowed. "Though my earlier words may show me too interested, sire, it is a plain truth she served you alone in the moment of crisis."

Raboros circled around to face Keladon. "Us alone? Did she turn the spell onto the traitor out of loyalty to us? Or to further the best interests of her son?"

He did not flinch from the king's sharp question. "The two motives were aligned during the claiming ceremony, sire. And they shall remain aligned for the rest of her life."

"You are a fount of wisdom." Raboros let out a weary breath. "And we are aware that, in part, our failings gave her cause to consider the traitor's words. We are not a typical husband to her, so be it; but we have failed to build any other tie between her destiny and ours. Here again we have botched and nearly lost our kingdom, and we have you to thank for your loyalty to us despite our flaws." His voice grew more thoughtful. "You, and her."

The king straightened his shoulders and resumed walking. "We also learned from the traitor that King Aril approved the plan to scald her son, and she was ignorant of her brother's plan until the traitor set the assurance cap on the claiming table. Do you think it likely she would forgive her brother for attempting to maim her son?"

Keladon looked straight ahead. "I do not, sire."

"We welcome your insight into the mind of woman," Raboros said. They approached a fork in the path and the king stopped. "We must take our leave, though we have one more thing to say. The traitor revealed an extenuating circumstance regarding Her Majesty's choice to keep his treasonous words to herself."

"Sire?"

"He led her to believe you conspired with him." The words trailed away before Raboros went on. "We shall see you under the pavilion, squire of Korobei."

The king's words partially closed the distance of the title. Keladon bowed and backed the requisite number of steps down the gravel path, then turned and hurried away.

THE PAVILION LOOKED ONLY a little different than it had two mornings previous. The claiming table and the statue of the Divine Couple had been removed. In their place stood two thrones, about eighteen inches apart. Raboros and Lilera sat, dressed in thick robes and crowned with golden circlets. They chatted amiably, then the king turned to the gentleman companion standing at his right shoulder.

The curly redhaired dandy wore a soberly styled doublet, slashed only on the sleeves, with fabric from his undershirt drawn out and creased. His sword had a hilt without jewels, and his expression showed solemnity. Where was Dobak?

The queen, meanwhile, murmured to Dalasa, then looked wistfully to Keladon in the first rank of the crowd.

From his place to the side, Melos went to the thrones and shared a few words with the king. Raboros nodded, and Melos gestured at a herald. The mirrors and horns set up for the claiming ceremony remained in place. Passers-by in the plaza would see and hear this audience. The herald's voice boomed, "Silence, all, and harken to the words of your king!"

The crowd under the canopy fell quiet. After a pause, Raboros lifted his head. "First, all our subjects know we have two days ago claimed our son, born to our wife and queen. It is fit and proper that a prince be guided in his upbringing by a man not related to him, who embodies the gentlemanly virtues. It is our free choice to name Barkelok, friend of the royal house, Mentor of the Child Prince."

The redheaded dandy stepped forward and knelt on one knee before the king. "I am honored, sire." His expression showed he believed his words.

"The honor comes not in being named to the office, but in acting to its purpose. Rise."

Barkelok stood and returned to his prior position.

Raboros turned to the light-passing mirror in front of him. "All our subjects know what treason was attempted against us, and how it was foiled by the actions of two people. It is our free choice to honor these people for their service to ourselves, our posterity, and our realm. To begin, is there present His Illustriousness, Keladon, squire of Korobei, and claimed son of our father, Radobom, First of that name?"

The silence of the crowd became even more profound. Keladon stepped forward and dropped to one knee. His lips parted and he blinked at moisture in his eye. "I am present, Your Majesty."

"Rise. As events have shown, a title does not make a man, but it may be the case that a man makes a title. You are a son of one king and a half-brother to another. We hereby name you Keladon, Prince of the Blood, with all the honors due that station."

Keladon blinked a few more times. "Thank you, sire."

"You are most welcome, Your Highness. Further, given that the recent treason led to forfeiture of the traitor's properties no less than his head, and our stewardship must focus on matters of national rather than local importance, we hereby grant you the properties of the Dukes of Vonen-Kiget in life tenancy."

"Again, thank you, sire."

"We cannot accept your thanks yet, as you must assent to the conditions of this grant. The properties in question pass to you for your life, but you cannot modify their inheritance. They can be bequeathed only according to Sodelerakan custom and law. Should you marry and have male issue, your son shall inherit them; should you never marry, or lack male issue, these properties shall pass to—your nephew. Under these conditions, do you accept this grant?" A hint of a smile touched Raboros' face.

The king knew Keladon would never marry. "I accept, sire."

"Very well. The Master of Offices has a request of you. It would please us if you were to hear it at this time."

A formality, to cement the decision he had made in the garden earlier. "I invite the Master of Offices to make his request."

On slow feet, Melos came closer. His face betrayed as little of his feelings as ever. "It is my honor and duty to offer you a position of great importance for the security of our realm. Do you accept the office of Master of Battlemages?"

Lilera sat up straighter and her eyes widened.

"I accept it, Master of Offices."

Raboros nodded. "Very well, Your Highness. You may step back."

Keladon did so.

The king went on. "We spoke of two people who preserved our kingdom against treachery. One of them is His Highness, Keladon, Prince of the Blood. The second, and in many ways the more astonishing and more worthy of praise, is our queen, Lilera. Armed with nothing more than knowledge of magegems gleaned from a few books, and a mother's unwavering love for her child, she turned the traitor's actions against him. We have it on one of the highest authorities—" Raboros glanced at Keladon. "—she would make an excellent practitioner of the magical arts. If she wishes to learn from His Highness while he serves here in the palace as Master of Battlemages, and if His Highness assents, she may take lessons from him." Raboros gave Keladon a leading glance.

"I would be truly honored to guide Her Majesty's learning, sire," Keladon said. He turned his attention to Lilera. "If you so desire, Your Majesty."

He read the fullness of her feelings from her eyes. She took a moment before speaking. "We would be truly honored to learn from a man so skillful and wise as you."

Raboros nodded. "And in the event His Highness may leave the Corps of Battlemages in qualified hands and retire to his school at Korobei, and if he assents, Her Majesty may take further lessons from him there. Though irregular, we would permit it, to allow Her Majesty to become the most glorious queen of Sodelerak the Divine Couple would allow her to be. The palace has confined her talents far too long. There would be, however, one condition for her to learn from him at Korobei."

Lilera spoke. "What is your condition, our husband?"

Raboros gave her, then Keladon, a regal and serene smile. He raised his voice to carry through the pavilion. "We must be allowed to visit Korobei from time to time." Gaze forward, he extended his arm to the side, and took Lilera's hand in his. Only then did he turn his face back to her. His voice remained firm and resonant, a true king's voice, as he said, "For so long as Samala may permit it, we desire to conceive more children."

ACKNOWLEDGMENTS

I thank Ari Goelman, Samantha Ling, Char Peery, and Connie Willis for reading and commenting on earlier versions of the story.

Raymund Eich
Houston, May 2013

ABOUT THE AUTHOR

I'M RAYMUND EICH. I use my Middle American upbringing as a launchpad for journeys to the ends of the Universe.

Growing up in the Midwest prepared me for my academic career, culminating with a Ph.D. in biochemistry from Rice University. It helps me help innovators prosper from their progress in medicine, biotechnology, and life sciences.

Above all, it inspires me to write science fiction and fantasy about ordinary people facing extraordinary wonders and horrors, battling enemies both foreign and domestic, and building better lives for themselves, their families, and their societies.

My last name has one syllable and is pronounced "eye-sh." I live in Houston with my family.

Connect with me at **www.raymundeich.com** or follow the QR code below.

Online and brick-and-mortar bookstores around the world list millions of books, with thousands more published every day. I'm glad you discovered this one.

If you'd like to know when I release a new book, instead of leaving it to chance, join my Readers Club. I'll email you every two weeks with publishing news, book recommendations, or a short personal update.

Yes, please! I'll go to **www.raymundeich.com/mailing-list** or scan the QR code below.

No thanks. I'll take my chances next time I look for your books.

OTHER BOOKS BY THE AUTHOR

Available wherever books are sold.

Learn more about these titles at our website, **www.cv2books.com,** or
follow the QR code below.

SHORT STORY COLLECTIONS

The First Voyages: The Complete Science Fiction Stories 1998-2012

From 21st century asteroid settlements to World War II Romania, from an Earth dominated by immortal aliens to Christ's empty tomb, a fresh, distinctive voice in science fiction will take you on journeys to the photosphere of the sun, the coding regions of DNA, and the complexities of the human psyche.

Stage Separations: The Complete Science Fiction Stories 2013-2018

In these pages, you can...

...race against time to solve mysteries hidden in a planet's vast desert—and in a woman's heart

...learn the true story of a president's assassination

...journey 14,000 miles to a high-tech fountain of youth

...win or go "home"—to an Earth you've never seen

and explore six other worlds created by a distinctive voice in twenty-first century science fiction.

Orbital Maneuvers: The Complete Science Fiction Stories 2019-2020

Come and join–

- A mission to terraform a lifeless, rocky planet
- A private detective uncovering the ultimate crime
- A woman called by an ex-boyfriend... who's been dead twenty years
- A President breaking his country's highest law
- A star athlete discovering the true price of a championship

And five more tales, in the third installment of the Complete Science Fiction Stories of Raymund Eich.

Extravehicular Activities: The Complete Science Fiction Stories 2021-2022

Leave the safety of your space capsule for the dangers of billion-year old alien derelicts, intelligent insects with mysterious motives, espionage in an alternate 1920s Paris, and rogue reconstructed dinosaurs. These wonders and more await in the fourth volume of the Complete Science Fiction Stories of Raymund Eich.

NOVELS

The Progress of Mankind

Stone Chalmers, Book 1
Complete four-book series available

Stone Chalmers. Spy. Assassin. Instrument maintaining Earth's dominion over all human worlds.

Opposing him? Hostile forces on colony worlds... and within the Earth government itself.

Take the Shilling

The Confederated Worlds • Book 1
Complete trilogy available

Tomas seeks an escape from his backwater planet and his widowed mother's rigid religious home.

'Taking the shilling' - enlisting as a space soldier - is only the start. The fates of worlds will turn on this uncommon soldier.

Exploration 2127

The False Flag War • Book 1

Two men from opposite sides of divided Earth make an interstellar discovery that could destroy Earth's fragile peace... unless they come in war for all mankind.

The Blank Slate

Neuroscience entrepreneur Clay Shieffer must stop a tyrannical president... because he unwittingly gave the tyrant power over the human mind.

New California

After New California's founder commits suicide, two men clash to rule the colony.

One, Ashwin George, supported by the colony's elite and the Chinese company dominating half the settled galaxy.

Against him, Desmond Park, nanotechnology engineer, armed with the most formidable weapon of all.

A single idea.

The Reincarnation Run

Skeptical spacejock Landry Krieger knows exactly how to smuggle the "reborn" spiritual leader of an oppressed people past their conquerors... but the boy's priests—and governess—shake up his orderly plans.

www.ingramcontent.com/pod-product-compliance
Lightning Source LLC
Chambersburg PA
CBHW020721130726
47899CB00011B/593